The echo of the door shutting hadn't faded before I scooped up the phone. I had to look up the number I needed, and then it took a few minutes to get someone. The hold music grated on my nerves as I mentally commanded someone to pick up. I had to be finished before she got back. Hurry, hurry, hurry. I think I was saying that under my breath.

"Hello, Department of Roommate Assistance. Sheila speaking." Finally.

"Yes, hello. This is Violet Peters, Price Hall 613."

I could hear typing on the other end. "Rooming with Ilse Teps?"

"Yes."

"What seems to be the problem?"

"Well, she's claiming to be a vampire."

"Yes, that's right."

It was almost a minute before I could respond. "What?"

"Ilse Teps is a queen vampire, a blood descendent of Count Dracula. She's probably one of the oldest and strongest among the student body. So she should have the best self control as well." There was a pause. "Though it might not be a bad idea to sleep with your door locked. Oh, and stock up on bandages." An even longer pause. "Is that a problem?"

I didn't even recognize my own voice. "No, no problem." The phone fell from my nerveless fingers. What had I gotten myself into?

THE PAWN'S PLAY

The Hyde Chronicles: Book I

By H. J. Harding

This is a work of fiction. Any resemblance to real people or events is a coincidence. Some places were borrowed, but were returned more or less intact. Hyde University is fictional, much to my dismay. If it really existed, it would be run with much more competence. If you actually read this, please email the author at **hjhardingbooks@gmail.com** and let me know.

Acknowledgements

Anyone who says they wrote a book on their own is lying. No book comes solely from one person any more than a baby appears from nowhere. This book was inspired by my sister, Katie; who asked me to write a vampire school story. Sorry, I wrote this instead. Proving that even I don't know where a book will go when I write it.

Thank you to everyone who read this book in an earlier form, particularly my family, the Critters community, and Petticoat Betty for proofreading.

Thank you to anyone who reads this book, buys this book, or persuades anyone else to read this book. If you've done all three, thank you thrice!

Last but certainly not least, thank you to my Lord and Savior. No accomplish can be made without You, and if it could, it would be meaningless. May this book honor You.

Chapter One
Rooming with Vampires

"Ready to go to Monster School?" Rose asked, popping into my room as I finished last minute packing.

I stifled a groan at her running joke. Ah, the height of thirteen year old wit. Could a five-year age gap really make that much of a difference? "It's not a monster school." I doubted this would be any more effective than the previous zillion times I told her, but reacting too strongly just encouraged her.

"But it's called Hyde University. Like from *Dr. Jekyll and Mr. Hyde*." There were times I really wished that hadn't been on Rose's summer reading list.

"Yes, I've read the book too. But the school was named for George Hyde Wollaston. He was a geographer. Brother to William Hyde Wollaston, a famous chemist." I thought the school was named for him anyway. The school was on an island in Wollaston Lake, which I knew was named for him, so it made sense that the school was too. I had told Rose all this before, but for some reason, she refused to give her older sister credit for her wisdom and knowledge.

"It was named Hyde because it's for monsters. Which is why you're going. You can be a mad scientist."

I shook my head. "Anyway, yes. I'm ready to go." I zipped up my duffle bag and scanned the room one more time. I hadn't forgotten anything, had I? No.

Mom had insisted I make sure the room was neat and orderly before I left, supposedly because it would be easier to tell if I had forgotten anything. That would mess up my organization system and make it more likely for me to forget something, but I didn't argue with her. After all, I'd be gone for a few months anyway.

The room looked different this way. My posters of the periodic table of elements, and taxonomical charts were still on the wall, though I had finally given Rose my poster of sleeping kittens that she had been eyeing covetously. The computer was off, where I usually kept it on during the day; and there were no papers or random CDs around it. The bed was actually made, something I rarely bothered with. My old gray teddy bear, Mendel, was sitting on the pillow. I had spent weeks debating on whether or not to take him. I had given Rose my cell phone, since I had been informed that there was no cell service up at Hyde. Apparently a combination of few or no cell towers, and magnetic interference. "Right. That's … everything." Was it possible to feel homesick before leaving?

"Violet! Rose! C'mon, it's time to go!" Dad's shout yanked me from my musings. Rose grabbed my suitcase and dashed for the stairs. I slung my backpack over one shoulder, and my duffle over my neck from the other shoulder. I got almost to the door before hurrying back, and quickly stuffing Mendel in my backpack.

Loaded down as I was, it was a little difficult to get through doorways, and the staircase was near impossible. I ended up knocking down a picture. School pictures from last year. Someone else would have to get it, because there was no way I could bend down to get it.

"Let's go, we don't want to be late!" Dad was outside by now.

Rose, picking up the picture so I didn't step on it, whispered to me, "Isn't your flight in three hours or something?"

"Yeah, but you're supposed to be about two hours early for an international flight. Then, there's travel time to the airport." I had to rearrange my bags so I could get past the newel post at the bottom of the stairs.

"It only takes twenty, maybe twenty-five minutes to get to Newport News International. And I've been in there. It takes less than ten minutes to walk from one side to the other," Rose muttered.

"That's in good traffic. When have you been in the airport?" Neither Rose nor I had flown before. Dad was a company vendor and flew a lot. We had picked him up a few times, but I wouldn't say I knew the airport well.

"School field trip. Last year." She tossed my suitcase in the trunk, with my bags following.

Taking our seats in the car, we buckled up, and Mom began 'mom-ing'. I wondered if she had made a list. Or maybe seen mine. "You have plenty of time between connecting flights, right?"

"An hour and a half between when I'm supposed to land in Chicago and when I leave. Close to that for the Saskatoon leg." Dad had been particularly adamant that I be careful with that.

"Do you have money on you?"

"In three places."

"Is your jacket in your carry-on? It's currently sixty-two degrees in Wollaston Lake. Besides airports can be chilly."

"Yes, right on top. I'll be fine." It had been in the nineties in Newport New for the past week, occasionally flirting with triple digits. Wollaston Lake was going to feel cold.

"I do wish we'd been able to visit the school at least once before you moved there," Mom said. The school was stingy on visitation days and we hadn't been able to arrange one. "When you come back for Christmas, you'll have to tell us all about it."

"I will," I promised. "Plus I'll write all the time. The school does have internet access." Internet, but not cell phone. Oh, well.

"You'd better." Rose wasn't quite looking at me, but I thought I saw a glint of possible tears. "You will be back for Christmas? Promise?"

"Already have my tickets."

Ninth grade biology had instilled two major concepts in me. One, I definitely wanted to be a geneticist; though I had been interested in genetics for years. Two, Hyde University was the best place to study for that. My biology teacher, Ms. Green, had attended and raved about what a wonderful and exclusive science program Hyde had. That part worried me some. I was a decent student, but I wasn't sure I could make the cut, or that I could afford it if I did. But I had to try, and I made sure to ask Ms. Green to write me a letter of recommendation. I applied several other places too, so I can say with some authority that the Hyde application has the strangest questions. Possibly because it was a Canadian school, I couldn't apply on a common application website. In fact, I couldn't even print out an application or apply online. I had to ask them to mail me a paper application.

I don't know what Ms. Green wrote, but it must have been impressive, because Hyde University not only accepted me, but they offered me a full academic scholarship for four years, contingent on my keeping my grades up. I was a little worried when it said I had to have an A average, until I learned that in Saskatchewan, there was an A+ grade, that was a ninety to hundred percent, an

A which was eighty to ninety, and so on. So it was similar to a B average, which was what I tended to get in high school. I had gotten some attractive offers from other schools but didn't give any of them much consideration. Hyde was my first choice, and with the scholarship, I could use my savings to fly home during breaks.

"How are you even getting to the school if it's on an island?" Rose asked.

"There's a ferry when the lake isn't frozen. When it is, the lake can be used as a road. Plus the school rents snowmobiles. I wouldn't be surprised if the town does too." On the banks of Wollaston Lake was a town, also called Wollaston Lake. Slightly less than a thousand and a half people living much closer to the Arctic Circle than people are meant to live. A large percentage were from the First Nation, Hatchet Lake Dene tribe. I had never heard of the Hatchet Lake Dene tribe, but that's what the information about the town said.

"How much of the time is the lake frozen?" Rose asked.

"About November to June."

College was going to be an experience, but it was definitely one I was looking forward to, cold weather not withstanding.

***

I had little experience with traveling. I had never left Virginia. Other than our yearly trip to stay at the beach for a few days, usually with Uncle Jack and Aunt Laura and my cousins, I barely left Hampton Roads. This was my first time ever traveling any appreciable distance alone. So, when I boarded the first plane, I was pretty excited. For the first hour. Then it got boring. Stale air, cramped seats, stuffed up ears, etc. I had a book, but finished it in O'Hare, and all the flight magazines were the same. I could read my student packet, but I had all but memorized it before leaving.

By the time I landed in Wollaston Lake, I had been in four different airports and three different planes. I was surprised by how worn out I was. Sure, it had been over eleven hours, but I had been sitting for at least nine of them, how bad could it be? Yeah, I was naïve. I disembarked from the final plane tired, sore, and with painfully stuffed up ears, but my excitement was rising again. I had finally arrived.

It was probably fortunate that both my first and last airports were nice small places that could be navigated with ease. I certainly wasn't up to navigating another O'Hare. At this point, I might not have been able to navigate a mall. Wollaston Lake airport, on the other hand, could have probably fit in my high school.

With everyone off the plane, there were still less than forty people total in the airport. It took less than ten minutes for me to claim my luggage; prove that I wasn't a terrorist, again; and get my passport stamped. I doubt they would have bothered with the last part if I hadn't asked. Then I was officially on Canadian soil. I think.

"American, eh? Well, it's a bit past the height of the tourist season," The lady at the exit desk said, as she handed me back my passport.

"I know. I'm here for the college."

"Heading to Hyde, are you? You're the only one today. It's odd, we hardly see students from there. Anyway, ferry's on the edge of town. About three kilometers. Just follow the signs."

I did some mental conversion. Three kilometers should be just under two miles. I could walk that on a normal day, but dragging luggage? "Is there a cab or shuttle I could take?" I asked, adjusting my suitcase strap so it didn't cut so much into my neck.

The woman thought for moment before turning to face a man about twenty feet away. Middle-aged, very dark hair, wearing a uniform, he was sorting through the mail sack that had come in on the plane. "Hey, Paul! You making a ride to town soon?"

The man looked up, letting me see the 'Post' badge on his shirt. "Yeah, about ten minutes. Why?"

"Give this girl a ride to the ferry?" She nodded towards me.

The man gave me a quick onceover. "Sure, not a problem. Truck's outside, you can load your bags in the back." Two envelopes in hand, he pointed at a side door.

"Oh, thank you."

"It's nothing. The ferry's practically on my way, anyhow. You can wait in the truck if you like."

It wasn't hard to find the truck. It had the same small boxy shape that American mail trucks have, but the paint was primarily cherry red, with bits of white and blue. In case I had any doubt, it proudly proclaimed 'Canadian Post' in both English and French. Well, presumably that's what it said in French.

I dug out my jacket and put the bags in the back. It was still above sixty degrees, probably, but that's cold compared to mid-nineties. Instead of climbing in the truck, I took a look around. Lots of pine trees, which I could have guessed even with my eyes closed. I could hear birds but couldn't see them. While not an expert on birdsong, it didn't sound that different from birds back home. There was a road sign for the road away from the airport. It was called Welcome Street. That made me smile.

Now that I had gotten some of my bearings back, I could wonder at something else. Why was I the only Hyde student on the flight? The school was small, and I was early for orientation, but there were only a few flights a day, so there ought to be at least a small handful. I could see being the only one on that flight, as it was the last flight into Wollaston Lake today, but she said I was the only one today. Both Dad and I had checked the dates and times repeatedly, and the school sent a confirmation email a few days ago, reminding me of my room assignment, when and where check-in and registration were, and my class assignment. I couldn't possibly be here on the wrong day.

The lady at the information desk said that they didn't see many students, but that made even less sense. This was the only place they could get to the campus. Well, maybe not. Wollaston Lake, the lake, is big but not huge. Wollaston Lake, the town, may be the closest bit of civilization, but it probably wasn't the only one. Maybe this was just the most convenient ferry, not the only one. Besides, a small school this far up north was probably made up of mostly local and semi-local students.

Paul came out then, tearing me from my musings. "You could have waited in the truck." He tossed in the mail bag before shutting and locking the back door.

"I'm fine. I've been sitting too long today." I climbed in.

He chuckled understandingly. "Paul Rutchkin." He offered a calloused hand as soon as he settled in the truck.

I shook it. "Violet Peters."

"Nice to meet you. So, off to Hyde? Little early, isn't it?"

"A little. Classes start the fifteenth, but freshmen and transfers have to show up a week early for orientation. That starts Monday. By showing up the Friday before, I have a chance to get used to the campus and learn my way around before it gets too crowded." It was August fifth, so he had a point. "Have you ever seen the campus?"

"No, they're pretty strict on security. Only students allowed. Can't even get on the school ferry without an ID. Every couple of years or so, you get a story of kids trying to sneak on, pretending to be students, or someone boating and trying to take refuge there in a storm or 'cause of mechanical problems. No one who isn't a student gets further than the dock."

"Wow, that's…" totalitarian, "odd. What do the students say about it?" It was more than odd. How did a college even survive without recruitment visits, publicity events, athletic games, etc.? Not to mention, why so stringent on security up in the boondocks of Canada?

"Not much. We don't see much of them. Most seem happy enough, but they don't talk about the school."

Okay, this was getting beyond odd into creepy. "Why not?"

"Don't know. Maybe you can tell me next time you come to town. I'm usually at the general store."

I hadn't been paying much attention to the town, but I did recall seeing the general store. We pulled off Welcome Street into the parking lot of the ferry and I had to stifle to urge to beg Paul to drive me back to the airport.

Paul must have read something in my face. "Look, I don't think anything's wrong at the school. I really don't. But if there's a problem, or you need a way out, at any time, here's the store number. You can reach me there or leave a message. I have a boat and can borrow a snowmobile. Okay?" He handed me a napkin with a hastily scribbled number on it.

As I took the lightly stained napkin, my paranoia faded, leaving me feeling silly. "Thank you, but I'm sure I'll be fine. There's bound to be a reasonable explanation."

"Look forward to hearing it. Don't lose that number."

"I won't." I tucked the napkin into my jacket pocket. Then thanked Paul again for the ride and for helping me with my bags. I tried to pay him, but he refused, insisting I get on the ferry before it left without me.

The ferry was a beautiful little boat; dark wood and gleaming brassy metals, even a riverboat paddle. But before I could embark, I had to convince the man sitting next to the plank that I belonged on the boat. He was a tall man, with an intelligent glint in his eye, and he seemed completely relaxed. However I had the strangest feeling that if I tried to get past him without my ID, I would end up in the hospital long enough to miss orientation. Not that I planned to try, I wasn't much of a risk taker or rule breaker.

My student packet included a temporary ID. Between that and my passport, I was able to prove my 'student-hood' and he let me on board. Just me. Paul had offered to help with my luggage, but the guard wouldn't let him so much as step foot on the plank. So, I again thanked Paul, took my luggage, said goodbye, and embarked. Once on board, I waved again. Then had to grab the rail as the boat jerked and started moving. Wow, I must have cut that one close.

The boat was maybe three times the size of the mail truck, including below deck, meaning it took under five minutes for me to realize I was alone with the ferryman. No other passengers. The ferryman was probably around two inches taller than me, so about five-nine, and my initial thought was that he was probably the skinniest man I had ever seen. Not that I could tell much because he was thoroughly wrapped in a coarse brown cloth so I couldn't see his face or any distinguishing features. Yeah, that wasn't creepy at all.

I scolded myself for making snap judgments like that and tried talking to him. "So, do you have many more trips today?"

"Last ferry 'till Monday." He rasped out in a voice that sounded like he had been eating glass, gravel, and sand for years.

I forced back a shiver, trying to concentrate on what he said instead of how he said it. Monday, huh? Then I was very lucky. Though, what if something happened at school during the weekend? We'd be trapped. No, stop it, Vi. If there was an emergency, the school would get the ferry running again. I would just have to plan ahead so I didn't need to go to town during the weekends. Perhaps the ferry was in limited operation because it was summer, and there might be weekend trips during the school year. Besides, I still had Paul's number if I needed it, but I wouldn't need it. "Are we close to the school?"

Instead of speaking, the ferryman raised a bony stick of a finger, pointing to an island in the middle distance, enshrouded by slate-gray fog. What had I gotten myself into?

***

Sudden and unexpected burst of cynicism aside, we arrived without incident. Another guard, a woman this time, required me to prove I was who I said I was, that I was supposed to be here, and to sign a huge stack of paperwork. They wouldn't even let me off the boat until I was finished. Mom was a real estate agent and had impressed on Rose and I to never, ever sign anything we hadn't read and understood completely. And I totally agreed with her. But I was so tired, sore, my ears made everything sound like it was coming through cotton, and by the time I had finished reading the first sheet (essentially saying that I was signing the following papers of my own free will and not out of coercion), I had a pounding headache. It didn't help that the words were tiny and written in legalese. I eventually resorted to skimming and hoping I wasn't agreeing to sign over all my worldly goods (which basically consisted of my luggage) and/or my firstborn. Finally I signed the last paper, and the nice guard lady, who I fully believe could have broken me in half, let me off the boat, and gave me a student handbook and a map.

"Don't I get a copy of those papers?" I should get a copy.

"When you check-in and get your permanent ID."

Okay then. Just as well. I didn't have a free hand at the moment. So, priorities. It was too late for check-in, and I needed to find my dorm. According to the map, the freshmen girls' dorm, Price Hall, was close to most of the buildings I'd want to go to often, such as King Library and Victor Science Building. Very convenient. Even more convenient, it was close to the dock. Good, I was enough out of it to start walking into things. Not that it would be difficult, the fog was only slight lighter on the island than it was from a distance. I could see movement from people within twenty feet, but I couldn't see anyone clearly. Price Hall was the first building I got a good look at, which again got me wondering what I was in for.

I knew it was a tall dorm, I was on the sixth floor. On an island that was only about two miles in diameter at the widest, it only made sense to build up instead of out. I had a catalog with pictures of various buildings, so I knew much of the architecture was gothic in style, made of dark gray stone. It was one of the details Rose had latched on to when declaring it a monster school. In the pictures, taken on what appeared to be a sunny, summer day, it looked lovely and historic. On a cold foggy day, it looked eerie.

Come on, Vi, you didn't come over a thousand miles to stare at buildings. With a deep breath, I walked semi-boldly up to the door, and promptly discovered I couldn't get in. Fortunately, the Resident Advisor on duty, a strawberry-blonde woman sitting behind a desk, spotted me at the door and pressed some button to unlock the door.

"Hey, miss check-in?" She asked, after I maneuvered my luggage and myself through the door. Her smile was sympathetic but amused.

"Yeah, I had to take a late flight." Her expression seemed to change, but I probably imagined it.

"Not a problem. Okay, name, and if you know it, room number?"

"Violet Peters, room 613." I know I didn't imagine the sudden look she gave me; but I couldn't interpret it.

She looked at a list, but didn't seem to be checking anything, before handing me a key on a key ring shaped like a moose. "Here you go. Your room key will let you call the elevator. Your RA is currently in a meeting, but will meet up with you as soon as possible. Your roommate has checked in, but I think she's out at the moment. I'm Risa Torney, third floor RA, if you need anything. I'm here until midnight, if you leave and need to get back in."

I nodded. By now I was bordering on drained and was more than ready to just drop off my stuff and collapse for a few minutes. Or hours. Risa showed me how to use the key to call the elevators, and I was soon in a huge, probably a freight, elevator. I wondered about that, but figured it was probably for moving furniture, like the beds.

Sixth floor was at the top. I exited the door and barely had time to look around when a door at the end of the hall opened. Out popped a girl, about my age, who was maybe an inch or two shorter than me. Her shoulder length honey-brown hair flounced in the air as she practically skipped over to me, huge grin etched on her face. "Hi, I'm Kara! Are you Denise?"

I blinked at her at least twice before my brain started functioning again. "No, I'm Violet Peters."

For a millisecond, she looked disappointed, then the grin was back full force. "Great to meet you, Violet. You're rooming with Ilse Teps, right?" I nodded, wondering how she knew that. Kara also pronounced it 'Ill-sa', where I had been thinking 'Ill-see', I'd have to see which one was right. "Awesome, you're right across the hall. Should have known you weren't Denise. Her stuff's in the room already. Need a hand?"

She didn't actually give me a chance to answer before snatching my duffle bag and trying to take my suitcase, only stopping when she realized she couldn't take it without strangling me with the cord. Silly me, I had put the backpack on over the suitcase strap.

"This way." Kara led me down the hall, giving me a brief tour of what she knew so far. Things like where the RA was (Room 606), where the lounge was (604-605, directly across from the elevators, with the laundry room attached), that there would be a floor meeting tomorrow night, and a bit about the other girls she had already met. 'Quiet' was an adjective that came up a lot, to my amusement. Unfortunately, my brain was too muddled to make much sense of it. I did manage to notice that the rooms had signs on them, telling who the residents were. Well, that was one question answered.

The hallway itself was dimly lit, and the walls were slightly textured under a paint that could probably be best described as 'oatmeal'. A well-worn carpet, gray with black and white flecks, lay on the floor. The doors were a medium brown wood, but I couldn't identify better than that. Room 613 was at the end of the hall, same side as the elevators. There was a purple sign that said VIOLET, and a red one that said ILSE. Across the hall was 612, with a blue sign for KARA, and DENISE in green.

Kara, in her enthusiasm, was trying to open the door before I could unlock it. I couldn't help laughing at that, but fortunately, she wasn't offended. I unlocked the door and Kara stopped on the threshold. "You don't mind, right? I mean, it's your territory. If you're tired or want privacy, I won't be offended. I know I can be a bit… energetic."

I laughed again before answering. Being tired does that to me. "I don't mind, though I haven't met my roommate yet, so I can't speak for her. But I doubt my room looks much different from yours or anyone else's just yet." Kara smiled at my permission and moved inside, allowing me my first look at my new home.

The room turned out to be a set of rooms. The hallway door opened into some kind of sitting room: a blue-gray couch and two matching chairs, a table, two bookshelves, a desk with a computer, a kitchenette (a sink with outlets nearby and a couple cabinets overhead) and three other doors. One door obviously led to a bathroom, but I had to go inside to see the others. The door towards the exterior wall had my name on it, while the door across the room had Ilse's name.

I hadn't bothered visiting other colleges, but I was pretty sure this wasn't the usual set up. However, when I mentioned this to Kara, she seemed surprised by my surprise. "Yeah, the whole college is like this. They say it's easier for students to get along when they all have their own territories. It reduces fatalities." She was still smiling, but I wasn't sure she was completely joking.

I also wondered slightly at her word choice. That was the second time she referred to rooms as territories, which seemed unusual. Still, I was making my first friend at college, and I certainly didn't want to mess it up over unusual wording.

Kara led the way to my room, again stopping just shy of the door. "Seriously, if I'm being a pest, just tell me. You look tired, and I won't take it personally if you want some time to yourself."

"No, you're fine." Honestly, her energy was making me even more tired, but I didn't want to be rude. I had enough trouble making friends. Kara nodded, and stepped in to drop off my duffle bag. I followed, shedding my backpack and suitcase before looking around. The room wasn't much. A bed, a bookcase, a desk without a computer, a chair, a dresser, and a closet. The woods were the same medium color, and the rug matched the one in the sitting room and the hallways, though it clearly hadn't seen as much wear and tear. The room was in a corner of the dorm, so I had two exterior walls, with a window in each, with wooden blinds. It wasn't much, but for now, it was mine. It was home.

After a minute or two of surveying my new realm, I realized I was ignoring my guest. I turned to apologize, but it wasn't necessary. Kara was smiling at me. Not the huge grin from earlier, but a smaller softer smile as if she knew exactly what I was thinking. Maybe she did.

"I'll let you settle in. Remember, I'm right across the hall. Stop by anytime." She paused, and I'd almost swear her ears picked up. "I hear someone. Maybe it's my roommate. Nice to meet you, Violet!" I sat down as she disappeared in a flurry. Well, I looked like I might have made a friend already. Great. If Ilse was half as friendly, I should be fine. Half as friendly was about all I could take!

***

I was just finishing up unpacking the things I would need for the next day or two when I heard the main door open. For a moment, I wondered if whirlwind Kara had come back, but she didn't have a key. So it was probably Ilse, my new roommate. Well, this was as good a time as any to meet her.

My first glance almost froze me. Ilse could be a model. She was tall, possibly a hair over six foot, making me look short. I had always wondered what alabaster skin meant, now I knew. My hair was dark enough that some mistook it for black, but her hair was truly black, with hints of blue. To top it off, she carried herself with such grace and poise that swans would probably look ungainly in comparison. "I am Ilse. You are Violet?" Her diction was formal, but not unfriendly. There was an accent that I couldn't place, but she did pronounce her name as ending in 'a'.

"Yes, um, nice to meet you."

"Likewise." She nodded gracefully at me. Okay, formal, but not unfriendly. I could work with that. Hopefully.

Unfortunately, it looked like neither of us knew what to say now. I broke the awkward silence by saying the first thing that came to my head. "So, why did you decide to come to Hyde?" Wow, that sounded even lamer than it did in my head.

I got the feeling that only extensive training prevented her from rolling her eyes at my stupid question. "It was never in doubt. Where else can a queen vampire attend school? Still, it gives me a respite from the council."

It was a strange statement, but only one word truly penetrated. "Vampire?"

She gave me a strange look. "Were you not informed?" I stared at her. "Have you spoken with the Resident Advisor yet?" I shook my head mutely. "I see. This was unforeseen. Wait here, I shall find her." She was gone before I could say anything.

The echo of the door shutting hadn't faded before I scooped up the phone. I had to look up the number I needed, and then it took a few minutes to get someone. The hold music grated on my nerves as I mentally commanded someone to pick up. I had to be finished before she got back. Hurry, hurry, hurry. I think I was saying that under my breath.

"Hello, Department of Roommate Assistance. Sheila speaking." Finally.

"Yes, hello. This is Violet Peters, Price Hall 613."

I could hear typing on the other end. "Rooming with Ilse Teps?"

"Yes."

"What seems to be the problem?"

"Well, she's claiming to be a vampire."

"Yes, that's right."

It was almost a minute before I could respond. "What?"

"Ilse Teps is a queen vampire, a blood descendent of Count Dracula. She's probably one of the oldest and strongest among the student body. So she should have the best self-control as well." There was a pause. "Though it might not be a bad idea to sleep with your door locked. Oh, and stock up on bandages." An even longer pause. "Is that a problem?"

I didn't even recognize my own voice. "No, no problem." The phone fell from my nerveless fingers. What had I gotten myself into?

Chapter Two
Dimensional Dementia

I had just enough time to consider calling Paul and begging him to get me far, far away from here when Ilse returned with a woman I assumed was the RA. She was a short woman, looking even shorter next to Ilse, with wavy brown hair, tinged with green, brown skin, and slightly pointed ears. An elf? No, stop it, Vi. This wasn't happening.

"Hello, Violet. I do apologize. I planned to catch you when you came to explain everything." The not-elf cast a quick glance to Ilse, who took the hint and disappeared into her room. "Right, now where to begin?"

"Is she really…?" I couldn't even say it, feeling ridiculous for even considering the idea.

"A vampire? Yes, and I'm really a wood elf." I stared blankly at her while a distant corner of my mind mused I had been right. The rest of my mind was shutting down. "Alright, to make a long story a little shorter, Hyde was built on a nexus point between dimension, or universes if you prefer. Beings of all sorts live and study here. It was built as a refuge. Every known dimension is represented, though due to various factors, some are more represented than others. For example, there are currently a fair number of vampires on campus, but there are far fewer wood elves. About a decade ago, that ratio was reversed."

"Dimensions? Like length, width, height, and time?"

"No, not like that." The RA huffed. "Are you familiar with the theory of infinite universes or dimensions?"

"A little." Physics wasn't quite my thing. Too much math. Throwing in quantum mechanics, well, that was just begging for a headache.

"Something like that. I'm not actually the best person to explain. Maybe your roommate would do a better job, and I know there are books in the library. For now, just take my word for it."

Great. Okay, don't argue with this. Just go with the flow and try to figure out information. "So how many humans are there?"

She hesitated and her ears twitched. "Your dimension has a decent number of representatives, but for some reason, there have been few humans in recent memory. I think you may be the only one on campus this year. There aren't any in the faculty or staff, and I know there were only two last year, neither of whom are still on campus."

"Only? But, but I met Risa, and what about Kara? Or the ferryman?" I paused. "On second thought, I'll believe he isn't human."

The RA chuckled. "Risa is a fire elemental. Nice girl, but don't get her riled up. Trust me. Kara, well, I'll let her tell you. Some are particular about who knows where they are from, or their precise species. As for the ferryman, I don't know if anyone knows what he is. We don't ask."

I heard her words. I could recite them back to her. But they made no sense to me. Fluff was invading my skull and conscious thought and reason slipped away before it. Evidently this was somewhat obvious. "I realize this is a shock to you. That is why we insist on having freshman come in so early. About a fifth or so of all incoming freshmen have little or no idea the school is so... diverse when they arrive. There is a special orientation for such students, to help with the questions that arise. They'll be able to explain the dimensions much better. Again, your roommate may be helpful. We try to arrange that each of the, surprised ones, if you will, is matched with someone who has dimensional experience. I believe Ilse has also had family attend."

A thought slammed into my head, jumpstarting the rest of my brain. "My family. They have no idea about this. They'll think I'm nuts!"

"They will not, because you will not tell them," The wood elf said firmly. "Yours is a shade dimension. One where the majority has no idea about the different dimensions and it is illegal to inform them. You are forbidden to share such details of the school with anyone who doesn't know about the dimensions and the types of inhabitants therein. That includes your family. It is a safety precaution."

This explained why no one at Wollaston Lake knew much about the school. "So, I can't say a word to my family, but I could to my biology teacher, who attended here?" I asked, trying to make sure I understood.

She flicked her hair back. "If your teacher truly attended, and you can check that in the student listing, then yes, you can discuss the school with him or her. But not with someone who never attended and doesn't know. There are those who know, but never attended, but that is harder to ascertain."

"How would you know if I did tell someone?" It wasn't like I would advertise breaking the rules.

"When you arrived on the ferry, you were given papers to sign, correct?"

"Yeah, loads of them."

"One of them was a magically binding contract agreeing not to give information about the school that isn't common knowledge or 'safe', to anyone in a shade dimension who isn't in the know. The consequences for breaking it are… unpleasant. You do not want to run afoul of a magical contract. Fortunately, that is the only magically binding contract you signed, be careful about signing others."

"Magic is real?"

"Certainly. I have some ability myself. Quite a few at the school do."

I shook my head. Don't get sidetracked. "What happens if you break a magical contract?"

"Depends on the contract. This one is pretty dangerous."

"So, all students sign this dangerous contract? How come no one objects? Is that even legal?"

"It is legal, and will continue to be legal as long as students from shade dimensions are in a minority. At no point is the student population more than one quarter made up of first generations from shade dimensions. Most students aren't affected by it at all." Which provided no impetus for change.

This was ridiculous. No, I was dreaming, that was it. During one of my flights, or even after arriving, I fell asleep. This was all just a dream.

The RA measured me with her eyes. "I know this is a lot to consider. Take time to think things over. I am available to answer questions. The orientations will also help. The ferry will not let you back on until a week from Monday, so you have time to adjust. Don't be alarmed, everyone is overwhelmed at first. My room is 606 if you need anything." She left then, my seat on the couch allowing me to see her almost bump into what appeared to be a red dragon before shutting the door.

I don't know how long I stared at that door, thoughts and fragments of thoughts racing through my head. If this was a dream, then sooner or later I'd wake up. But what if it wasn't? Then I was really here, and had a conversation about magic, dimensions, and strange beings with someone who claimed to be an elf. I could have gone crazy, but that didn't seem the most logical answer. It could be some kind of prank, but it was awfully elaborate. Or it could be... Perhaps it would be best to stay calm and go with the flow while getting more information. Just stay calm and cool.

I promptly almost had a heart attack when Ilse left her room. We watch each other warily for a moment, unsure how to respond to each other. Ilse spoke first, breaking the increasingly awkward silence.

"I am going to the cafeteria now."

I blinked at the utter normalness of it. Automatically, I glanced at my watch. "It's almost nine. Will it still be open?"

"Hyde has a significant number of nocturnal students. As a result, most buildings have late hours."

That actually seemed very logical. Now there was a question of 'how much do I really want to know about vampire feeding patterns' even if this wasn't real. "Mind if I join you?" Did I just say that?

Before I could say anything to back out of it, Ilse smiled at me for the first time. "By all means, please do." Her voice seemed a bit warmer too.

I stood up and grabbed my jacket before I could change my mind and possibly offend her. Yes, I was nervous. Last time I checked, a vampire's main diet was blood. Also last time I checked, I was a convenient source of said liquid. On the other hand, if Hyde was supposed to be an integrated refuge for beings of different dimensions to learn together, there were probably rules about not attacking or eating your fellow students. Besides, if Ilse wanted to attack me, it would probably be easier for her to do that in a private dorm room than in the public cafeteria. And, I would get more information about what was going on in the cafeteria than I would in my room.

Like the dorm, the cafeteria was a wide gray building, but much wider and not as tall. According to Ilse, my native guide, it was three stories above ground and at least two or three below. The three middle levels (two above ground, one below) were the cafeteria itself. The top level was offices. She didn't mention what the bottom level or levels were. This seemed unnecessarily large to me, but it made more sense when I saw all the different sections it was divided into. I could see at least seven before I was fully inside.

To get fully inside, the doorman had to let you in. The doorman was a three-foot-tall, blue, scaly I-don't-even-want-to-know-what, with three arms, the third coming from the middle of the top of his upside-down triangle head. Ilse called him Bob. Bob would swipe student IDs to access their meal plan. Unfortunately, I still didn't have my student ID and wouldn't be set up with a meal plan until I checked-in tomorrow. I told Ilse this, and moved to head back to the dorm.

"Nonsense. Bob, you can swipe my ID twice, can't you?"

"Yes, I can do that," Bob sang in a high soprano voice. He did so and handed Ilse back her card before I could say anything.

"Um, thanks," I said, trying to look around without gaping like a fish. This place had even more sections than I thought, presumably to cater to many different diets. Seeing one counter that appeared to hold spoiled meat garnished with live worms (and may well have been), I could see why this was necessary. Ilse's voice caught my attention.

"Think nothing of it. Perhaps you will return the favor at some point. Now, my section is over there," she pointed out a table close to the near wall that was mostly covered in little foil drink packs, "If memory serves, you will likely want that section over there," She indicated a group of counters near the other end of the building. "There is a vegetarian counter and one with meat products. You may have to specify to what degree you wish your meat cooked, if at all. Once you are finished, we can meet there. Acceptable?" Ilse pointed to a table on the second level, which seemed like a large balcony. Looking up also allowed me to notice that some of the counters were only accessible by air.

I quickly agreed, and wandered over to the section she directed, trying to hold back a shudder at the thought of raw meat. The thought passed quickly as I got my first real glimpse of a large selection of the student body. Most didn't even look close to human. One counter was surrounded by flying beings ranging from a few inches tall to about three feet. I made a mental note to be careful about 'mosquitoes' here. Another counter had what appeared to be feathered bi-pedal seal people in varying colors. Near the back was a pool that opened to the lake. Since the lake was frozen for two-thirds of the year, that seemed odd, but there was definite movement in the water, and the school was very old. So, chances were that they knew something I didn't. This was evidence against an elaborate prank; too much time, effort and money involved. A dream? Well, I'd see.

There were so many things to see that I might have been gawking forever if I hadn't nearly walked into some guy. He looked human, from the back at least, so I was probably near the counters Ilse mentioned. The food looked pretty edible, and the other people around looked human enough for me to decide I was probably in the right place. Ilse had been right about needing to specify that I wanted my meat cooked. To be on the safe side, I just took two slices of pizza and a soda. I had my food and was turning to leave when I nearly bumped into someone standing behind me. "Oh, sorry!"

I looked up to see who I had almost smacked with my tray. To my surprise, it was the same person I had nearly walked into not two minutes before. A guy, probably about five-eleven, black chin-length straight hair, intense green eyes, and wearing all black including a duster. He just stared at me, eyes piercing through me.

Swallowing my nervousness, I tried again. "I'm terribly sorry about that." No response. "Um, I'm Violet." I tried to maneuver my tray so I could offer a handshake, but that just made me almost spill my drink so I gave up. He didn't offer his name. He didn't say anything at all. If anything, he was staring at me even harder.

This was getting incredibly awkward. "Right, sorry again." I tried to leave, but now I was stuck between the counter and a support pillar. Without the tray, I could have squeezed through just fine. With the tray, well, that wasn't happening. "Uh, would you excuse me, please?"

For a moment I thought he would just keep staring at me, but after a few seconds he swept to the side with a grace I could only envy. "Thank you," I said, while carefully moving past him.

As I was almost out of earshot, I thought I heard a voice from his direction, "My name is Adrian." I turned around, but he had his back to me. Having a strange feeling he was watching me anyway, I gave him a nod and left to find Ilse. I wasn't sure what to make of that encounter. It wasn't that big a school, we would probably run into each other again.

Ilse had, unsurprisingly, made it to the chosen table first. She had several labeled foil packets. One of them said A+, and I studiously ignored them after that. That's my blood type. Even if this wasn't real, something I was having trouble believing, I really didn't want to think about that.

"Were my directions inadequate? You seem to have been delayed."

"No, I found it. I just had a slight distraction." I briefly explained the encounter.

"Hmm," Ilse pondered around a straw. Yes, it seemed surreal that a vampire used a straw instead of her fangs, but there was no way I was going to say anything. "Many humanoids in the school would gravitate towards that area, but the ones eating this late at night are more likely to be Weres or shifters."

"What's the difference?"

Ilse choked on her drink. "Keep your voice down," she commanded in a low voice, looking around quickly. This prompted me to look around too, even if I didn't know what I was looking for. "Good, it would appear you were not overheard. I must say it's a good thing you asked *me*. Weres and shifters tend to be insulted if confused for each other." She leaned in, lowering her voice, "Though, in all honesty, it seems to matter more to them than anyone else."

Moving back to proper posture, she continued, "To begin, Weres. This is generally a genetic trait, though there are ways it can be contracted. Contraction is difficult though, and cannot be accomplished quickly or accidentally. Weres change during their lunar phase, and only their lunar phase, which is almost always full moon. There are rumors of ways they can shift at other times or not shift with the moon, but as far as I am aware, those are mere stories. There are several different types of Weres and they prefer not to intermingle. I'm told it has to do with not liking the scents of other types. It also prevents any possibility of hybrids. They are known to avoid your dimension."

"My dimension?"

"Yes, 13A if you were wondering. Weres are generally from 13B or one of the 14s. Now, shifters are often in your dimension. This is a term for those who shift into a specific animal. General shape shifters are usually called 'morphers'. This is purely a genetic trait. Should a shifter marry a non-shifter, the children are almost always shifters. In addition, while werewolves will always give birth to werewolves, and werebears to werebears, related shifters will likely not turn into the same animal. A family of four shifters may well each turn into a completely different animal. While there are several theories, no one has a definitive answer as to why. Shifters can change at any time, unless they get stuck, which does happen sometimes. Again, I do not know why. They may be stuck in human form, animal form, or somewhere in between. This typically lasts from a few hours to a few days. The record, if I recall correctly, is three months. While this can happen to any shifter, and does, it is generally considered very embarrassing, so the shifter may try to hide the fact."

The information she gave me, valuable as it was, hit my skull like a cascade of pebbles, leaving me with only a headache. "I think I'm more confused than when I started. Okay, how about we start with dimensions. The RA said she couldn't explain it properly." Maybe if I could grasp that, I could understand the rest.

"Very well. An excellent place to begin. Are you familiar with the theory of infinite universes or dimensions?"

"A little."

"Good. Now, try to picture a series of dimensions, or universes, stacked on top of each other like chessboards." She waved a hand at various heights. "The closer any two dimensions are, the more similar they are likely to be. The further away, the more different. For example, while you are human, and I, a vampire, physically, we appear to be very similar in the basics. That implies that our dimensions are probably very close to each other. Which they are. You are from 13A, and I am from 12B, with only 12C standing between your dimension and mine."

"What is the difference between 12B and 12C? If they are separate dimensions, then why are the names so similar?"

"Because 12A, 12B, and 12C were once all one dimension that gradually separated. This also moves to my next point. The barrier between dimensions, and sub-dimensions, isn't equally strong in all places. Sometimes it's weak or non-existent. That is how beings from one dimension can deliberately, or sometimes accidentally, slip through to another. Search the folklore of any dimension, and you will find examples of accidental dimensional travel, one way or another. Then, there are places that exist in more than one dimension." She moved the salt shaker and waved her hand to illustrate two or three 'dimensions' that supposedly intersected the salt shaker.

"And those are called 'nexuses'? And Hyde is one of them?"

"Nexus points, usually. But you are right about Hyde." Ilse saluted me with her foil packet. "Hyde University is one of three places that intersects all known major dimensions."

Interesting wording. "So, if there are major dimensions, does that mean there are minor ones?"

"Yes, but most of them are unimportant. With one exception, minor dimensions are uninhabited and generally used as temporary storage, or a brief wormhole for travel. The exception is for the council. You'll learn more about the council later."

I nodded, wondering how much more my brain could take before it spontaneously combusted. "So what are the other two places?"

"One is the Library of Alexandria."

"But that was destroyed centuries ago!"

Ilse smirked slightly, "No, it was *hidden* centuries ago. It is difficult to access from your dimension, but it definitely still exists. There will be a trip to visit during Junior year. They'll teach you how to get to it from your home dimension then. I've been once before, but that was over seventy-five years ago."

I ignored the obvious implications of her age for now. "How about the third?"

"There is a market place in the area you call 'The Bermuda Square'?"

"Triangle. You know, that almost makes sense."

"Triangle. Must be another that uses square." Ilse muttered under her breath.

"So, does that mean I could cross from one dimension to another here?"

"Yes and no. It can physically be done, though you are unlikely to do so accidentally. But more importantly, when you stepped foot on the ferry, a spell was placed on you that restricts you to your natural dimension. By the time you graduate, you'll know enough that you can safely travel through the dimensions, and the spell will be removed."

"They do that to everyone?" I did not like the idea of spells placed on me without my knowledge or permission. Actually, I didn't like the idea of spells period.

"Everyone who isn't a natural Jumper. One who is capable of traveling dimensions on their own power. Near the end of sophomore year, you should be ready for careful, supervised trips to safe dimensions."

"What makes a dimension safe?"

"Ideally, a 'safe' dimension is one that is not more than two or three dimensions away from your home dimension, not currently involved in internal or external fighting, and is fully aware of the possibility of Jumpers. But that isn't always possible. For you, there is a good chance you'll travel to my dimension. You should like that."

"External? Dimensions can fight each other?"

"As long as at least one can access the other, dimensions can fight."

Looks like some things never changed. Before I could ask anything else, I was distracted by a green flash of light a few tables away. We glanced in that direction to see where it came from. Probably where the eight-foot-tall cake was sitting now. "Magic flare," Ilse confirmed, "A magicus changed someone briefly into a cake.

Watch." Another flash of light, yellow this time, flew from the hand of a human-looking woman, turning the cake into what appeared to be a beam of white light. "See, no harm done. It was likely accidental. Younger races are especially prone to such."

"So, he's supposed to look like that?"

"It. Solurts despise gender separations. Yes, that is their normal form."

"Magic. Fun."

"You don't believe in magic?" Ilse asked sympathetically, picking up her previously abandoned foil packet.

"I didn't. But then again, I didn't believe in vampires either. Still, I came here to study science, and magic goes against science." I wasn't sure just what I believed right now.

Ilse took a sip before continuing. "Science, you say? Well, perhaps this will help. Every day scientists learn that something they thought was true, isn't, or something they didn't think was true, is. Also, don't certain things appear to go against the rules of science? How did you get to Hyde? Did you take an airplane?"

"Three of them."

"I've never actually seen an airplane, but they are large, heavy, metal objects, correct?"

"More or less." I tried to picture having never seen an airplane. Newport News was close to an air force base. Between that and the airport, jets were flying overhead several times a week.

"Yet they defy the laws of gravity."

"That's because other scientific laws have stronger effect. Aerodynamics, thrust, things like that."

"But I'm sure it seemed impossible in the beginning." I nodded. "Magic has rules as well. People have been studying for some time to integrate the laws of science and magic. You can read about it in the library."

I shook my head, lightly dazed. "I have a lot to learn, don't I?"

Ilse smiled at me. "Is that not why you came?"

We had finished our dinner by now, so we left the cafeteria and headed back to the dorm. Ilse pointed out various buildings along the way. I had to take her word for it about the extensive underground tunnel system, allowing people to get almost anywhere on the island without ever coming to the surface, and the modifications for aquatic students.

She walked me to the dorm, but wasn't ready to turn in herself. I decided to ask her later about whether or not vampires really couldn't handle sunlight. In any case, she promised to be quiet when she did come in, so I said goodnight and went in. I was exhausted. That wasn't good evidence for my dream hypothesis, but I hadn't given it up yet.

Risa was still behind the desk, and I waved to her as I went in, but I admit I was paying far more attention to the three-foot tall sparkly girl with purple and red butterfly wings watching TV in the lounge, and the brown unicorn heading down the first floor corridor. I was just going to go back to my room and get some sleep now. Then I would be able to make sense of everything. Good idea.

I shared the elevator with a six-and-a-half-foot girl with green scales and pink hair. It worked surprisingly well for her. She didn't talk much, if at all, and I (barely) resisted staring. She got off at the fourth floor and I had the elevator to myself.

Of course, almost the instant I stepped onto the sixth floor, I caught Kara's attention. Apparently the self-appointed welcoming committee was still going strong. "Hi, Violet. Did you meet Ilse yet?" Kara bounded over to ask.

"Yes. She seems nice. How about you, meet your roommate yet?"

"Yeah! Denise is a dragonfly shifter. From the Bahamas. Isn't that cool?"

"Amazing." I just had to get to my room. Get to my room, shut the door, and somehow, everything would resort to something logical.

Kara slowed her bounce so she didn't leave me behind. "I met the girls next to you, too. They're ice elementals. Twins."

"Twins, huh? Are they identical?"

"By looks, yeah, they're pretty close. By scent, they're pretty distinct. Oh, right. You aren't a Were, so you probably wouldn't notice." She paused to look at me. "You did know I was a werewolf, right?"

I mutely shook my head. Kara shrugged. "Well, I am." We were at my door now. "You should get some sleep. You look tired." I restrained my laughter because I wasn't sure I'd be able to stop if I started.

"Sounds marvelous. Goodnight, Kara."

"'Night, Violet." Kara flounced off, undoubtedly to find more friends, while I took three tries just to unlock the suite door. Once in, I dragged myself to my room, shut the door, and stared at the wall. If this was real, I had a lot to think about. Not to mention a lot of unpacking. If I decided to stay. If it was a dream…. Actually, I was just too tired, and sore to think about it. The bed looked inviting enough. Maybe if I just lay down for a few minutes, I would get some energy. Just a few minutes….

Chapter Three
An Unpopular Minority

When I opened my eyes, it was morning. Very early morning according to my watch, which meant it was even earlier. Wollaston Lake is two hours behind Virginia, and I hadn't adjusted my watch yet. When I realized I had fallen asleep, I realized two other things. One, if I woke up at Hyde, then my dream hypothesis was completely discredited. Two, if the sun was going to shine in my eyes at not quite five in the morning, every morning, then I was going to have to invest in some curtains. Or at least make sure my blinds were shut.

An inarticulate lump of a person, commonly known as Violet under better circumstances, stumbled out of bed and shut the blinds. There, that was better. Now I was awake enough to think. Hyde couldn't be a dream, or I wouldn't have woken up here. Hallucinations probably wouldn't make this much logical sense. If it was a prank, it would have to be an extremely expensive, elaborate one. Not to mention, it probably wouldn't have gone on this long. Which meant, unless I wanted to go on under the paranoid belief that someone was playing a long, complex, expensive trick on me, I had to at least consider that this was real.

Okay, if this was real, I had a lot of adjusting to do. I would have to adapt to living and studying with beings I never suspected existed. This was going to take a special kind of tact, and a lot more information than I currently had. "Okay, Vi. Play this cool. Take things as they come, and for heaven's sake, try not to be rude or offensive. Also, try not to let people catch you talking to yourself."

First thing I needed was more information. The best place to start would probably be the library. There was also Ilse, and the RA, whose name I had never learned. So, register at check-in then hit the library. Good plan. I would like to say that I took that half-formed idea and turned it into a real plan before promptly getting organized and implementing it. However, that would be a total and complete lie.

The first thing I did was go back to sleep. After all, it was five in the morning, and I figured nothing would be open. When I did get up and go to check-in, at about nine-thirty, I discovered I was wrong. Check-in had started at four. In fact, I was just in time for a shift change.

Check-in was in the Barker Central Building. Not exactly the center geographically, but it was the main hub of the campus. This building was actually built of white stone, limestone I think, but still looked a lot like a European castle or cathedral. It was the only building on campus made of white stone, so it was easy to find. At least four stories above ground, I don't know how many below, Barker held the auditorium, most of the administrative offices, and rooms large enough to hold most or all of the school at once. Ilse mentioned last night that the easiest way to cross dimensions was in Barker.

Check-in involved standing in lots and lots of lines; one for almost everything under the sun. The first line was just to get a paper to tell me which lines I had to go through. Since these were individualized lists, I suppose it was necessary; but the whole thing was a slow, frustrating process. I hate waiting.

I did learn some interesting things, though. For one, in addition to the spell keeping students from crossing dimensions, there was also a translation spell on everyone to make most languages sound and appear to be the native language of the student. If I paid very close attention, I could sometimes tell when something was supposed to be in another language. There were occasional mistakes and some languages resist the spell, but for the most part it worked well enough to allow beings from however many dimensions to live and study together.

I also learned that human looking beings were rarer than I originally thought. Most students, though not nearly everyone, had a body shape that appeared at least semi-human (though at times the wrong size, color, texture, and/or with more or less appendages). But people who could be mistaken for human if they walked through the streets of my home town seemed to make up closer to ten percent of what I was seeing, instead of close to a quarter like I thought last night. Then again, it was possible that neither occurrence was a true representative sample. I would have to wait and see.

I also learned one other important thing. I was in my third line, meal plan or health insurance or something, and behind me was a girl with bright blue eagle wings, equally blue hair, a slightly bird-like face, and an outfit that seemed better suited to the Caribbean than Canada. She was obviously unimpressed by her surroundings and current company, but it was a slow line, so she deigned to talk to me, asking me where I was from.

"Newport News, Virginia."

"Never heard of it." She waved a hand, as if brushing away a dust mote.

I tried giving a brief geography lesson, but she wasn't interested. I was quickly interrupted with, "So, what are you, anyway?"

Personally, I found that more than a tad rude, and it wasn't like I couldn't return the question; but I decided on a hopefully more neutral approach. "Human." I gave a questioning look, hoping she'd volunteer her own information.

"Oh, you're the human." And with a fluff of her wings, she turned around and started talking to the centaur behind her. Well, alright then. I ignored her the rest of the time in line, which luckily wasn't much longer.

I would have written Bird-girl off as an isolated snob, but I had similar reactions three more times before I finished my last line (class schedule and the name and office number of my advisor). It was a very awkward feeling. Yeah, I might be weird to them, but they weren't exactly shining examples of normality to me either.

By the time I had my new plastic student ID, I was giving serious thought to slinking home without a word of this to anyone. I was surprised by how disappointing the thought was. Once I had gotten past my shock and convinced myself it wasn't a dream, I had started looking forward to all the cool things I was sure to learn.

Maybe I was being too intimidated. Yes, I had been rejected by four of my fellow students based on nothing more than being human, but I had made friends last night. Ilse clearly knew I was human, and wasn't bothered by it. Kara probably knew, and she didn't have a problem. It wasn't like I had been Miss Popularity before. But I had never been a total outcast either. Could I really deal with all this?

Deep in my musings, which were definitely not to be mistaken for moping, I got turned around and found myself lost. Paying attention now, I looked around and discovered I had wandered into the offices part of the building. Barker was built like a maze, a characteristic that apparently most of the non-dorm buildings shared. Trying to get my bearings, I noticed that the door closest to me had a nameplate that just said 'TARIA' in deep purple ink. That name seemed vaguely familiar, so I checked the papers in my hand. Sure enough, Taria was listed as my student advisor and one of my teachers. Well, at least I knew where her office was. Or would once I got myself un-lost.

I was about to leave when a voice called from behind the door, "Come in, Violet." I paused and looked around before turning to face the door. It was still closed, and no one was in the hallway. I lightly tapped the door, partly hoping no one would answer. "Come in," The voice called again, sounding amused.

Now very hesitant, I cracked open the door and peeked in. A purple humanoid woman, with wings that I couldn't identify as bird, bat, or insect as they kept changing shape, was smiling at me. "Um, hi." I stepped inside at a rate that may have rivaled glaciers. Slow ones.

"Hello, Violet." She folded her hands on top of stacks of paperwork.

"Sorry to disturb you, I just got a bit lost."

"It is no bother. I am always available to my students." She still sounded like she wanted to laugh.

"How did you know I was there?" Or my name for that matter? I eyed the door, looking for anything that might identify visitors in the hallway.

"I am a telepath. I heard you thinking about me." Her wings stretched over her like a canopy. "I have been the faculty advisor to every human student for approximately one hundred years. If you have questions or concerns, I would be the ideal person to ask."

"You read my mind?" I tried to force back a shudder, but probably looked more like I was caught mid-flinch.

"I heard my name. From there, I learned your name. I am aware that something upsets you, and while I can guess at what that may be, I will not invade your privacy to find out. My scans are surface only, non-invasive, and completely confidential barring emergencies or disciplinary investigations."

I nodded slowly. That made sense, but I still wasn't comfortable with the idea. Her smile broadened as butterfly wings stretched out at her sides. "There are study groups and classes that can teach you basic shields against telepathy. I even teach a few." My surprise must have been pretty obvious. "A lot of noisy minds aren't pleasant for anyone. Nor am I the only telepath on campus. While certain ethics are expected, it would be terribly naïve to expect every telepath to take their responsibility seriously without thought of personal gain."

Okay, that made sense. "I don't mean to offend you, it's just…"

"That non-telepaths are never automatically comfortable with the idea of someone reading their thoughts. Believe me; you are far from unique in that regard."

That reminded me of something I *was* apparently unique in. "You said you were the advisor of every human student?"

"For the past hundred years, yes. Before that, there were enough to have more than one advisor."

"Am I really the only human on campus?"

"If by 'human', you mean an inhabitant of one of the 12s or 13s who is not a shifter, Were, vampire, elemental, or magicus, then, yes, you are. Some would argue that some of those classifications can be considered human, but they are not officially counted as such."

"Why am I the only human?"

Taria sighed. "Make no mistakes, there are many, many humans. Possibly more than any other race. At one time, there were a good many humans attending. There have always been humans in Hyde, and always will be. Yet, because your dimension is a shade dimension, we have to keep, how do you put it? 'A low profile?' While people know Hyde exists, we are in a location that is not very geographically accessible, and we try to avoid having much in the way of publicity. In addition, we screen our applicants very carefully. After all, they are in for quite an adjustment. Most people really aren't suited to having their world changed and then going back after school is over and pretending it never happened. Nor are all capable of staying here or moving to another dimension that is not shaded."

I swallowed hard at that. Could I do that? Taria continued. "For this semester, we received one hundred and five applications from humans. Of those, seven were deemed suitable to attend. Of those seven, only you accepted and currently attend."

"The only one? Why?"

Taria shrugged, I think, and her wings, currently looking like ribbons, stretched back and did a reverse loop. "They decided to attend elsewhere, or not to attend college at all, I presume. No one requires them to tell us why they will not attend, only that they won't."

I hesitated to ask, but I really had to know. "Why do certain people seem to look down on humans? I had four people snub me in about an hour."

Taria went very still and didn't say anything for a minute. "Tolerance is the most important quality for any being at Hyde. We are all so very different from each other that without tolerance and attempts to understand each other, the whole society would disintegrate. Lamentably, it is also one of the most difficult virtues to practice. There is not one being on campus, student or faculty, that isn't despised or looked down on by someone else, simply for being an 'inferior' race. That is an unfortunate truth. Also unfortunate is that, 13A being a shade dimension, we get few humans. Of those we do get, not all adapt well. Last year, we had two humans. One graduated. A nice girl, but not one who stood out in a crowd. Not someone who will be remembered for long. The other was expelled for dangerous intolerance. It caused a big scandal near the end of our spring semester. I assure you, you will hear many rumors about him, and what happened. Don't take them too seriously as no one, myself included, knows everything that truly happened. I apologize, but the fact is that you may well have to live down his reputation and the reputation of every human like him."

I didn't say anything, but couldn't help thinking that was hardly fair. I must have thought too loudly.

"No, it isn't fair. Intolerance never is. May I offer a suggestion?"

"Please." I certainly wasn't sure what to do.

"I have been at this school for a very long time and have watched many students and the paths they have taken. Some try to fade into the background, not get noticed. Some try to act less human, and more like some other race for acceptance. Some try to have others conform to their standards. Rarely, you have students who try to prove everyone's worst fears. None of these paths help the students or the school at large. The students that do the best, for themselves and the school, are the ones who recognize the prejudice, both their own and that directed towards them, and strive to rise above it. To learn more about others without rejecting their own past. Be the best you can be and don't be overly concerned with what others may think. You may, of course, come to me with any problems or questions."

Recognizing the subtle dismissal, I thanked her for her time and advice and left. I had a lot to think about. As soon as I figured out how to get out of here. "At the end of the hall, turn left, and then right at the end of the corridor," Taria called through the door. Yup, lots to think about.

***

After a quick and early lunch, I went to the library. The next special orientation for shade dimensions was at two and I didn't want to miss it. But I felt that I would have a better chance at understanding the orientation if I had built a foundation first. I had gotten a glimpse of the library last night, but I had been tired and it was really foggy. Good thing it was much brighter today, allowing me to see buildings and beings clearly. At least, I think it was a good thing.

The library, like most of the school, was dark stone gothic architecture, but there were stone gargoyles here. At first I thought that was just part of the design, until I saw they were moving. I must be adjusting to Hyde. That thought barely surprised me.

The inside of the library was darker than I expected, using candles instead of the electric lights I had seen so far. While I could understand using dimmer lighting to protect some of the ancient-looking books, candles seemed like a fire hazard. Then again, what did I know?

Books were absolutely everywhere in seemingly haphazard stacks, filling the building with that musty, old book smell. I know libraries pretty well, usually able to find what I need in either Dewey Decimal or Library of Congress systems easily. It took me about five seconds to figure out this library was using neither of those, nor any other system I had ever heard of, and the whole place was built like a labyrinth. Clearly, I wasn't going to find anything here without help. So I went looking for a librarian, catalog, or a map. Or at least a ball of string.

What I found was something I originally took for an abstract sculpture that had possibly been dropped from a great height. Say, an airplane. It turned out to be the Head Librarian's desk. The shape made more sense when I met the Head Librarian, a thirty-foot long chartreuse dragon named Ms. Grazletz, or Ms. Graz for short. She had been Head Librarian for at least four hundred years according to her achievement plaque. It stood to reason that if anyone knew how to find things in the library, it would be her.

Ms. Graz was not surprised by the question. Since twenty percent or so of incoming freshmen come from shade or semi-shade dimensions, many come to the library for more information. They even had a special section for it.

"Go up those stairs, turn left at the statue, and look for the section marked 'Hyde's History'. I recommend starting with 'Dimensions Made Easy' and 'A Tale of the School'. Those should be the easiest to understand." She peered over her pink spiked glasses at me while gesturing to the stairs with her tail.

I thanked her and headed off to find the books. I was almost to the stairs when I realized that I had just initiated a conversation with a dragon, without stammering or staring, fully expecting we could communicate. I hadn't even been here twenty-four hours yet.

Even with directions, finding the books wasn't easy. For starters, 'up the stairs' led to the second floor and another flight of stairs. Had she meant the second floor, or was I supposed to go to the top? Since I was here, I decided this was a good place to start. I found lots of statues, but no place labeled 'Hyde's History'. What I did find was rows upon rows and shelves upon shelves of books that I could swear moved when I wasn't looking, for the express purpose of tripping me up and getting me lost. This floor was brighter than the first. There were overhead lights, and while it was still dim for a library there was at least enough light to read by. After about twenty minutes of wandering the maze, I was back at the stairs, though I'm sure the path hadn't led there originally. Still, not one to ignore a good thing, I decided to try another floor.

The stairs weren't making things any easier. They were stone, uneven, steep, and homicidal. Sometimes I get a weird vertigo when going downstairs, like I will lose my balance at any moment, fall and break my neck. Never have, but I still get the feeling. This was the first time it was triggered by heading upstairs.

I checked the third floor briefly, more because I was there then because I expected to find the right section. I didn't find it, but I did briefly get trapped by the bookshelves. Literally. For a moment, there was no open path.

When I finally got back to the stairs, I considered going down and asking the librarian to find the books for me. I didn't because that just seemed pathetic. So the bookcases moved. It wasn't like they were attacking me or anything. So I headed up to the fourth floor. I'm not in terrible shape. I was on the girls' lacrosse team in high school. I wasn't great, but I made the team for three years. These stairs had me wheezing like I was asthmatic within one flight.

At last, I reached the fourth floor, caught my breath and looked around. There were fewer books and more people, primarily gargoyles and other flying beings. Off in one corner was a computer lab, and this floor, like the one below it, had small study rooms. Trying to shake off a headache, I decided that the books better be here and they'd better be worth it. Checking every statue, I finally found the right section.

That was about when I discovered an interesting wrinkle in the translation spell. If the book had been written in say, French or Spanish or Atlantean, it would translate the book to (mostly) understandable English. However if the book was written in English, say five hundred years ago, then the spell registered it as my native language and left it alone. Pity English was never my best subject.

I discovered this when at least two of the more promising beginner books turned out to have been written centuries ago. Others were written is such complex jargon that I had to check to make sure it really was English. There were a few possibilities though. In the end, I skimmed 'Dimensions Made Easy' and decided to check out 'A Tale of the School' and 'The Dimension Jumper's Guide to Emergency Survival and Etiquette'. Now, back to the evil stairs.

I was passing the third floor when I felt something insubstantial hit my back. Before I could even register what happened, I was unbalanced and falling. Down a stone staircase. Face first. This was going to hurt.

Chapter Four
Friends, Enemies, and those In-between

I didn't have time to scream, or even really panic when something black appeared at my side. One and a half blinks later, I wasn't falling. In fact, someone was holding me upright. I had slid a step, maybe two, my books were a few steps in front of me, and other than a few twinges in my ankles and a weird tingling in my back, I wasn't hurt at all.

Turning to see who rescued me, I was surprised to see the guy I had bumped into last night. He looked me over once and let me go, apparently satisfied I wasn't going to fall again. Then he agilely scooped up my books and handed them to me with a rumble of, "You had better be careful. Inattentiveness is dangerous around here." So it *had* been his voice I heard last night.

I took the books hesitantly, unsure if that was supposed to be a subtle threat, a warning or small talk. Still, he had saved me from a nasty fall or worse, so I shouldn't be rude. "Thank you. I'll keep that in mind." I wasn't sure if I was thanking him for saving me, the books, the 'warning', or all three, but he seemed to understand.

One final glance over and a nod later he stalked upstairs. It wasn't until I was nearly to the ground floor that I realized absolutely no one else had been on the stairs when I started to fall. In order for him to catch me, he would have to have the quickest reflexes I'd ever seen or heard of, and/or known I was falling before I did. The only ways he could have gotten there would be to either jump the staircase or teleport. In any case, he would almost have to be watching me. *Stop it, Vi. He just saved you. Cut him some slack.* No point in being paranoid just because things were unusual. Otherwise I'd be in a permanent state of paranoia around here.

***

The special orientation for shade students was held several times during the first week. Curious as I was, I wanted to take the first available one, hoping to make sense of things as quickly as possible. It was quite an experience. To my relief, the information I had already gathered gave me enough of a foundation that I was not completely lost when exposed to new information. This new information, in turn, would help give me a foundation for the more complex books. I was also relieved to learn that I wasn't the one having the worst time adjusting. For example, the orange cat-mole-plant guy next to me kept muttering that it was all a trick. I wondered if he'd last the semester. Though, considering that less than a full day ago, I was trying to convince myself it was all a dream, I didn't have much room to judge.

The basic explanation on how everything worked was mostly an elaborate explanation of what Ilse told me. I discovered that geography tended to be very close in most dimensions. Not country borders so much, but if there was a river in one dimension, it was probably in at least the three to five closest dimensions as well. It might be bigger or smaller or it might have slightly different turns, but there was probably a river.

There was also a beginner's explanation to the Inter-dimensional council. There was one councilman for each group of dimensions, like one council member for the 1s, one for the 2s, etc. Council members were elected for life, or until they resigned, unless voted out by five-sevenths of the other council members. However, no one really knew who was elected. There wasn't an explanation for that. Anyway, the council worked, and sometimes lived in a particular minor dimension. They had very little say in internal issues a dimension had, but a lot of authority in inter-dimensional issues. Now that I was 'in the know' I could vote the next time it came up for my dimension. I made a mental note to look that up some more.

We were also informed that our grades and transcripts would reflect what would be acceptable for our dimension. That was why I had to get 'A's', because that is how a normal college in Saskatchewan in my dimension would grade classes. We were given handouts on how certain things were kept track of. Grades, units of measurement, money, etc. After all, we had to use Interdimensional standards. Well, in most cases. Money, the school made up a currency, called 'Hydeonians'. Our sheet for that was self-updating, so we always knew the exchange rate. Right now, one Hydeonian was worth $4.82.

Also of practical use was the list of easily misunderstood phrases and gestures, and where you should avoid using them. This was attached to a cheat sheet about what beings were from which dimension, a little information about them, and where to find more. I decided to memorize this as soon as possible.

For whatever reason, many of the middle dimensions were just about perfect conditions for humans to live in. Not that humans did live in all those dimensions, but it was possible. Which explained why most the inhabitants of Hyde were at least vaguely humanoid. In fact, humans were considered baseline medically, with other races considered plus or negative in certain areas (such as strength, senses, magical ability, etc.) depending on how close or how far they were from humans. Unfortunately, that led to some calling humans 'zeros', which was considered a slur.

On Monday there would be a general orientation for all new students, and tonight was the first meeting for our floor of the dorm. I will admit to feeling apprehensive about that. Other than Kara and Ilse, I hadn't met anyone on my floor yet and I wasn't sure how friendly they would be. Sure, the two I met were friendly enough, but my anti-human encounters were steadily rising. It seemed statistically unlikely that at least one of my new floor mates wouldn't feel that way. On the other hand, there was nothing I could do about that. I did have a head start in making some friends, so I decided there was no point in borrowing trouble.

The floor meeting was an… *interesting* experience. To our mutual dismay, Bird Girl from check-in shared my floor. Appropriately enough, she was a harpy. As the rest of us inferior beings were unlikely to be able to properly pronounce her name, she condescended to be known as Arie. Her roommate was a seven-foot-tall pink-skinned, purple-haired troll named Klocka. Neither seemed impressed with the other. They might have been only two doors down from my room, but I doubted I'd spend much time in or near their room.

Between us were the twin ice elementals; nearly identical girls with blue-tinged blonde hair and incredibly blue eyes. They were Krystal and Bria. It would probably be a while before I could figure out which one was which.

I knew Kara and had heard about Denise, but this was my first time meeting the dragonfly shifter. Denise was a pretty girl, with darker skin and braided hair. She was petite, friendly, and very laid back. The last trait was probably important when it came to rooming with someone like Kara. She barely spoke at all during the meeting. Kara was in her element, being able to make lots of friends at once.

I had indeed seen a dragon earlier. She lived next to Kara and Denise, sharing the room with a fairy. Or was it the pixie? One of them. The other roomed with the leprechaun, near the other end of the hall. I lost track of who lived where, but also on the floor were two more elementals who weren't related or even the same type, another Were (werecat, I think), a gargoyle, a chimera, another shifter, and a dryad. I think that was everyone, but my brain was threatening to explode by then.

We played some 'get to know you' games which only Kara seemed to like. The RA introduced herself (her name was Thylica), and went over the rules. Finally, we were dismissed to go back to our rooms, ideally to get to know our roommates better.

More information was likely to make my brain ooze out my ears, so I gratefully agreed with Ilse's suggestion that we just relax for a bit instead of talking just yet. I more or less collapsed on the couch while Ilse took a more poised seat on one of the chairs, and we basically stared at each other for a few minutes.

I was actually the one to break the silence. "Okay, I know you have an older brother, but you still seem really knowledgeable about Hyde, and well, everything. Why is that? If I may ask."

"No need to apologize for curiosity. My home dimension is not a shade dimension, and I have grown up with knowledge of various dimensions, even traveling to a few. In addition, my family is part of the vampire council. It is an aristocracy of sorts. As such, I know more than the average citizen of my dimension."

"This is different from the Inter-dimensional council, right?"

Ilse smiled, but didn't laugh at me. "Quite. Though I admit that many of the rules and protocols are borrowed from the Inter-Dimensional Council. The vampire council only has authority among vampires. It is hereditary, instead of elected. In addition, everyone knows who is involved on the vampire council."

"Why don't people know who is part of the Inter-Dimensional Council?"

She just looked at me as if I asked her to explain why ice was cold. "That is the way it is done."

Right, okay, change of subject. "If the vampire council is hereditary, will you be part of it someday?"

"My brother, Wilhelm, stands to inherit the Teps house seat. I could take part if Wilhelm were to step down, or even to a limited extent if he doesn't, but have no desire to. I am instead training to be an ambassador."

"Wow, an ambassador? You'll probably be good at it. You've certainly helped me."

That's when I learned that vampires can blush. A little anyway. "My thanks. What of you? What career do you seek? Do you have siblings? Your parents, what of them?"

"I have a sister, Rose. She's five years younger than me. Ever since she learned the name of the school, she's been calling it a monster school." I paused, realizing both that it was truer than Rose suspected and I could never tell her, and that the statement could be considered offensive. Fortunately, Ilse seemed amused.

"I suppose your sister might well consider some of us monsters. However, I doubt you wish to know how reciprocal the feeling is."

"No, probably not. Anyway, my parents. Dad works in sales. He travels to companies to convince them to buy his company's products, mostly paper. Mom is in real estate, selling houses. My dad's brother and his family live near us, so we get together often. I have three cousins. There's Jesse. He's a couple years older than me. Their daughter, Charlie, short for Charlene, is Rose's age. And they adopted a boy, named Lesley. He's four. I'm a biology major, hoping to be a geneticist." I smiled. "Mom wanted me to be a nurse or a doctor. I did some volunteer work in hospitals, took some first aid classes, but I really didn't want to go down that path. I like that I know what to do in an emergency, but I don't want the pressure of having lives depend on me like that. Not particularly fond of blood either. Or needles. Or hospitals." We both laughed. "What can I say, I'm more of a researcher than a doer. I'm pretty boring, actually."

"Oh, I don't think that at all."

It seemed to be true, too. As we exchanged information, Ilse seemed as interested in my tales of home and high school as I was about her family and the council. I finally asked her what a queen vampire was. The full explanation went over my head, but the gist seemed to be that it was a gender neutral term for the ruling class of vampires in her home dimension. They were blood descendants of Count Dracula, who really was a vampire. It had something to do with parts of Transylvania overlapping dimensions. They also had legends of an older, stronger, type of vampire called king vampires, also a gender neutral term, who were descended from an older vampire or demon or something. In any case, if they ever existed, they don't now.

We compared the vampire council to high school and found a disturbing number of similarities. There were the cliques, the popularity contests, the fake friends who would turn on you the second you lost your edge, and there weren't even teachers to regulate things. Ilse was clearly disenchanted with the whole processes. I hesitated to point out that being an ambassador would probably be pretty similar but she brought it up first. Apparently there are only so many 'approved' pathways for someone in her position and she preferred an option that at least let her see new places and learn new things.

Ilse was older than the average vampire student for a couple reasons. First, vampires who could join the council had to go through additional schooling, so she spent at least ten or fifteen years studying politics and history on top of regular school. In addition, vampires of her class were supposed to spend at least a decade in indentured servitude to learn humility. She had spent her time working under a potter, and enjoyed it so much that she spent twenty years instead, and was still in touch with her.

I learned that she seemed distantly fond of her often-busy parents, and was devoted to her brother who was twenty years older than her. She told me about the first time they went dimension jumping on their own, and she got trapped in a basement belonging to a ghoul in a shade dimension, so they couldn't be seen. Wilhelm broke a few windows in the back of the house for a distraction. When the ghoul investigated, Wilhelm snuck in and got Ilse out. The two barely made it out of the house and back to their own dimension in time. Then they got grounded for a year because they weren't supposed to be dimension jumping in the first place.

Ilse clearly enjoyed telling that story. Her voice lost a few of her more formal patterns and she smiled more. I was a little disappointed that she reverted to normal when finished, but I didn't say anything. It was my turn for a story.

I might never have jumped dimensions behind my parents' backs, but I did sneak two toads into Bobbi Fisher's locker in seventh grade after she told my crush that I had warts. Needless to say, Bobbi and I weren't friends after that, even if she couldn't prove that was me. Ilse seemed amused at that, though she looked slightly wistful when I mentioned that Bobbi and I had been friends for years before that.

"So who was your best friend growing up?"

"Friendship depends on trust. Trust is a rare commodity in a governing body. I trust Wilhelm. All others, well, one learns quickly that others usually have their own agenda."

"That's... really sad."

"That is life." I didn't agree with that, but wasn't sure how to debate that. It didn't help that I was trying to stifle my third yawn. It was almost two. "Perhaps you should get some sleep."

"Yeah, maybe I should. Goodnight, Ilse." I had almost closed the door, before giving in to an impulse. Turning back, I looked at her. "Hey, Ilse?"

"Yes?"

"I don't need anything from the vampire council." Slightly embarrassed by my impetuousness, I murmured a quick goodnight and shut the door.

It came a few moments later, but I definitely heard her reply back. "Goodnight, Violet."

***

I started to settle in pretty quickly after that. Ilse and I never mentioned our late night chat, but the vampire was less formal and friendlier when I was the only one around. We usually had dinner together, and would often talk late at night.

She was good at helping me keep from completely humiliating myself. I could ask her questions that might have gotten me in trouble with other people. She also gave me a special perfume that was more of a scent concealer than a scent. Apparently, among many races that have a better sense of smell than I do, advertising certain times of month is considered 'ill-breeding'. That was an embarrassing conversation, but I'm sure it saved me from much more embarrassment later.

Orientation was an interesting mix of things that I suspect are similar in every school (rules, sports and clubs, extra-curricular events, etc.) and things that were probably unique to Hyde (what to do if you can't breathe oxygen, where to repair magical accidents, telepathic etiquette, etc.). On my second full day, there was a hall meeting where we met all the RAs of the dorm. First floor was Twislow, a unicorn. Second floor was a magicus named Rachael. I had already met Risa from third. Grewlizt, a goblin, and Jarwel, a hydra, were the forth and fifth floor RAs. The Resident Director, or RD, was a centaur, but due to some kind of mix-up, she wasn't available to show up for the meeting.

My current policy of going with the flow helped a lot. By this point, it didn't make sense to claim that so and so or such and such was impossible. So what if a giant snake liked to hang out in our lounge, or that I had to be careful not to get caught in the middle of spell fights between the pixie and the fairy of our floor? It also helped with more mundane things, like people's eating habits. I often ate breakfast with Kara and Denise, and learned quickly not to pay much attention to Kara's food. Being a werewolf, she liked her meat quite a bit rarer than most.

Denise tended to collect our silverware and sometimes dishes to build sculptures with them. She was also prone to random subject changes that left most of her listeners lost. Ilse built scale models of famous buildings of all dimensions out of toothpicks. Kara was already trying to join as many clubs as she could, especially a very aggressive Frisbee Tag league called 'Ultimate Frisbee Deathmath'. There were corners of the campus where something strange was always happening. Though strange quickly became relative.

Actually, within a few days, the weirdest part about Hyde was writing home. I emailed my family about once a day the first few weeks and it was feeling increasingly like torture. How could I tell them about school without giving away all the information about what made Hyde so unique? Even if it wasn't illegal and potentially dangerous to tell them, my parents would never believe me. I had no idea if Rose would or not, but I couldn't tell her. Christmas was going to be *fun*, I could tell.

I compromised by describing things in vague terms, giving names (sometimes) of my fellow students but little else, and only a few hints about how different things were from what I was expecting. It wasn't perfect, and they kept asking for more information, but I did what I could.

Still, I was adjusting. By the time orientation was finished and classes were ready to begin, I thought I knew what I was getting into. It continues to amaze me how very naïve I can be.

***

By the end of the first week, I knew classes would be a challenge. Of course, I expected that going into college. What I hadn't expected was some of the teachers. Professor Argus, for example, was a very short humanoid in olive green, with four arms, and eyes literally in the back of his head. He was very strict, and used those eyes to make sure students behaved themselves at all times. No talking unless called upon. Two times being late made an absence, three times absent dropped you a letter grade. Spelling and grammar were vital, but if you could prove that you had been right in your own language and it was a flaw in the spell, you could get the grade put back. IF you could convince him. He taught Foundations of Literature, a class dedicated to literature of various dimensions so we could analyze the similarities and differences. Judging by the syllabus, the teacher had a fondness for Shakespeare. Lit was never my strongest area, but it was a required class.

To increase the fun, Arie, or Bird Girl as I still called her in my head, was not only in the same class, but due to the seating chart, was practically right next to me. This allowed her to look down her beak at me whenever I got an answer wrong or asked a particularly stupid question. She was, of course, one of the best students in the class. It took less than fifteen minutes of my first day to decide that F of L would not be in the running for my favorite class.

Basics of Interdimensional History was a little better. Many of my floor mates were in the same class. It was also a required class, taught by Taria. Maybe she didn't teach as many classes as Professor Argus, or maybe there were more literature teachers, but Interdimensional History was a much bigger class, closer to two hundred than the twenty in F of L. There was even a deep water trench in the back so mermaids and water sprites could attend. Still, students learned quickly that it's hard to misbehave in front of a telepath. Taria could be strict but she didn't have the same aura of grouchiness that Professor Argus wore like a coat. She had a sense of humor and was very patient, especially to students who stayed after class to ask questions. She was also friendlier outside of class. It would probably be an interesting class if I managed to wrap my head around the subject matter.

Fitness for Life was taught by Coach O'Rater, a leprechaun who was also the football coach, if several classmates weren't playing a practical joke on me. That in mind, I expected to end up playing football or soccer. I was mistaken. No, Coach O'Rater started us out on river dancing, something he apparently did every semester. I was lousy at it, but it was fun, if extremely tiring. Coach O'Rater was not an open and friendly person, and was always scolding someone for various flaws in posture, but he was fair, didn't play favorites, and he laughed a lot.

Math class almost made me break my rule about not reacting when I first saw Professor Pod. A seven-foot centipede who walked upright, shiny black exoskeleton, huge compound eyes, and large front limbs that I knew were poisonous on all centipedes. I'm not terrified of bugs, but I will admit that centipedes always gave me the creeps. Still, I swallowed my scream (not everyone managed that), and actually got used to him and the way he talked (with lots of clicks and whistles mixed in) pretty quickly. He was a little boring and tended to use concepts a little too advanced for the class, but I was good at math so the class shouldn't be too bad.

Music was taught by Medusa. Well, a medusa. Apparently the Greek myth was inspired by one who accidentally slipped into our dimension. Professor Shale was a cool teacher; friendly, laid-back, and passionate about her subject. If one ignored the snakes for hair, the slight green-brown cast to her skin, and the elaborate sunglasses she wore to keep from turning people to stone, she looked very human. One of the first things she mentioned in the first class was that there was a way to counter the whole 'turned into stone' thing, but personally, that was one experiment I was not eager to test. The little snakes in her hair ranged from a few inches to nearly a foot long. They were mostly brown and green patterned and were very lively. Whenever music was playing, which was often, they would dance. It was pretty funny. I'm not musically inclined, but we didn't have to write or even play music, just listen and analyze it. Even though class was at eight in the morning, it was one of my favorites.

My favorite class, no comparison, had to be Biology 1. Good thing, considering it was the foundation for my major. Bio 1 was taught be Doctor Gronk, a large, bright orange troll who was obviously brilliant. To my shock, he had even published some (very well known) texts in my dimension under a pseudonym. Maybe when I went home for Christmas, I could get my copy and see if he'd sign it. Dr. Gronk was friendly and clearly loved working with students, especially those who enjoyed biology. Though, we did have to watch out for pranks.

Apparently there was a lot of pranking among the science division. The lab was incredible and equipped with devices I had never heard of. To make things even cooler, we were starting out by learning how closely different dimensions inhabitants were to each other taxonomically. Bio would be a challenge, but it was one I was definitely looking forward to.

Classes wouldn't be easy, but I was prepared for that. What I wasn't prepared for was the other students. It wasn't how different they could be. I was learning to expect that and it was getting rarer and rarer for me to be caught completely flat-footed. No, it was the other students' reactions to me. It all started with the rumors.

Chapter Five
Rumors and Relationships

I went to public school. I was never popular, but I wasn't a complete outcast either. Mostly, I was kind of invisible. As a result, I was rarely, if ever, grist for the rumor mill. That didn't mean I didn't know how it worked and I definitely knew it when I saw it.

The whispers started two days after my arrival. They would get quiet when I was near, and start up again as I left. Then came the whispers I was meant to hear. Kara, Ilse, and I started to compare the more interesting rumors. Ilse knew the most about rumors, the politics behind them, and how to deal with them. Kara came because the rumors bothered her, probably more than they did me, and laughing at them with me proved I wasn't hurt and she could be friends with me and with some who believed the rumors at the same time.

We all had our favorites. Ilse seemed charmed by the one that claimed I was trying to take over my home dimension and was here so I could be stopped, or (depending on who was telling the story) to raise an army. According to her, I would make a lousy dictator. I'm inclined to agree. Kara preferred the one about my being in some kind of Interdimensional Witness Protection Program. My particular favorite was the one that said I was a descendent of Victor Frankenstein. I can't prove it, but I think Arie started that one. That rumor surfaced the same day I leafed through a copy of Frankenstein in the library, and I know Arie saw me there.

As orientation ended and classes began, Kara and Ilse stopped telling me about the rumors, claiming there was nothing new. They were lying through their slightly pointed teeth. Kara was no good at lying. She couldn't make eye contact and would mumble a lot; very different from her normal cheerful attitude. Ilse was much more subtle, though I did notice she would occasionally lick at her fangs. Since that wasn't something she normally did, it was probably a nervous tic. Had Kara not been involved, Ilse might have fooled me. Except I knew she was lying, because I heard the rumors. They were getting more and more vicious. Still, I pretended to believe them, and they pretended to think I was fooled.

Along with the increasingly nasty rumors was an epidemic of sudden deafness among certain students whenever I tried to talk. Or when I tried to sit next to someone, there was often someone already there, evidently invisible judging from the lack of visible beings showing up later. Most didn't go further than that, but I did have to make sure not to leave any belongings lying around, and avoid walking near certain students to avoid onsets of clumsiness. I could deal with it, but it did get discouraging.

That wasn't to say I didn't have friends, because I did. Ilse was a definite friend, probably my best friend at school. We spent many nights talking, exchanging information about different things, causing me to stay up way too late. Talks with her helped me avoid constantly embarrassing myself with one *faux pas* after another. Not that I didn't still embarrass myself sometimes, but much less often than I might have. When we were alone, she dropped a lot of her formal persona, though Kara was making steady in-roads with her too. Kara was also a good friend. Loyal, friendly, and exuberant. Problem was, she acted the same way with everyone, so I wasn't exactly sure where I stood with her. Denise would sometimes tag along with Kara, but I rarely saw her on her own.

I was also on decent terms with some of the other girls on the floor and a few classmates. It wasn't much, but we'd exchange greetings, talk a bit, and they wouldn't claim the seat next to them belonged to an imaginary friend. Some of them, I know, were just trying not to be rude to my face. But I thought some might, if pressed, even call me a friend. Sort of. So I wasn't Miss Popular. So what? I got overwhelmed if surrounded by people all the time anyway.

Besides, school was too interesting an experience, with animals attending classes, the ongoing prank war between the biology professors and the chemistry professors, and the magic war on our floor, for me to worry much about being unpopular. And then Kara came up with one of her 'brilliant' ideas.

***

It was the Friday of my second week of classes and I was sitting in the lounge trying to finish my Lit homework. I was almost done when Kara bounced in, saw me and grinned. I suddenly felt cold shivers go down my spine.

Kara often acted as if she had some form of ADHD, and I rarely saw her not smiling. Still, both her hyper-ness and her smiles had degrees. For example, her usual level of hyper-ness was about three cups of coffee in an hour hyper. Actually, I'd never seen her drink caffeine, and she seemed to eat less sugar than I did, but that was still how I kept track. At the moment, I would have no trouble believing she had guzzled down three bags of chocolate-covered espresso beans with two liters of Red Bull. Her smile would not have looked out of place on some mad scientist who had just come up with some plan sure to destroy the world.

"Violet, there you are! I was looking for you!"

"You found me. Congratulations." I smiled back warily.

"What are you doing tonight?"

"Homework."

"Besides that?"

"Not much. I was thinking of seeing if Ilse wanted to play some ping pong." The dorm lobby had a ping pong table. At some point during orientation, probably because Ilse said it was low class, Kara talked Ilse and me into trying it. Neither of us had played before, but ended up loving the game. We had played a few more rounds since.

"It's Friday."

"Has been all day. To my knowledge, that doesn't mean I can't play ping pong."

"That's boring."

"I'm boring." I shrugged.

"No, you aren't," Kara sounded exasperated. "Look, Violet, I need a favor."

"Oh?"

"Yeah, I have this friend, you see? He's in my math class. Really nice guy, and his weekend plans are about as boring as yours."

"Hey, I like ping pong. What's your favor?" Kara couldn't be suggesting this. She really couldn't be trying to set me up with a complete stranger, could she? Who was I kidding? Of course she would.

"You two have a lot in common. You're both smart, really nice. I think you could get along great. You could see the durchy game; maybe get a coffee at the café afterwards. It'll be fun."

"You're setting me up on a date with someone I've never met?" I had never really dated in high school. Closest that came was hanging out with friends in groups, and one time a guy asked me to go to the movies with him. Turned out to be him and a group of friends and he didn't say two words to me after we got to the theater. I even had to call my parents for a ride home because he forgot about me. I wasn't big on dating, and I certainly wasn't interested in dating a stranger, particularly on a campus where I was disliked.

Kara frowned. "Doesn't that happen in your dimension?"

"Well, sometimes. But it can be very dangerous too."

The werewolf rolled her eyes. "I wouldn't set you up with someone dangerous. Besides, you're going to be in the middle of campus."

She had a point there. "But I've never met the guy." I don't do well with strangers, particularly when I'm already in a large group.

"You're about to. I told him you'd meet him at eight."

An automatic glance at my watch revealed it was almost seven-thirty. "You said yes without asking me?"

I had started to stand, something Kara took full advantage of, ushering me to my room. "Given half a chance you'd back out. This will be good for you. Come on, you need to get ready."

"Get ready?"

"You can't go on a date like that." She gave me a quick onceover. "Wear your blue sweater. It accentuates your eyes." In my confusion, she got the key from me and unlocked the door. Once in the suite, she steered me to my room. "Hurry, the darker blue sweater, not the powder blue. And tie back your hair, the way you tie back the sides. Then come out so I can do your make-up."

"I don't usually wear make-up."

"That's why I'm doing it."

Ilse wandered out at this point, wondering what all the commotion was about. We must have woken her up. I was a bit nervous, having learned early on that it's not a good idea to wake sleeping vampires. Fortunately, she seemed more curious than upset. "What's all this about?" Ilse rubbed at her eyes.

"Violet has a date."

That woke her up. "You never mentioned a date."

"I didn't know I had a date. Kara, I really don't think this is a good idea."

"Do you trust me?" She sounded a little hurt.

"Yes, of course…"

"And you don't want to hurt his feelings by not showing up, right?"

"No, but…"

"There you go. You don't have time. Hurry. Blue sweater." Kara bounced impatiently. I obeyed, listening to Kara explain. Fortunately, I knew exactly where my sweater was and it didn't take more than a minute or two to fix my hair. It still wasn't quick enough for Kara. I had no sooner stepped out of the room when she dragged me to a chair and started pulling out more make-up than I would have thought possible from a small bag.

"Now, Kara, let's not go overboard." I gripped the chair arms and leaned away.

"It'll be fine. Trust me. Close your eyes." I did so, wondering why I was going along with this. Probably because I didn't have enough friends in Hyde that I could afford to alienate one of my closest. And Kara was so excited about this, I couldn't ruin it just because I was scared. Besides, she had a point about not wanting to hurt anyone's feelings. As soon as I closed my eyes, Kara began applying foundation while holding a cryptic conversation with Ilse.

"This one or this, do you think?"

"Hair that dark? Definitely the second. And this."

"Oh, perfect. Here, choose a lipstick. Yes, I agree. Violet, open your mouth a bit, good, now close. Yes, what do you think?"

"She still needs something. Wait here." A moment later, Ilse returned and I felt a weight on my neck. "You can return it when you come back." Oh, great. Now Ilse was lending me jewelry. Her cheap pieces cost more than all my jewelry put together and probably most of my mother's as well.

"Thank you, Ilse; but I'd rather not borrow your necklace. What if I lose it or it breaks or something?" I tried to be diplomatic about it.

Ilse waved off my concern. "Nothing will happen. Even if it does, don't worry. It's a mere trifle." In other words, it probably cost more than my parents' wedding rings. With maybe my mom's engagement ring thrown in.

"Oh, it's perfect." Kara clapped. "Okay, Violet, time to go, or you'll be late. He'll meet you at the gym. His name is Tim."

Fitness for Life met at the gym, which was how I knew that the quickest route was almost a mile. I had about twelve minutes. Either fortunately or unfortunately, Ilse and Kara were literally pushing me out the door to make sure I got there on time.

"Remember to tell us everything when you get back!" Kara called as I dashed to the elevator. I hadn't even had a chance to see what I looked like. Arie poked her beak out, probably wondering what all the fuss was about. She took one look at me, raised a perfectly groomed, feathery eyebrow, sniffed disdainfully, and shut the door again. Of course that could have meant anything.

I wished I knew more about this guy who Kara had considered a good match for me. I really wished I knew what I looked like. The elevator's shiny doors were not reflective enough to be a true mirror, but I could tell I looked reasonably normal. No gaudy face painting, or extreme colors. That was a slight relief. I also got a look at Ilse's necklace. Several deep blue sapphires and decent sized diamonds in the shape of a starburst. Evidently my initial estimate was far too conservative. This probably cost more than my house.

Before I could freak out about that as well, the elevator opened, letting me off at the first floor. I waved to the RA on duty, Rachael from second floor. "Where are you heading?"

"The durchy game," I called back as I reached the door.

"Have fun." I heard as I left and started sprinting towards the gym. Because of the distance, this quickly became a jog.

There were a lot of people heading into the gym. Hyde might not have sports competitions with other schools, but it did have a thriving inter-mural sport program. Durchy was one of the most popular sports if you excluded the gladiatorial type matches. I had tried to research it once, but got too confused and gave up. Most of the people going in were in groups or obvious couples. No single guys looking confused.

This 'Tim' did know about the date, didn't he? Maybe Kara had pushed him into it, just like she had me. Maybe he had decided not to come. Would that be a relief or a disappointment? Did Tim know I was human? That had become an important consideration when interacting with other students. Most seemed to know or figure out quickly that I was 'the human' but reaction to that varied a great deal. Kara hadn't paid it the slightest heed and expected everyone else to do the same, but not everyone did, and she sometimes seemed oblivious to that. Tim might very well mind that I'm human. Come to think of it, I didn't have a clue what Tim was. Another Were, like Kara, perhaps?

Maybe I missed him. Maybe he was inside already. Maybe he didn't show up. Maybe if I didn't calm down, I would have a panic attack. I took a few deep breaths, trying to force myself to relax. I'd wait ten more minutes. If I couldn't find him by then–

"Excuse me, please. Would you be Violet? I'm Tim." A deep, gentle voice startled me from my musings, proving I hadn't actually managed to relax that much.

I turned, answering, "Yes, I'm Violet. It's nice to… meet… you." My voice trailed off as I caught sight of Tim. *Kara, you could have mentioned he was a yeti!*

Chapter Six
A Date with a Yeti

Long, shaggy white fur tinged with blue, standing about eight and a half feet tall; I had no doubt I was looking at a yeti. That was what my first glance showed me. My second glance, however, revealed intelligent brown eyes, a stance that tried to radiate a non-threatening attitude so much that it had become automatic, and the slightly wary expression on his face as he waited for me to gather my wits and possibly run away screaming.

Instead, I straightened up, my smile only slightly forced. "Did I keep you waiting? I'm sorry, I wasn't given much notice." Tim had come from the direction of the gym. I still thought I had gotten there first, but it was all I could think of to say.

I hadn't realized he was so tense until he relaxed. It made him look almost exactly like a giant teddy bear; a thought I was careful to keep to myself. "I just arrived myself. Yes, our mutual friend can be a force of nature." So he wasn't involved in the idea either. "Shall we go in?" He offered his arm, and I am quite proud of the fact that I took it with no signs of hesitation.

The game wasn't a ticketed event, but there were a lot of people going. I thought we'd have trouble finding seats, but I was mistaken. It appears that one of the quickest ways through a crowd is walking at a yeti's side. Even at Hyde, Tim was one of the larger beings on campus. Crowds melted in front of him, letting us get in and find seats faster than I thought possible.

Alright, if I was on a date with someone who might be as nervous as I was, I should probably try to make small talk, right? "I have to admit, I've never seen a durchy game. I'm not even sure how it's played."

"Athletics are hardly my forte either. Though I do believe I have at least a rudimentary understanding of the basic regulations."

I gave him a sideways look. "You're a Lit major, aren't you?"

Tim laughed, revealing a frightening set of canines. "Guilty as charged. And yourself?"

"Biology, with a concentration in genetics."

"Ah, the building blocks of life." He might have said more, but the game was starting then.

Hyde has no official mascot for many reasons. Considering the diversity of the teams, I imagine getting everyone to agree on a team mascot is tough. So, the teams at Hyde often use colors or numbers as names. Tonight, it was the Blue team versus the Orange team. After a quick whispered conversation, Tim and I decided to root for the Blue team, for the highly thought out reason that we both prefer the color blue over the color orange.

Tim occasionally filled me in on the rules, when he could. Having watched the game, I still don't know the rules; Tim certainly didn't know all the rules. I'm pretty sure no one knows all the rules.

Basic premise involved getting a triangular shaped ball into one of the several goal spots, some on the ground, some floating, which would disappear without warning and show up somewhere else. There were seven people on each team, except for the times when there were nine. That much I could get. Then it got weird. The rules changed depending on the number of letters in the name of the day, the phases of the moon, the tide, whether the goals were North and South, or East and

West, how many flying players there were on a team, and whether or not the ball was yodeling. The yodeling made me glad that I have relatively dull ears compared to most people at Hyde. Tim was clearly wincing. Players who didn't fly wore rollerblades, and everyone had some kind of padded club that seemed to be more for attacking the other team than to direct the ball. In fact, they may well have been using telekinesis to move the ball, because I rarely saw anything directly touch it.

When the game was over, I had to ask who won. So did Tim, which made me feel a little better. But seriously, the score was Indigo to Cricket. Fortunately, referees announced the Orange team to be the winner. Tim and I, as emotionally invested in a Blue victory as we were, looked at each other and shrugged.

By unspoken decision, we waited until the gym emptied out a bit before leaving. I was used to crowds being difficult to travel through, and preferred to avoid them if possible. I wasn't sure of Tim's reasoning, but he didn't seem to like people being afraid of him.

"That was fun. I still don't know how durchy is played, but that was fun," I admitted.

"It was fun. I've played before, and I still have trouble with the rules."

By the time we got outside, most of the crowd had dispersed. We were walking down the path when I heard a loud cracking sound, and saw something move out of my peripheral vision. I jumped backwards, more in surprise than anything else, but I must have tripped on something when I landed because I kept falling. Before I could hit the ground, I found myself actually going up, while leaves brushed by my cheek. It took me a moment to figure out what happened.

A huge branch had come crashing down, and probably would have hit me if I hadn't moved back. Actually it might still have hit me if Tim hadn't caught me and moved me further back.

"Are you alright?" Tim asked.

I took a deep breath. That had been close. "Yes, I think so. Thank you." My voice was steady. I was proud of that.

"Good."

"Um, Tim?"

"Yes?"

"I think you can put me down now." My feet were still about eighteen inches off the ground. Yetis must be really strong.

The fur made it hard to tell, but I think he blushed. "Ah, yes. Of course. My apologies." He set me, very gently, back on the ground. If I had been made of spun sugar, there wouldn't have been a crack.

Well, that was a bit embarrassing. I looked around to see if anyone was staring. Fortunately, most people weren't paying us much attention. Maybe it wasn't that obvious, or maybe they considered the excitement over. There were a few people still watching us. I recognized the other vampire on my floor, I think her name was Celeste.

She mouthed something that I'm pretty sure was asking me if I was okay. I gave her a smile and nod, so she smiled back and left. As she left I spotted Adrian. He had the oddest look on his face, took a few steps towards us, then stopped.

Tim was talking to me. I turned and looked at him. "Are you sure you are alright?" He asked with the air of someone repeating himself.

"Yes, fine. Just a little shook up." It was true, I was getting jittery, and there was no good reason. It was over, no one got hurt. Why was I suddenly so shaky?

"Come, I'll buy you a coffee. That will help."

"I'm fine. Really." C'mon, stupid nerves, knock it off.

He didn't believe me. At least he was nice about it. "Oh, indubitably. But you will feel better with a hot drink in you."

"Well, I'm not one to turn down a free coffee." I smiled at him before taking a look around to see if we were still being watched. We weren't.

I shivered, and it wasn't just nerves. Had it been that cold before? It was still August, but the nights were chilly. Tim noticed and put an arm around me, forcing me to walk close to him. I looked up (and up and up) at him with a questioning look.

"Please, do not think me too forward; but you must have noted the decrease in temperature. As you appear to have neglected a jacket, this is the best way to keep you warm. You risk a bad chill if you don't take precautions." It was much warmer, so I didn't argue with him.

The café was close to the gym, which meant that many of the other students who had gone to the game had the same idea we did. We looked at the mass of people in dismay; I wasn't sure Tim could even fit in there. I could, but it would be a nerve-wracking experience.

"The library has a coffee shop. Maybe they won't be so crowded," I suggested. The library was closer to my dorm anyway. Considering the temperature, I wasn't looking forward to going home without my current fur 'jacket' Last time I was going out at night without a jacket or coat until spring.

"A rather perspicacious idea, I believe." I didn't ask what that meant only because Professor Argus liked to use that word. It seemed to mean 'smart' or 'wise'.

At our speed, the library was about a fifteen-minute walk. We probably could have made it faster if I wasn't half-walking into Tim to stay warm, but other than the cold, it was a nice walk. We talked a little about Tim playing durchy, and I mentioned playing lacrosse. He knew about as much of lacrosse as I knew of durchy. We finished that subject as we got to the library coffee house, which was fortunately, much emptier. We were able to get our coffee and find seats within minutes.

I was surprised at just how interesting a conversationalist Tim was. True, I didn't fully understand his explanation of metaphysical poetry, and I'm not sure how much he got out of my ravings about Gregor Mendel, but we had fun. We talked about everything: classes, sports, Kara, philosophy, literature, durchy, roommates (ours specifically and in general), science, the school, several of the professors, etc.

One thing we didn't discuss, but I inferred anyway, was that being a yeti on campus was not much easier than being a human on campus. I don't think Tim was the only yeti here at the moment, but there clearly weren't many. Tim briefly mentioned something about yetis having a reputation for being not terribly bright. As in, 'do rocks make good food', not terribly bright. That surprised me as Tim was clearly intelligent, possibly smarter than I was.

"I try not to listen to rumors. According to them, I'm a dangerous, delusional megalomaniac who's out to conquer or destroy the world, reveal Hyde to my native dimension, and/or I collect dust bunnies to teach them tricks." The dust bunny rumor was at least partially my own fault. I had been telling Kara and Denise how I had difficulty keeping my room neat, and joked that by the end of the semester, the dust bunnies would take over. It was Denise who suggested I train them to clean up the room. Two days later, I was hearing rumors about an army of dust bunnies.

Tim chuckled. "Then shall we defy rumors and expectations together?"

"Sounds like fun. We're not the only ones you know. According to stereotype, Ilse should be imperial, commanding, cold and unfeeling, and she's really not. And Kara!"

"Yes, Kara is Kara. Definitely beyond explanation."

Even at Hyde, werewolves were expected to be aggressive, territorial, and isolationist. Kara seemed to be making a determined effort to be friends with everyone on campus, and had the philosophy that her room was there to invite friends over. She was a little more considerate about other people's rooms. Also, I had never seen or even heard of her being angry. I wouldn't tell anyone, ever, but I thought she was closer to a were-golden retriever.

Ilse didn't defy the usual stereotypes on first meeting like Kara did, but when she got comfortable with someone, it was obvious. Still, at least in Ilse's case, I could see why someone who didn't know her might believe the tales. But that was why it was stupid to judge someone from first impressions.

"Yes, we can but be ourselves, regardless of what others assume." Tim took a sip of coffee, grimacing slightly. Not surprising, it was probably as cold as mine by now.

"This above all, to thine own self be true." I quoted, feeling probably more pleased than was warranted to quote Shakespeare to a Lit major.

"Indeed, the Bard usually does say it best."

"Excuse me." We both looked up at the squid-armed barista. "We're closing now."

"Already? I thought you didn't close until two. Oh, it is two." I looked at my watch. Wow, when did it get that late? The café was open twenty-four hours, as was the library proper, but the coffee shop in the library closed from two a.m. to ten a.m.

"*Tempus fugit,*" Tim sighed, standing up and taking my trash.

I blinked. "When did you learn Latin? And why wasn't it translated by the spell?"

Tim smiled, ushering me out. "Did you understand that phrase before coming here?"

"Yes."

"That's why it didn't translate. You already understood. I learned it before coming as well. Through a tourist, actually."

Okay, that made some sense. Especially why it didn't translate. I was still a little surprised that he had picked up a little Latin before coming here. Oh well.

"Let me escort you to your dorm. Price hall?"

"Yeah, sure. Thanks."

I took a deep breath as we got outside. Which I regretted because it was about forty-five degrees. It was much warmer walking with Tim, something I was grateful for. But now I was really nervous.

One of the things encouraged during orientation was to learn the mating and courting cultures of the various beings on campus. It helped avoid mistakes where one thought they were friends where another thought they were practically engaged or equivalent. I hadn't spent much time studying that, and had barely skimmed the section on yetis. One thing I did recall, while we were talking at the coffee house, was that yetis didn't do much casual dating. Two dates and you were practically engaged. What was Kara thinking?

I had a great time with Tim tonight, and liked the idea of having him as a friend. But I was not ready to get serious with anyone, particularly someone I could never possibly introduce to my parents. There was so much difference, I doubted I could manage. Besides there was no chemistry. But I didn't want to hurt him either.

Alright, calm down. Just because yetis don't usually do much casual dating doesn't mean he's interested in getting serious either. He had been pushed into the evening too. Don't panic until there's a reason.

Tim did walk me home, all the way to the lobby. Was it my imagination, or did he look a little nervous too? What do I say? "Tim-"

"Violet-" We started at the first time.

"You go first." Again in unison.

This time I just shut up and looked at him. After a moment of patting down patches of fur, he began. "Violet, I would like you to know that tonight was truly a delightful experience. I hope you feel the same." I nodded encouragingly. "I am most thankful that Kara arranged this, as I am not certain when or if we might have met otherwise." He took a deep breath. "I hope that we will remain friends-"

"You want to just be friends?" I interrupted without thinking, then I blushed. That may have come out a bit too strong.

"I think that might be for the best. I do hope you will not be offended."

"Oh, good! I mean, no. No offence taken." I stammered out, hoping I wasn't offending him.

Tim smiled again. "Then, until we meet again; goodnight, Violet."

"Goodnight." Just as I had stopped blushing, I started over again, as he kissed my hand. No one had ever done that before.

I watched him leave before going upstairs. It was late enough that the RA wasn't on duty anymore, but I was clearly not the only one awake. I wasn't surprised Ilse was waiting up for me, and only slightly surprised Kara was there. I shouldn't have been, though. "Don't you have class in half an hour?" I asked Ilse.

"I do indeed. Which is why I am glad you returned before I had to leave. I might have had difficulty concentrating if you hadn't." Ilse sounded amused as I returned her necklace.

"Wow, two-thirty. That's a late night for you," Kara teased, leaning on the edge of her seat. "So, how did it go?"

I had ducked into the bathroom to wash off my make-up and brush my teeth. Wow, I really wish I had known I looked that good before I went out. When I came back out, they were still waiting for an answer. I gave them a huge smile. "Orange won. Goodnight." With that, I went to my room, shut the door, and went to bed, ignoring cries of protest.

***

Ilse, for whatever reason, was willing to drop the subject completely. Maybe she considered it rude to pry. Maybe she assumed if I wanted to talk about it, I would. Maybe she wasn't that curious, though I doubted that.

Maybe she was afraid that if she seemed too interested Kara would arrange a date for her. Whatever the reason, when I thanked her the next day for lending me her necklace, she accepted the thanks gracefully and other than asking if I had a good time, didn't ask a single question about the night before. Though she did say she'd listen if I wanted to talk about it.

Kara, sweet girl that she was, had never learned the art of subtlety. She spent two days almost hounding me for information and getting nowhere. Probably not my best personality trait, but I can get awfully stubborn when I feel pushed. I wasn't mad at her, if fact, part of me was at least a little grateful. I had made a new friend out of the deal. I think Ilse finally went and talked to her. Monday, Kara actually came and apologized.

She looked contrite, sheepish, and possibly a trifle depressed. I had never seen her look anywhere near that upset. Before I could ask what was wrong, she started to talk. "Violet, I'm sorry for putting you in what may have been a difficult situation. I just figured you two would have fun together. You have a number of things in common, you're both nice people, and it seemed like it would work. I just forced things together without thinking it through. I do that sometimes. I didn't mean any harm. But looking back, you obviously weren't comfortable with it, and maybe he wasn't either. I should have just mentioned the possibility to the two of you, instead of making plans and forcing you to go along. Are you mad at me?"

At this point, I was willing to say almost anything to get her to stop seeming so sad. It was just wrong. I could hear a few of Ilse's phrases in the apology but the sincerity was pure Kara. But there was one more question. "Did you know that yetis rarely do casual dating?"

She winced a little. "Sort of. Tim didn't seem in a hurry to court anyone, so I didn't think one date would lead to anything permanent. But I knew it was a possibility."

"Yeah, really, really not ready for marriage yet." I was eighteen. I didn't even want to think about that yet. "No, I'm not mad. But please don't try to arrange my love life again?"

"Deal. But you had fun?" Some of the old Kara exuberance was peeking through, like the sun through clouds.

I sighed. "Yes, Kara, I had fun."

"And…?"

"And I'm pretty sure he did too."

"And..?"

"And what?"

"Are you going to see him again?"

"As a date? No, probably not. We had fun, but there was absolutely no chemistry. We decided to just be friends. Before you ask, it was a mutual decision."

Kara sighed. "Oh, well. I guess it's not too surprising. You made a new friend at least. That's good. So, what were you doing out until two-thirty in the morning? Violet? Where are you going? Violet!"

***

I didn't see Tim again until the following Thursday at lunch. It was a bit odd; I usually had dinner with Ilse, as long as I was willing to wait until about nine or ten. I often met up with Kara and Denise for breakfast after my eight o'clock on Tuesdays and Thursdays, and a similar time on other days. But I never seemed to run into anyone I was on friendly enough terms to join for lunch. Unfortunately, lunch was also the most crowded time in the cafeteria, so it was difficult to find a table.

This time I lucked out and managed to quickly snag a table as the previous occupants were leaving. I hadn't been there two minutes when I spotted Tim weaving around, looking for something.

I waved at him while swallowing my chili. When he looked in my direction, I asked, "Hey, do you need a seat?" Surprisingly enough, he actually heard me over all the background noise. Either that or he was good at guessing.

After making sure I had no objections, he sat down very gingerly. I think he was a trifle paranoid. While the table and chairs weren't designed for someone of his height and probable weight, there were sturdy, just not necessarily the most comfortable. There were a few tables that were specifically designed for beings of vastly different size or shapes, but the ones for the larger students were full. "Thank you. I was wondering where I might find room. I also wondered when we might meet again."

I smiled at him. "Glad to see you again, too." He seemed almost a little surprised that I was happy to see him again. Perhaps I had come across as a bit rude when I was so eager to just be friends. I hadn't meant to be.

Meal times at Hyde could be an adventure. I had learned quickly that it wasn't always a good idea to pay much attention to what others around me ate. Kara was particularly bad, as the Were in her didn't like cooked meat, and she wasn't a vegetarian. Ilse's was fine as long as I didn't think about what was in those little foil packets. Though I had learned it wasn't all human blood.

Apparently vampires can drink the blood of any non-vampire sentient being. Students could earn money by donating blood for that purpose. A thought that made me extremely grateful for my scholarship.

Denise had fairly normal eating habits except for her tendency to drink salad dressing, and put relish on almost everything. Even chocolate cake and ice cream. Despite knowing it was a bad idea, I was suddenly very curious about what yetis ate. The answer, today anyway, was some kind of a green stew with a fishy scent, and a cherry snow cone. And coffee, of course.

Lunch was fun. A lot like our date, actually, where we discussed everything and nothing and lots in between. One of the things we discussed was our schedules. It turned out that most days we were both free for lunch at close to the same time. While we didn't come out and say we'd get together for lunch, that was definitely the implication. That would be nice.

Altogether it was a very pleasant time. Unfortunately, it was mostly overshadowed by what happened almost immediately afterwards.

Chapter Seven
Tricks, Traps, and Illusions

Tim left to get to class, but I had an hour to kill. I left the cafeteria mentally debating if I should go to the library or my dorm when I bumped into Ilse. Almost literally. "Ilse? What are you doing here? It's daytime." It would take something serious to bring her out in the middle of the day. But what? She should be asleep.

"There you are! I need to talk to you. It's urgent."

This was odd. "Alright, what's up?"

"Not here. Meet me in the gym. Third floor, the large room at the end of the H wing. Make certain you aren't followed." Then, after looking around suspiciously, she left, presumably for the gym.

I'm not a suspicious person. I've been accused of being too trusting. Many, many times. I was suspicious right now. Ilse, who shouldn't even be awake right now, was pulling some kind of cloak and dagger stunt, wanting to meet with me secretly? That didn't make sense.

Was that even Ilse? Something like one being in twenty-five was supposed to be capable of shifting or using illusions to look like someone else well enough to fool an observer visually. Magic users could use spells to see through that kind of thing, Weres and many shifters could often smell the difference, and the rest of us could buy certain enchanted items to let us see through illusions. Unfortunately, they were unbelievably expensive.

On the other hand, Ilse was part of the ruling vampire class. I knew she knew how to be covert, but why would she need to draw me in? Why would she even want to? Anyway, Ilse or not, I wasn't going to get any answers standing around here.

I didn't spend much time making sure I wasn't followed. For one thing, that would probably draw attention. For another, I doubted I'd be good at spotting tails anyway. I did glance around a few times, when I could do it discretely. No one seemed to be paying much attention to me.

As I got to the gym, I wondered why she would tell me to meet her there in such a short time period. If someone was trying to follow her or me, the fact that we talked briefly and then both directly headed off to the same place, separately, would probably seem suspicious. Well, maybe not if we went to our dorm room. Why not meet in the dorm room, anyway? Of course the fact that she was up at all was unusual but wouldn't it make sense to pretend she was meeting me to go somewhere and then we went to wherever it was safe to talk, together? Then again, what did I know about spy stuff?

Getting to the gym wasn't a problem. Finding the third floor wasn't hard. Finding the H wing, that was a little more difficult. Finding the last room in the H wing; that was a challenge. Somewhere along the line, when the school was being designed or redesigned, or being rebuilt, someone fell in love with mazes, labyrinths, and possibly the works of M. C. Escher. Or maybe Escher attended Hyde and was inspired by the architecture. The dorms, well, Price Hall at least, was straight forward. The library was a labyrinth, though I had learned how to keep the bookcases from surrounding me. This floor was even worse. It didn't help that a side effect of sharing dimensions meant that many of the buildings were actually at least a little bigger on the inside than they were on the outside. On the plus side, I was now sure that no one was following me.

When I got to the room, I didn't see Ilse anywhere. Maybe she was inside. I peered in to check. The room was completely dark, and there was no light switch by the door. "Ilse, are you here? Where's the light? I can't see in this." Maybe she could, but I couldn't.

I thought I heard something inside, so I walked in, still feeling for the light. Then the door slammed behind me. "Ilse?" This was such a bad idea. "Ilse, are you here?"

Something from the floor or the wall threw me what had to be at least a few feet. I was still on my feet, but only barely. What was that? "What's going on? Who's there?"

My only answer was a flash of light that I only identified as a laser after moving away from it, with a rather hysterical screech. Okay, it was definitely not Ilse I ran into. Unless Ilse secretly wanted me dead. Awkwardly side-stepping something that sounded suspiciously like a wheeled saw, I realized where I had to be. Hyde had some advanced training rooms for some of the strongest beings on campus. Humans were definitely not on that list. I had to get out of here before I got killed. A spurt of flames less than a foot away forced me to back up, screaming. I didn't know where the door was or what the terrain to get there would be. But I couldn't stay here.

Risking a dash to the wall I hoped the door was in, I was knocked off my feet when something hit me square in the back. It stung like blue fury, but I didn't seem to have any broken bones, or even blood. I tried to push myself up, but all my muscles seized painfully.

Come on, Violet. Get up and run. You've been hurt worse than this playing lacrosse. Get up and run! I staggered up and hobbled. Nothing came out of the darkness at me before I reached the wall, though I could hear threats in various directions. I found the wall, mostly with my nose, but unfortunately, not the door. Left or right?

I tried right first, flinching at every noise. Finally my wall met the next one. Okay, try left. Was it my imagination or was the floor tilting? It had to be my imagination. I revised my opinion as I started skidding. Hands on the wall, I managed to stop my skid as I found the door.

Handle, handle, where was the handle? Found it! And it did absolutely nothing. The room must lock when in use. "Help! Let me out!" I pounded on the door. Come on, *someone* hear me. I would almost certainly be in trouble for being somewhere I obviously wasn't supposed to be. But I could deal with that, with any trouble I got in… just as long as I didn't die here! I rattled the handle, pounded on the door, and screamed as loud as I could. Why wasn't anyone doing anything?

I could hear something building up behind me. I was going to die. "Someone let me out!" No one was going to come. The noise came closer. Growling, metallic, deadly. Despite the dark, my eyes shut of their own accord. I braced myself, just feeling it come closer. It was right on top of me. I tensed, waiting.

Then it stopped. The room was quiet, and just felt less threatening. Before I could react to that, the door opened and an arm literally dragged me out. Green eyes, black hair, all black clothing. And very angry. "What were you doing in there?" Adrian demanded. He had rescued me. He also showed a disturbing ability to be around when things got weird.

"Nearly getting myself killed, apparently!" I snapped back, trying to stop shaking. Come on, legs. Time to stand. Then I realized I was being rude to someone who had probably just saved my life. "Thank you for your help."

He ignored both comments. "You aren't even supposed to be back here. The training rooms are far too advanced for humans. You could have been killed."

"I didn't know what it was!"

"Whatever possessed you to go in there?" Why was he so angry with me?

"Long story." He snorted and kept staring at me. "Incredibly bad advice?"

"Be more careful who you trust."

"I'll remember that, thank you." That was still a little snappish, partly because the adrenalin was wearing off, and partly because, as a direct result of the former, the pain in my back was coming back. I straightened with a small noise. It wasn't a moan or a groan or anything like that. Just a small gasp. Well, maybe a cry.

Adrian muttered something that sounded decidedly rude under his breath. "You're hurt," he accused.

"Got hit with something. Threw me a few feet, I think. I'm fine."

"Do you know what hit you? Or if it has any secondary or lasting effects?"

"No, not really?" It came out more of a question than a statement.

"Probably a magical blast of some kind. Means it could be more damaging than you know. Have you been to the infirmary?" I looked at him blankly. He just pulled me out, how could I have gone anywhere? He rolled his eyes. "I mean, since starting Hyde."

"Oh. No, not yet."

"Do you know where it is?" He ground out, like I was an exasperating child.

"Yes?" I wasn't completely sure, but he was annoyed enough, and I wanted to get away before I completely broke down in hysterics. I'd find it on my own.

Adrian looked skeptical. "Which way?"

I pointed in what seemed the most likely direction, though I had gotten so turned around in the gym that I wasn't sure where anything was. "That way?"

"You don't have a clue, do you?"

"Not really."

He growled under his breath. "I can take you part way, but then you're on your own. When you get there, try to make sure you see either Dr. Zyloas or Nurse Persephone. Either of them will fix you up without asking too many questions. Just tell them you think you got hit by a random magic blast. Happens a lot. Probably don't want to tell them you were in the gym, certainly not here. Do not, under any circumstances, tell them I was here." There was iron in the last part as he escorted me out of the gym. Well, more of dragged me, but since my feet weren't working properly, it was probably understandable.

"Why not?"

"That's not your concern." I was going to ask more, but he cut me off. "Consider it payment for saving your life. And I *did* just save your life. You didn't run into me. I was never here."

Was it just me, or did this day just keep getting weirder. I didn't think it was me. Why was he so adamant about this? Maybe he wasn't supposed to be there either. Or maybe he didn't want flack about helping the human. Well, in any case, it seemed harmless enough. He could have just left me to die, and no one would have ever known. At least he wasn't calling in a life debt. Many on campus would have. "Fine. I wasn't there. You weren't there. Neither of us were there."

"Good." We were outside by now and he was, very briskly, taking me down back paths. Just as we were getting to a clearer area, he stopped. "That's the back of the library, there. Head in that direction until you get to the huge oak tree. Turn right, keep to the path, past the science center and the cafeteria. When the path forks, take the left one almost to the edge of the island. Just on the waterfront is the infirmary. It's marked. Stay on the path, sometimes there are hazards on the sides." He pointed out various directions in turn. "Remember, Dr. Zyloas or Nurse Persephone. You need to be careful where you go. Hyde holds dangers for all of us, but perhaps for you most of all." His eyes were out of focus when he said that, like he was thinking. Then they refocused on me. "Why are you still here? Go. Don't stop if you can help it. Scram!"

I scrammed. As I was leaving, I thought I heard him say, "Alright, Allison. You win." But when I turned to look, he had disappeared.

The directions he gave turned out to be less complicated than I had initially feared. The distance was also less than I was afraid of. Though not so close that I wasn't highly tempted to stop and rest a few times. I resisted the urge though. Adrian was right. I had no idea what I had been hit with or what the effects were. Orientation taught us that when dealing with unknown magical effects, you wanted to get them taken care of as quickly as possible. Normally, I wouldn't have had a problem, but my back was really throbbing.

Fortunately, just as I was about to ignore the danger and rest a minute anyway, I spotted a squat two story building, clearly marked 'Griffin Infirmary'. Hoping that didn't mean it was only for griffins, I went in. Sure enough, it was the general infirmary. I was glad it was labeled as I wasn't sure I could brave another mystery place.

The infirmary was on the waterfront, some distance from the rest of the school. Perhaps it was so it could accommodate aquatic students more easily, perhaps it was to have some distance from the normal craziness of the school. It was noticeably bigger on the inside than the outside, more so than the other buildings I had seen so far. It was also painted in fluorescent pinks, oranges, and greens which I'm sure was for some better reason than to keep people out of the infirmary. Or making those who had to be there wish they were blind. Don't ask me what that reason was though.

Hyde had made me pretty open-minded. My favorite class was taught by a troll. Another class by a giant centipede. Last night, while waiting for my vampire roommate to wake up, I spent hours playing card games with a werewolf (Kara), a shifter (Denise), a dragon named Phyna, and a leprechaun named Veronica. I figured there wasn't a whole lot that could surprise me anymore. All the same, finding out that Dr. Zyloas was an actual zombie was enough to give me pause. Was that sanitary, even if she didn't have open wounds?

Therefore, I was very relieved to be in the examination room (which wasn't quite as blinding as the waiting room) being treated by Nurse Persephone, instead. I wasn't sure what she was, but she clearly wasn't a zombie. Instead, she was a bright medium-blue humanoid with magenta hair, standing about six foot tall. This was far more typical of the school.

"A random magical blast, huh?" She asked in one of those 'what are you trying to pull' voices.

I really hoped Adrian wasn't setting me up for something. "That's right." I came so very close to telling her everything, but I bit my tongue. Literally. Maybe it was some kind of power of hers. Or maybe I'm just lousy at keeping secrets.

Her eyes glowed white for a moment. "Pain centered in the middle of your lower back, scrapes on your hands and left knee?"

Huh, hadn't even noticed the scrapes. I sure did now, though. "Yeah, sounds right."

She circled around me, and touched my back, right where I had been hit. A weird tingling exploded in me and my back arched involuntarily as it changed to a watery feeling. I think I moaned as my muscles went limp.

"Better?"

"I think…" A few test stretches. "Yeah, a lot better. Thanks."

She nodded. "It wouldn't have intensified, but it would have lingered for hours, possibly a day or two. Treat any stiffness as usual muscle soreness, but come back if there's actual pain. The scrapes aren't serious. Do you have any antibiotic ointment? Good. My removing the magic blast will help them heal slightly faster, and you can take your normal over-the-counter pain medication if you need to. Alright, be careful and avoid magic blasts."

"Oh, believe me, I intend to." I stood up and my eyes feel on the bright red fire extinguisher by the bed.

"Huh, I haven't seen any fire safety measures anywhere else in Hyde."

Nurse Persephone followed my gaze. "Most of the campus has sufficient fire suppression wards to prevent damage to anything serious, while still allowing fair freedom for any fire users. However, fire users have less control when sick or injured, and the fire suppression wards interfere with the healing wards of the infirmary. There are limits to how much magic can be layered on to a place or object."

"Makes sense." Plus now I knew the campus was safe in the case of fire. Maybe. I seemed to recall reading in the school's history, there had been a big fire that caused most of the school to have to be rebuilt a couple hundred years ago. Well, perhaps they now had upgraded wards.

"Did you need anything else?" Nurse Persephone spoke up, reminding me that I was still staring into space.

"Oh, no. Thank you again." I was more than glad to get out of that color monstrosity. Besides, I really needed to talk to Ilse.

***

While it was probably a ludicrous thought, it struck me as unfair that after all this, I was still in time to go to class. Not that I wanted to be late to Foundations of Literature; Professor Argus was so harsh about punctuality. But it just seemed so anti-climatic. One hour I'm nearly killed, I think, and the next I have to go to class and pretend everything is normal. I wasn't that successful. I even tried to tell myself to skip class because I was in shock. Problem was, I didn't think I was in shock. A little jittery, colder than usual, but I was thinking clearly, mostly about how it was a bad idea to skip class.

F of L, not my best class on a good day, seemed even more obscure and esoteric than usual. If Arie's reaction was any indication, I was denser than usual, as well. I certainly felt stupid.

Math, which was right after, went a bit easier. There was no class discussion to participate in, and I already knew the principle we were working on. Besides, I could work from the book as easily as I could from the lecture. Maybe even easier.

Finally, after endless lifetimes, both classes were finished and I could hide in my room. My drive to talk to Ilse hadn't diminished at all, but she wasn't likely to wake up for hours yet. I considered, very briefly, waking her before deciding that I really wasn't in a hurry to visit the infirmary again. Still, I did hate waiting. Especially when I was already so keyed up.

Staring at her door, trying to bore holes in the wood through glare alone wasn't working. Not very productive either. So, I decided to do my homework. Although, to be accurate, it was more like flipping through pages, staring at them randomly, and then flipping through more pages. Giving up on this, I went back to staring at her door. When I got bored of that, I went back to 'doing homework'.

I have no idea how many times the cycle repeated itself, but I was at the staring at the door part when the door gave way to a not-quite-awake Ilse, rubbing her eyes. Catching sight of me, Ilse quickly woke the rest of the way up. "Violet? Whatever is wrong?"

"Were you awake at all today?"

She frowned slightly, thinking. "I do not believe so. I certainly didn't leave the room. Why?"

"Are you sure?"

"Absolutely certain. Why ever would you ask?"

"Because someone wearing your face tried to kill me today."

Chapter Eight
Gathering Information

I may or may not have exaggerated the case, but it certainly got Ilse's attention. I never even saw her move. One moment she was at her door, the next, she was perched over the couch armrest, trying to ask me a hundred questions at once. Rather than answer each one individually, and probably confusing us both, I told her everything from the beginning. Everything except who pulled me out. I just said that someone passing by pulled me out and told me how to get to the infirmary. Ilse was silent as I explained, her features becoming more and more tense. At the end, she looked like someone had chiseled her out of granite.

"You were very lucky. Those rooms are completely soundproof to almost all of the school. How did this passerby even know you were there?"

"Soundproof? Really?" I thought he heard me scream. If he hadn't heard me, then how did he know? He certainly wasn't surprised to see me, or that I was in trouble.

Ilse dropped the question, seeing I had no explanation. "Perhaps a telepath or empath. Or someone who could hear a little. It matters not. Someone imitated me to lure you into danger. I do not like this. Not one bit. Rumors are one thing, but you could have been killed. And they used me to do it!" She kept licking at her fangs, and her fingers formed into fists until she noticed and forcibly relaxed. Then as she stopped paying attention, her hands fisted up again. "You need to report this."

"Who would I report? They looked like you."

"Point. If we are unable to identify anyone, the school might have trouble narrowing it down as well. Hmm. The person who rescued you, would you be able to identify him again?"

"Why?"

"Because, perhaps it wasn't an attempt to kill you, but just to scare you. If so, then there would have to be someone to put a stop to things. Your 'rescuer' may well be in on the whole plot. If you can identify him-"

"If he wasn't under an illusion too." I doubted that was the case. While I certainly couldn't claim to know Adrian well, he seemed to be acting mostly the same as before. Besides, I had promised not to tell anyone he rescued me.

Ilse deflated. "Again, you have a point. So basically, we have nothing."

I nodded sadly.

Ilse worried her lip, before coming to a decision. "Wait here." She came back a moment later, carrying a small red velvet bag, like a fancy jewelry bag. "Wilhelm gave me this as a going away present. It's a fortune stones set."

"A what?"

"A way of casting lots. Trying to predict the future, answer questions, etc."

"Kind of like tarot cards?" I figured she was more likely to know about that than a Magic Eight Ball. Ilse nodded. "You actually believe that?" Ilse's eyebrow rose. "Sorry, didn't mean it quite like that. I just, well, you don't seem the type to believe in that kind of thing."

The vampire ignored me, shaking up the pouch and pouring two gems into her hand. "Hmm, the smoky one, that's metal. It signifies conflict. That's the major stone. The minor one, the clear, that's balance. Together, it could mean that the balance is changing or that we have to maintain the balance."

Personally, I thought that seemed far too vague to be useful. Was there ever a time when there wasn't conflict, or the 'balance' wasn't changing? Still, no point in offending Ilse. "So, how does it work? The fortune stones?"

Apparently that was the right question. Ilse beamed as she poured the rest of the stones into her hand. Each stone was a different color with a symbol engraved on it. The only ones I could have guessed were the wavy lines on the blue stone for water and the scale for balance. "This one is fire. A danger sign, warning that problems will soon occur." She discarded the orange stone and picked up a green one. "This is earth. It stands for strengthening foundations or defenses, sometimes it means finishing a major project. The blue is water, a warning to be cautious. The red is blood. Time to expand, do something new. Air is this yellow one, something good is about to happen. To use them, I start with them all in the pouch, think of my question or dilemma, and then pour two into my hand. The first to fall is the major stone, while the second is the minor, to modify the first."

Ilse had told me a little about vampire folklore, and leant me a book to learn more, but I hadn't had time to read it yet. I had learned that those were the traditional elements in vampire lore, with an emphasis on balance. So, I wasn't terribly surprised they were part of a vampire divining set. Still, I didn't lend it much credence.

"What do you think?" Ilse asked.

"Of the stones? They're very pretty." They were pretty. I just wasn't ready to credit them with knowing the future.

"Thank you. But I meant the attack."

"I think we've spent nearly an hour getting nowhere. Before you woke up, I spent several hours with my mind going 'round in circles. It's time to take a break. Let's get some dinner." Ilse was showing some of her hunger tells, like darting eyes and licking her lips; and I was starving. Usually I had something light in the late afternoon to tide me over until Ilse woke up. Today, I had been so preoccupied that I hadn't even thought about it.

"Dinner? You can think about eating? Now?"

"I've had almost seven hours to deal with this. Whatever stuck Jell-O in my legs wore off hours ago. Never mind, human reference. The point is, you're hungry, I'm hungry. Taking a break to eat won't change what happened. Maybe we'll have some new ideas after a break and some food." I was actually beginning to think of an idea, but I needed time and luck to pull it off.

Ilse muttered something in Romanian, I think, that the translation spell didn't quite pick up, but we left for the cafeteria. I'm pretty sure that Ilse was trying to keep an eye on me, even after we split up. If so, her task was easier because there were a lot fewer students than normal in my section. Yes, it was after ten, one of the quieter times, but it wasn't usually this empty either. For a change, I made it to 'our' table before Ilse did. We were both a little surprised but Ilse figured out the explanation first.

"Ah, yes. Tonight is the full moon. Most Weres won't be here."

"What do they do about full moon?" I had been curious for a while, but wasn't sure it would be right to ask Kara. While she was very open and honest about most things, every once in a while something would affect her the wrong way, and she'd get all quiet. Ilse, at least, was very used to my dumb questions.

"To my understanding, when in a non-Were community, they take a powerful herbal mixture that makes them sleep through the night. It's called *zealopor*. Kara takes it; I've seen it in her room.

"Are they asleep right now?"

"Some might be, but most are unlikely to be. Weres simply are not very hungry the day of full moon."

"That's odd. I remember Kara saying it took a lot of energy to change. Shouldn't they be especially hungry today?"

"One might think, but the fact is; while their minds know they shall spend the night asleep; their bodies expect to be hunting. Tomorrow they'll be ravenous. Wiser ones make a point to eat well today anyway. It mitigates some of the effects." Ilse paused, then looked at me. "I know you usually break fast with Kara in the mornings. You may wish to avoid that tomorrow. Or at least be very cautious around her until after she's eaten. Weres are near their most dangerous when hungry."

Like vampires? I thought but knew better than to say. Ilse tried to keep it under control, but I had learned early on, that it was best not to say anything… questionable about vampires in front of her. She got huffy about it. Besides, it was sound advice.

"What about when they aren't in a non-Were community? Like at home? Would they take the zel-op-er then?"

"Zealopor. No, according to our ambassadors, most prefer to spend the night awake and hunting when possible."

We finished dinner and left the cafeteria. "I'll walk you back to the dorm," Ilse said.

"You usually do."

Ilse didn't say anything to that. We were passing the science building when I saw the chance to put my plan into action.

We happened to pass Adrian. I nodded to him, and while he didn't nod back, his look was intense enough for Ilse to notice. Once we were (hopefully) out of earshot, she turned to me. "An acquaintance of yours?"

"Sort of. I've seen him around a few times. I think his name is Adrian." I mentioned when I'd seen him other than today at the gym.

Ilse had extensive training not to give away her emotions easily. But I was still very certain she was angry. "I don't like this. He could be stalking you. Give me a few days, I'll find out some information about him."

I smiled and thanked her. That had worked perfectly. Ilse had contacts everywhere. If he had been hiding under a rock for the past five years, Ilse probably knew someone who could tell her what kinds and the names of the insects he shared it with. All I had to do was wait.

***

It took longer than Ilse had expected to get the information she wanted. What she anticipated to take two or three days ended up taking nearly a week. It didn't take nearly that long for me to decide that Adrian hadn't been stalking me before, but he definitely was now.

The first time I noticed anything was the next day, when I got out of history and happened to spot him in the hallway. He didn't look at me; in fact, he seemed to be examining something on the wall. For all I knew, he was counting windows. I made a mental note to tell Ilse, since she had made me promise to keep her informed, but otherwise ignored him. He stopped counting windows or whatever he was doing when I left, and we exited the building about the same time.

I tried telling myself it was a coincidence, but even I didn't believe it. Especially not when he followed me to the library, sat three or four tables away, staring at a book I'm sure he wasn't reading, only to leave when I did. Subtle, he was not.

I was supposed to meet Tim for lunch, but I wanted to lose my shadow first. Going back to my dorm was partially successful. Adrian couldn't come in the girls' dorm without being let in by a girl, and didn't even try, but didn't leave either. I figured it was because he could see me in the lobby. So I took the elevator to my floor and watched from the balcony of the lounge. I did a lot of staring at my watch, mentally urging him to leave. I was going to be late. Finally, after almost seven minutes, he wandered off, apparently satisfied I wasn't coming back out yet. Or maybe he had class or something.

I wanted to hurry up and leave as soon as he started to go, but I forced myself to wait until he was almost out of sight. I was late meeting Tim, enough so that he had been slightly concerned. This grew to greatly concerned when I explained why I was late.

"I could talk to him. Convince him to leave you alone." Tim gave me a smile that was probably supposed to be reassuring. The fork he had torn in half length-wise before crumpling into a ball, told me otherwise.

I smiled. "I'm sure I'll be fine." Adrian wasn't going to do anything in the middle of a crowd, and hadn't done anything to hurt me when he had the opportunity. I certainly wasn't pleased to be followed, but I doubted it was dangerous.

Hopefully it was an isolated incident. I considered waking Ilse up to tell her everything, but decided against it. It would take too much time to wake her up, tell her, and calm her down before Bio. When I spotted him in the hallway after Bio, I wondered if I had made a mistake. He followed me to the gym, but was gone when Fitness was over.

While I didn't see Adrian for the rest of the day, I dutifully reported everything to Ilse and Kara, who had heard about my new shadow and wanted to know more. Kara thought it was romantic. Ilse thought it was worrisome.

Over the weekend, I stayed pretty close to the dorm, and barely saw him at all. On Monday, however, Adrian was again outside waiting for me after History and Bio, went to lunch when I did, sitting a few tables away and ignoring Tim glaring at him. He even showed up at the café when I went on an impulse trip. All without ever saying a word to me or making eye contact. Kara agreed that maybe it was a bit spooky. Ilse offered to bite him.

Within a couple days, Adrian had proved to be consistently nearby whenever I finished History, Music, Biology, and Math, occasionally the other two classes, and sometimes when I went to class as well. He was also around a disturbingly high number of times when I went out for meals, library trips, walks around campus, etc. Most of which were not planned in advance, or at least varied in time. I was beginning to wonder when he went to class. Even if he took night classes, he would have to sleep sometimes, wouldn't he? How did he always know when I was leaving anyway? Had he slipped a tracer on me, or maybe a magical equivalent?

Kara got concerned enough to encourage the girls on my floor to walk with a partner when we went out. Safety in numbers. No one said anything, probably because it was hard not to like Kara, but everyone knew why she was doing it. When I went out at night, it was almost always with Ilse. During the day, I usually had Kara and/or Denise offering to walk with me. Phyna and the ice elemental twins (who I still couldn't tell apart), walked with me sometimes too. I had cut down on unnecessary travel, which I'm sure helped.

I was grateful for their care, their help, I really was. It was very kind of them. But honestly, it could be a little grating sometimes. I never needed a lot of interaction with others, and constantly being surrounded with people was a bit much. But the alternative was staying in my room, or at least my dorm. I got restless. Sometimes, very restless. I hated having to schedule my whole life around this.

Was Adrian even a threat? He had at least two opportunities to do nothing and let me get hurt, and each time he had interfered. Right now, yeah, his behavior was disconcerting, but it wasn't threatening. He hadn't even gotten within three feet from me since the encounter in the gym room.

I was really hoping Ilse got some information soon. I think I was expecting that to calm things down a bit. More proof of my naivety. I had just come back from a trip to the library, where amazingly enough, I had been alone the whole time. No stalker, no escorts. I was almost giddy. Mind still on Shakespeare and tomorrow's history test, I was startled to see Ilse wide awake in the sitting room, waiting for me. Since she wasn't usually up for another hour, I was instantly concerned. "Ilse?"

"His name is Adrian Char. He's a second year, a shifter. He's dangerous and you need to stay away from him."

Apparently I had spent too much time in the library and my mind was fogged up. I didn't immediately grasp what she was talking about. "What? Adrian?"

"Your stalker. You've heard of last year's…" She trailed off, staring at the wall over my head.

"Fiasco?"

"Good enough. My sources tried to find out exactly what happened, but were unable to. What they did find was that Adrian was a friend, of sorts, to Charles Morris, the human who was expelled last year near the end of the school year. As the year went on, Morris became more and more intolerant of other students, especially the ones who didn't appear human. This did not increase his popularity, as you can imagine. Then came the fiasco, as you called it. No one knows quite what happened." Ilse seemed quite upset to admit that. "I do know that Morris and Char were found in one of the training rooms in the H wing, surrounded by the remnants of a dark ritual gone wrong. Char was unconscious and bleeding, it looks like Morris turned on him. Both had memories of the event blocked, to the point even the faculty couldn't tell exactly what happened. They certainly tried. Morris was expelled and Char is on disciplinary probation. Afterwards, Char became rather vocally anti-human, though he seems to have cut back this semester. Probably to avoid being expelled."

"Why was Morris expelled? Why is Adrian on probation? What if he was a victim? Unconscious and bleeding, it doesn't sound like he was willingly involved. Who blocked their memories?"

Ilse held up a hand to stop my thinking out loud. "No one knows who blocked their memories except the one who did it. There was enough evidence to expel Morris, presumably enough to suggest Char wasn't a complete victim. Besides, look at what he's doing now. Report him for stalking and I imagine he'll be off campus by breakfast. I'll go with you if you like."

I sat down slowly, dropping my books on the table. That was a lot of information and I wasn't sure what to deal with first. "You really think he'd be expelled?"

"Well, normally there's a warning first, especially as he hasn't tried to make contact. But with him on probation, it would probably be enough to expel him. I looked into it." I bit my lip. Ilse continued, "It has to be *you* to make the report. Because of the nature of the action, unless there is sign of a threat, no one else can make a complaint."

I couldn't do that. He'd saved my life, possibly twice. Though it was also possible that he was involved with putting me in danger. Still didn't he deserve a chance? "No, I think we should wait."

"Wait? Why? For what? For him to hurt you?" Ilse stood suddenly.

"He hasn't done anything yet; just shown up where I am. While I'd love to know how he's doing that, he hasn't threatened me, tried to hurt me or anything. He won't even talk to me. Heck, he barely looks at me." Ilse didn't look convinced. "The school had someone read his mind a few months ago, right? Maybe they couldn't see his memories of that night, but they would have seen lots of other things, and they decided to give him a second chance. Let's see what he makes of it. Consider it giving him enough rope to hang himself. I promise, he makes one attempt to hurt me, or even threatens to, I'll report him so fast he won't know what happened."

Ilse shook her head, and her shoulders quickly rose and fell, kind of the vampire equivalent of a sigh. "Very well, we'll try it your way. For now. But you must be careful."

"I will, I promise."

"Good. Dinner?"

"Sure." We were almost out of the building when a thought caught up to me. "Wait a second; you said this happened in a training room in the H wing?"

"Correct. Oh, isn't that where the imposter lured you to? Hmm. I don't like that at all. Maybe it was an attempt to discredit you. Make you seem more like Morris."

That was an interesting theory. But I was more interested in what Adrian was doing there to rescue me. Suddenly his harmless request not to mention him didn't seem so harmless.

***

Ilse's information came on Thursday. I hadn't been completely sure of my decision then, and it wasn't taking much for me to question it. Ilse wanted more of an explanation for my reluctance, so I just said I owed him. I had mentioned the staircase incident, so she assumed that's what I meant.

"He might have had something to do with your fall."

"I fell when something that wasn't solid hit me in the back. You said it was probably either wind or magic. You also said Adrian was a shifter. Do shifters typically have abilities like that?"

"No. Sometimes shifters have psychic abilities, but not telekinesis," Ilse admitted. "This is still a bad idea."

I was close to agreeing with her. The whole business was starting to wreak havoc on my nerves. I felt like spring wound too tight. Then came the weekend.

It was Saturday, and I decided to go to town and do some errands. The ferry did run during the weekend when school was in session, which was useful. It was my first time in town since arrival. However, I would have to go alone. Denise had an all-day lab, and none of my other friends were from my dimension or natural jumpers.

The town was nice, but small. There weren't many stores, so not much variety, but the prices weren't too high. Maybe they'd be higher in the summer because of tourists. September was definitely not tourist season up here. It was weird, though, being in a place where everyone (probably) was human. Writing home was hard enough, trying not to talk about vampires, unicorns, trolls, and the like. Now I was face to face with other humans and I almost didn't know how to react anymore. I was never the most socially graceful, but at the moment I'd be lucky if I didn't convince anyone I was idiot-savant, possibly minus the savant part. Christmas was going to be very interesting this year, I could tell.

I did make it a point to find Paul and assure him that I hadn't fallen off the face of the planet. He was in the general store, manning the counter. He seemed glad to see me. Perhaps I should have come earlier; I had been at Hyde nearly a month now.

"So the school doesn't make the students vanish. I was beginning to wonder."

I smiled, thinking of the six hours I had spent invisible last week, after getting caught in a prank. I discovered it is extremely disconcerting not to be able to see yourself. It also makes classes interesting. But that kind of thing happens often enough, that the teachers just roll with it. "Well, it's easy to get so involved in school life you forget there's an outside world." Wasn't that the truth?

"That's why they call it the ivory tower. Speaking of which, you ever find out what all the secrecy is about?"

Yes, but if I told, I'd run into some rather nasty consequences. "Well, if I told you…" I joked, stalling. "In all honesty, it's mostly security. They are a bit paranoid, but they also do some positively amazing things in the science department, maybe a few others as well. That and I know some of the students are children of important people. One of my friends, her parents are very important in her home government. Things have to be safe for them."

"Some dinky little college up in the middle of North Nowhere attracts celebrities?"

"Only the ones who want some anonymity."

Paul shook his head. "Never would have guessed. How about you, eh? Are you famous?"

I smiled. "Not yet. I'm here for the science department."

My purchases had been rung up, but we were still chatting. "Say, he goes to the school, doesn't he?" Paul indicated a window with a nod.

Following the movement, I was shocked to see Adrian. Moving slightly so I couldn't be as easily seen through the window, I noticed that he didn't actually seem to be looking for me. This must be his home dimension too. "I've seen him around."

"Friend of yours?"

I almost laughed. "Not really. He doesn't seem to be the social type."

Paul gave me a strange look. "That's odd. The kids here love him. Watch." Before my astonished eyes, Adrian pulled a long balloon from his pocket and started to blow it up. Before he was halfway done, he was being mobbed by a crowd of children. He turned the balloon into something, I think it was a giraffe, before handing it to one of the kids. Immediately, they were all clamoring for one, loudly enough to be heard indoors. Fortunately, he seemed to have every intention of giving everyone a balloon, and candy. Once everyone had their balloon, he started telling a story, borrowing various balloons as props.

He was happy. On campus, I had never seen him look less than completely serious; but here he was playing with children, looking like a big kid himself. "Does he do this often?"

"Least once a week, weather permitting. Buys a bunch of cheap candy to pass out, usually from here, but sometimes the school, then goes where the kids will gather. Think he's been hired for birthday parties a few times, because of the balloons. Like I said, the kids love him. Call him 'Uncle Adrian'."

I shook my head in disbelief. I never would have expected something like this. It didn't seem faked at all, and as far as I could tell, he had no idea I was here. What would the others say if they could see this? I wasn't going to find out. It seemed almost an invasion of privacy that I knew. I couldn't tell anyone else. "Guess he doesn't want to ruin his reputation as a loner."

"Well, you know now."

"Don't tell him? I doubt he would want me to know."

"If you say so." Paul nodded towards the window. "But you may want to leave. He's coming in."

I slipped out the side door just before he came in the front, and wandered a bit until the ferry came back. Adrian must have been catching the same ferry, because we met at the dock. He seemed surprised to see me. So he hadn't followed me this time.

There was hardly anyone on the ferry, and ignoring each other didn't make sense. Besides, it was hard to be scared of someone after watching them perform a complicated pantomime with a balloon flower.

"Did you have a good time in town?" I asked.

He looked at me, startled. "I did, thank you." A pause. "And you?" It was as if he only just remembered it would be polite to ask.

"I did. Thank you for asking."

Neither of us were sure what to say for a moment. "Have you tried Mama Rose's diner? They have the best soup." Adrian asked.

"No, not yet. I'll have to keep that in mind."

We both stopped, not sure what to say. "Are you from here?" I asked. It was a lame question, but we were having a civil conversation and I didn't want to lose that.

Adrian blinked at me? "From Wollaston Lake? No. But I am Canadian. From the outskirts of Toronto actually. And you are from the States."

"That's right, Virginia." I had no idea how to continue from here.

"Are you dating the yeti?" Apparently it was his turn to ask an inane question.

For half a second, I considered saying yes. It would probably get Adrian to stop following me. But I don't like lying and I couldn't do that to Tim. "Tim? No, we're just friends. Why?"

"You have some good friends."

"I think so."

We were coming in sight of the dock now. Tim was obviously waiting for me, and I thought I could just make out Kara, too. Yes, that was definitely Kara. From the looks of it, they could see Adrian talking to me. He noticed too. "Tell your bodyguards that there are much worse dangers in Hyde than me."

I turned around, trying to think of a response, but he was already slinking away. Almost, I went after him. But before I could think of what to say, we were docking. I may not have known what to do about Adrian, but I could at least keep from being rude to Kara and Tim.

"You're alright? He didn't do anything, right? I had no idea he would go to town. Someone should have gone with you," The werewolf said, almost in one breath, while apparently trying to set the ship on fire through glare alone.

"Nothing untoward happened, correct?" Tim asked, looking me over and gently leading us away from the dock.

"I'm fine. I don't think he was following me this time. He seemed surprised to see me waiting for the ferry back. He was even polite. Though… He did say to tell my bodyguards that there were much worse threats at Hyde than him."

"If he threatened you…" Tim began.

"I think he was warning me." That got me a few skeptical looks, but no one said anything. Adrian disembarked quietly as we left, gave me a small nod, and slipped off in another direction. I followed Kara and Tim back to the dorm, absently listening to them debate the issue, and realized that as far as I could tell, Adrian didn't seem to have any friends on campus. I wondered if he was lonely.

***

Watching how a person interacts with children is not a foolproof sign of character. I knew this, and wondered if I was basing too much off of that, as he still kept showing up wherever I was. Yes, he had pretty well implied he wasn't someone I had to worry about, but even I wasn't naïve enough to think he'd tell me if he was planning on hurting me. Plus, since I wouldn't tell anyone what I saw, no one understood why I had suddenly relaxed some. Basically, I was back to wondering what to do.

Monday morning, I was pondering my dilemma instead of paying attention in Inter-Dimension History. I realized this might be a particularly poor choice on my part when a voice in my head nearly made me jump. '*Violet, please stay after class.*' Taria was not quite looking in my direction. When she made eye contact, I nodded.

Class dismissed soon after, and I lagged behind, gathering my things slowly; both so the room would clear out and because I was more than a little apprehensive. Finally there was no one else left in the room, and I was at her desk.

"You were very preoccupied today, and not with my lesson."

I winced. "Sorry, Professor. It won't happen again."

To my surprise, Taria laughed, purple wings stretching and circling. "That's not why I wanted to talk to you. Skies above, if I kept behind everyone who let their mind wander in class, we'd never leave. No, as long as you do well on your assignments and tests, and aren't disturbing anyone else, I can forgive a little cloud gathering. I'm more concerned with the subject you were preoccupied with. Adrian Char."

"You could tell?" I started thinking about elephants. Ilse had taught me that when I was concerned about my mind being read, I should concentrate on something very different. She suggested animals acting unusually or songs. Or both.

"I'm not oblivious to his current attention to you." She was serious now.

"You know? You're just ignoring it?"

"As are you. Should you file a report, action will be taken. But without you taking the first step, unless he oversteps the rules, there is little I can do."

That made sense. "Do you think I should do something?"

"That is a very good question, with few answers. If you are apprehensive, you should, by all means, ask him to stop." She paused. "For many reasons, I cannot violate his privacy any more than I would yours. However, I can tell you that whatever his current motivations are, they are not malevolent."

I thought about this and nodded. It was reassuring to hear I wasn't making a giant mistake. "Thank you for telling me."

"You are quite welcome. Do you have any further concerns?"

"Well, there are a lot of rumors about him." Now that I knew a little about him, I had heard plenty of them, enough to realize that what took Ilse's contacts so long to report was they had too much information to go through, not too little. Denise had been a rather surprising source. "I know I can't trust rumors, but there are a lot."

"Very true. He is the center of many rumors. Almost as many as you, yourself are. Do you have any specific suspicions? Anything you wish to discuss?"

Elephants. Red and purple elephants. River dancing and doing cartwheels. To the 1812 overture. Complete with artillery. I ignored Taria's raised eyebrow and muttered comment about it being impossible to river dance to that piece. "I think I'm fine for now. Thank you."

"You are welcome. I believe he is waiting outside."

Sure enough, when I left the classroom, fifteen minutes after class got out, Adrian was standing there, apparently reading a bulletin about fire evacuation procedures. Time to deal with this. My way. "Hi, Adrian."

He looked at me, clearly surprised I was talking to him before nodding in acknowledgement. Usually we both pretended he wasn't there.

"I'm going to the library. Is that where you're headed?"

His startled look faded a little faster. "I think I might, yes," He answered slowly, as if testing ice to make sure it wouldn't break under him.

"Great! You can help me carry some of these." I shook the textbooks and notebooks in my arms, smiling at him.

He stared at me for almost a minute before shaking his head. Giving an almost laugh, he took the two heaviest textbooks and gestured for me to lead the way.

Chapter Nine
Lines are Drawn

I would like to say that things settled down after that. That Adrian didn't feel the need to follow me around and that my friends didn't think I needed bodyguards. I would love to say that I was no longer *persona non grata* to a significant portion of the campus anymore. However, that would be an utter lie.

Adrian did continue to follow me, but at least he sometimes acknowledged my presence, especially if I started it. We weren't exactly having heart-to-hearts, but we'd exchange 'hellos' and he sometimes offered to help me carry things, always with a smirk. That was probably why Felicity, a werecat who lived in 607, who had ignored me before, now glared lasers in my direction, especially when Adrian was around. My friends were annoyed too, but I told them what Taria said, so most just ignored him.

The rumors hadn't gone away, but they hadn't intensified either. I kept hoping that if I waited it out, the rumor mill would stop. I wasn't that interesting, so they should get bored soon. Unfortunately, it appeared I didn't need to do anything.

Ilse had night classes, but one day one of her classes was moved to late afternoon to allow for some teachers' meeting. It didn't affect my schedule, so I never caught all the details. I was writing an email home when Ilse barged in, eyes wild. She stopped when she saw me sitting in the corner, hand over my heart, staring at her and trying to get my pulse back into human range instead of hummingbird.

"You are alright? Not hurt? You've been here the whole time?" The words poured from her mouth in a barely understandable torrent.

Puzzled, I answered her questions. "I'm fine. No, I never left. What's wrong? What happened?"

Ilse took a deep breath and donned what I called her 'council face'. "Nothing is wrong. Everything will be fine. Stay here while I find a Resident Advisor."

"Ilse, please don't treat me like an idiot. Yes, you are. You can't come in panicking, tell me you need to get an RA, and still convince me that nothing happened. I have a right to know." I was guessing on the last part. Maybe I really didn't have a right to know, but judging from her reaction, I was probably already involved.

I have no idea if I convinced her or if she planned to argue more, but the sound of Kara quickly becoming hysterical in the hallway threw a wrench in her plans. I couldn't make out what the werewolf was saying, but it was definitely her voice and she sounded scared. Then she actually forgot herself enough to try to open the door, which had automatically locked when Ilse shut it. As a werewolf, Kara had a deeply ingrained reluctance to trespassing on another's territory without permission. If she forgot that, then it had to be big. Two seconds of trying the handle, she then started pounding on the door. Ilse winced and let Kara in, presumably before she tried to break down the door.

"You're both alright? What happened to your door? Who would do something that awful? Why?" I wondered briefly if she could breathe, she was talking so fast. Then I deciphered her words.

Now that I had a direction, I started towards the door. Ilse blocked the door. "You don't wish to know."

"I have to." Neither of us backed down for a few minutes. Kara was shocked silent, watching us. Finally, Ilse moved out of my way.

"Really, you don't have to see this. You can stay here while I find Thylica or another RA and…" She trailed off at my gasp.

Someone had attacked the door. There was no other word for it. Deep gouges and long scratches were interspersed with carved insults, clearly meant for me. I was accused of being a slut, a coward, a freak, and several other things, some of which I didn't recognize, at least a couple that made Ilse really mad. I did recognize 'zero', an insulting term for normal humans. I had heard it a few times. Dr. Gronk had thrown a fit when someone wrote 'Zero, go home!' on my textbook and did something to make the pages unreadable. I had never seen him so angry. He gave a lecture on tolerance, and threatened severe consequences if this happened again. Then he kept me after class, and gave me a voucher for another text book.

I don't know how long I stared at the door before Kara pulled me inside and made me sit on the couch. Ilse had left to find an RA and Kara was trying very hard to use my electric water heater to make some hot chocolate. I pulled out of my numbness enough to help her before she destroyed the kitchenette.

"You can't pay attention to that. Don't let them win. Don't give them power over you. It's just the ranting of some bigoted idiot."

"Some bigoted idiot who was angry enough to vandalize our door. Some idiot who–" I cut off, not willing to mention that they might well live on this floor. Kara was probably friends with everyone on the floor, and the last thing I wanted was to provoke an argument.

So I sat there, drinking when prompted, and staring off into space. "I was here. The whole time Ilse was in class, I was here in the sitting room. Why didn't I hear anything?"

"It's probably a good thing you didn't. If you investigated, you might have been hurt." I looked up to see Risa, the third floor RA, examining the door. Ilse must not have been able to find Thylica.

"Still, shouldn't I have heard something? I have pretty good hearing. Well, for a human."

The fire elemental shrugged. "No idea. The walls and doors are charmed to cut down on sound to insulate and keep things quiet. It won't block everything, but it does help." She closed her eyes and held up a hand. After a few seconds, the hand was glowing orange and she began to press it to the door. She stopped about a quarter-inch from the door and seemed to push, but never got any closer. Risa withdrew her hand, which quickly stopped glowing. "That doesn't make sense. The charms are still active."

"The ones to keep down sound?" I asked.

"No. To cut down on accidental and deliberate destruction, most doors, windows, walls, and furniture are charmed to resist anything damaging. They can be overpowered, and there are safeties, ways to remove the charms when one absolutely has to break a door or window, etc. but in either case the charms would be gone completely."

Kara bit her lip. "So what does this mean?"

"I'm not sure. Either that something destructive got through the charms without them kicking in and raising an alarm, which shouldn't be possible; or that someone managed to take down the charms, which raises an alarm, damage your door, and fix the charms, which raises an alert, all without being noticed. Which shouldn't be possible." Risa glared at the door as if blaming it for her confusion.

"Well, if neither of those options are possible that the damage isn't really there?" I got a lot of confused looks. "I mean, could it be an illusion?"

Risa raised a skeptical eyebrow. "I won't deny that it would be easier to set up an illusion than to fool the charms, but I can feel these scratches." She cocked her head. "Someone hand me a piece of paper."

She took the sheet Ilse handed her, and put it against the door. Immediately, all the scratches and insults on that section of the door showed up on the paper. She ran her fingers over it. "Now that's quite an illusion. How did you guess?"

"It's not my first encounter with illusions. Besides, when you eliminate the impossible, whatever's left, no matter how improbable, must be the solution."

"Sherlock Holmes would be proud. I'll get a magic user in right away to take this down. Thylica will probably be back within the hour. I'll tell her what's going on."

Risa left then, and the three of us went back into the room as we noticed the attention we were attracting. Everyone on the floor would know about this within hours, I could tell.

"Alright, you understand politics best. What will likely come of this?" I asked Ilse.

"The door will be fixed quickly. No matter what, the school won't want that left unattended. Risa was muttering about calling a meeting, so at very least the resident advisors will discuss it. Whether they'll try to do something or brush matters under the rug depends on individual personalities, most of whom I know little about. Because it happened on Thylica's floor, she will have the most say, and I do not believe she will ignore it."

"Why would they ignore it? Wouldn't they want to deal with it quickly?" Kara asked. From what I had learned, werewolves are usually very direct in their dealings. When one is wronged, it is dealt with quickly before a vendetta can be formed.

"In case it makes them look bad," I answered, picking up my hot chocolate. Well, tepid chocolate by now. "Especially since we don't know who's responsible, it's easier to make a few pretty comments about tolerance and then pretend it never happened. So, I'm still learning. What kinds of beings would be capable of illusions like this?"

Ilse leaned back, closing her eyes to think. "For a freshman, it's rather remarkable. Perhaps an older student, but they would have to be invited into the building. A strong enough magic user of almost any type can do illusions of a kind, but this is advanced work. Leprechauns, like Veronica, and light elementals, like Lumina, are both known for their illusions. Fairies and Pixies specialize in illusions, and we have one of each on the floor. Even some dragons are capable of it. Because the targeted base for the illusion was wood, it is possible that a wood elf, like Thylica, could have done it. Some magici specialize in illusions. But to my knowledge, tactile illusions are near impossible for all of them." She opened her eyes. "Perhaps we should make a list."

"I think we should wait. See what the RAs do. Last thing we need is to interfere with an ongoing investigation," I countered.

Within an hour, two of the faculty came over to disassemble the illusion. Apparently, rather than just end it, which would have been quicker and easier, they wanted to keep what they called a 'magical signature' so they had a better chance of finding the culprit. That made it more complicated and time-consuming.

I wasn't due to take Magic for Non-Magic Users until next semester, so I didn't know what they were doing, but the light show was pretty impressive. Judging from the fact that most of the floor was watching, I probably wasn't the only one to think so. Thylica came by about halfway through, but she didn't stop to watch. She did announce that there would be a floor meeting that night, and just to be sure there were no excuses, she hung up a few signs.

Arie, who had been watching the proceedings with interest, glared at me when she heard about the meeting. So did Felicity, but that was normal. Apparently they were blaming me for the loss of their evening. Considering I hadn't vandalized my own door, I didn't think that was fair, but I didn't bother telling them that.

The floor meeting was at nine. Shortly before the meeting, Kara told me that at least half the dorm knew, and chances were the rest would learn within a day. Swell. Interestingly enough, despite the fact that everyone knew exactly what happened, Thylica never came out and said it. She just kept going on about a case of vandalism against one of the girls on the floor, and that kind of cruelty and intolerance was unacceptable. Anyone who knew anything was strongly encouraged to tell Thylica, one of the other RA's or the Resident Director of the dorm.

I had met the RD for the first time today, a centaur named Ralyinth. She made a point of expressing her sincere sympathy and her distaste that such a thing could happen in her dorm. I thanked her and didn't say anything about the fact that I suspected she was more upset that it happened in her dorm than that it had happened.

Anyway, no one said anything, so Thylica dismissed the meeting, again reminding us that we could talk to her at any time, especially if we had information about the event. I wasn't counting on anything coming to light that way, and went to bed early, wondering how the rumor mill would twist this one.

***

I hadn't expected things to go much beyond the dorm, but that was another example of my naïveté. The next morning I had music class at eight o'clock. As usual, I had spent a little too long waking up in the morning, and was in a hurry to get to class before I was late. While I was almost sprinting to the music room, I was stopped when someone came up behind me and actually grabbed my arm. It didn't hurt, but I did stop in shock. I stiffened in surprise as Adrian looked me over with a frown.

"You didn't get hurt? Or were you healed already?"

"What are you talking about?" It was too early in the morning to be cryptic and I was going to be late.

"Yesterday. I heard you were attacked."

"I wasn't attacked, my door was. I'm late. We can talk later." I pulled out of his unresisting grasp and dashed to class. It wasn't until half-way through class that it occurred to me to wonder how he heard about yesterday.

By the time music was over, Adrian seemed to be back to his normal self. All the same, I made a point of telling him the basics: that it was an illusion, not an actual attack. He didn't say anything, but he did seem a bit more relaxed. I also apologized for being rude, but he didn't react to that.

"So, I'm going to meet Kara and Denise for breakfast. Do you want to join us?"

That surprised him. After a moment, he gave me a blink-and-you'll-miss-it smile. "Thank you for the invitation, but I must decline. I think it would be more comfortable for everyone if I wasn't there."

I considered arguing, but wasn't sure how to without out and out lying. Kara was as friendly as they come, but she was as loyal as she was friendly. As long as she thought Adrian was a threat, she was going to be hostile to him, no matter what anyone else said. Since I was the only one defending him at the moment, it would probably take a while. I wasn't sure about Denise; I still had trouble figuring out her emotions.

I didn't mention inviting Adrian at breakfast, which was probably just as well. Kara told me that rumors had spread beyond the dorm, which I knew. That things had been distorted to claiming I had been hurt, which I guessed; and that most didn't know who had been attacked. Just that it was a student in Price Hall. How odd. Adrian clearly knew I was involved, even if he didn't know exactly what happened. I had figured that any rumors would have included that it was 'the human's' room. Being the only human on campus, that narrows things down a lot.

"I wouldn't worry too much," Denise said, snagging my spoon now that I no longer needed it, and adding it to her dish tower. "They'll get over it in time. Are you done with that cup? Thanks." The cup extended the base. The dragonfly shifter put Kara's yellow plate on top, before staring at it for a moment. "Do you ever wonder what yellow tastes like?"

I blinked a few times. "Can't say I ever thought about it. I probably will now, though."

Denise smiled. "You're welcome."

***

The next day, I had history. Taria kept me after class again. Once we were alone, she spent about fifteen minutes ranting in some language the translation spell didn't work on, before asking me why I hadn't come to her about this.

"The thought never occurred to me."

"I am your advisor. If there is a problem, a concern, or a threat, I should be informed. Preferably as quickly as possible. Something like this should never have occurred. But since it did, you should have come to me. Do you not feel comfortable coming to me with your problems? Would it help if you had different advisor?"

"No, that's not it. I just, well, never thought about it. It's not like we know who did it."

"That's my job. One of the places where being a telepath comes in useful. Now, have there been any other occurrences I should know about?"

Reluctantly, I told her about the fall in the library, trying to make sure I only thought about the library. Taria took it much more seriously than I had.

"Skies above! A fall on those stairs? You could have been killed! How were you not hurt?"

"Someone caught me."

"Adrian Char caught you? That was good of him. It also explains a few things. Yes, he does have amazingly quick reflexes."

"Um, I never said any of that."

"No, but you were thinking about it. Anything else?"

I started running 'It's a small world after all' in my head. "Nothing I'd like to share at this time."

Taria steepled her fingers. "Perhaps I shouldn't have said anything. I know you are hiding something, but I won't invade your privacy. I just want to remind you that I need to know about threats to my students. It is perhaps more important than you realize. Be careful and stay safe."

I thanked her and started to leave. "You're doing well, but one of the study groups would help you to keep your thoughts more private," Taria's voice trailed after me.

It was almost forty minutes after class, and I was due to meet Tim in about twenty minutes. Probably best to just go to the cafeteria. Adrian was waiting for me, which didn't surprise me. What did surprise me was that he broke the silence first. "You didn't tell her."

The gym, it had to be. I had promised not to tell anyone, and while I wasn't sure that was a good idea anymore, I had promised. Deliberately letting a telepath read it from my mind felt like breaking that promise. Turning, I looked him in the eye. "There was nothing to tell."

"You've heard by now."

"I've heard many things, from many sources that disagree wildly. I've learned not to believe everything I hear."

"So what do you believe?"

"When I figure that out, I'll let you know." I shook my head and continued walking.

My feet were on the steps to the cafeteria when I heard the quiet, "Thank you." I spun around but he had once again vanished. What kind of shifter was he, anyway?

***

Even after the defacing of the door, I still hoped that the news would run through campus and then die out. Maybe it would have. Except for the fact that three days after my talk with Adrian, Willow and Lumina, the dryad and light elemental in 601, found their door vandalized like mine.

The target wasn't clear, the insults more generic, and apparently not as harsh as what was on mine. It could have been against either or even both of them. Willow was extremely upset, but calmed quickly when Thylica confirmed it was just an illusion. Apparently the thought of wood being damaged like that hurt more than the insults.

I knew Willow. Not well, but she had occasionally acted as a buffer, someone to walk with me 'in case', plus she was in my biology and history classes. Apparently she was a biology major with a concentration in botany, so we'd probably share other biology classes. Lumina, I did not know, other than a few surface details. She had a tendency to keep to herself. But it was easy to tell she was currently very angry.

Lumina stood guard, glaring at any onlookers and changing the lighting around the door so it couldn't be seen clearly. Willow was supervising the removal, making sure the wood didn't get damaged. When I went over, Lumina eyed me carefully. "Yes?" Her greeting was sharp, but not quite rude.

"I just wanted to say how sorry I am. I know an attack like this is very... disconcerting, even if it isn't dangerous. In a way, that almost makes it worse. You feel like you shouldn't be so upset, but you are. You can't help it."

She softened. "How did you deal with it?"

"I have good friends who reminded me I should listen to them instead of cowardly, bigoted idiots."

Lumina smiled a little, the first time I have ever seen her do so. She was really pretty when she smiled. "A sound plan." She pushed some white-blonde hair back, sighing. "I know I didn't say anything before, but none of what was on your door was true."

"Thank you. I haven't seen your door, but I'm sure none of that is true either."

Willow came up then. "I don't know who did this, but when I find out, they're going to discover what termites are like. Thank you, Violet. Don't worry, I'm not going to stop being your friend just because some cowardly piece of sawdust thinks I should."

I swallowed bile. I should have thought of that. While they hadn't necessarily been targeted because Willow and I were on good terms, it was possible. Lumina winced. "I hadn't mentioned that."

Willow gasped in horror, flowery eyebrows disappearing into leafy hair. "I thought you knew! I'm so sorry."

"No, I'm sorry. I never thought that someone else would be targeted because of me. That should never have happened. I appreciate your comments, but if you do decide that you'd rather avoid me, I'll understand. There's still time to get another partner for the Bio report—"

"Not happening. I know you aren't a dryad, but us plant girls have to stick together."

"Willow…" What did I even say to that?

"I wouldn't bother arguing." Lumina smirked. "She's stubborn. You have to be stubborn to be dryad living on the top floor of a tall building. As for me, well, I know we haven't been friends, but I think that maybe I've been listening to some of the wrong people. I'd like to change that."

Lumina and I hadn't been friends, but it was more lack of interaction than anything else. She didn't claim the seat next to her was taken when it wasn't, and if she was involved in the rumors, then I didn't know about it, and didn't want to.

"I'd like that."

***

Two days later, I got back from class to see a crowd gathering at the end of the hall, near Kara and Denise's room. Suddenly nervous I hurried over to see what was wrong. A couple of the girls gave me cold stares, but I tried to ignore that. I could hear Kara's voice, so she was alright. Good.

Then I managed to get a look. It wasn't Kara and Denise's room at all, it was the room next to them. Phyna and her roommate, the fairy. What was the fairy's name again?

"It will be okay, Setrai. They'll have it down in no time. Right, Phyna?" There was Kara. Always the peacemaker. Setrai. That was the fairy's name.

"Of course." The dragon seemed much less concerned about the mess of their door.

"I don't need you trying to give me training wings. What do you care about this anyway? Everyone knows you're friends with the human."

I could just see Kara looking confused. "So?"

"So, this is her fault!"

Kara immediately denied it, and others were raising their voices too, on both sides. I was shocked silent. My fault? What in the world was that supposed to mean?

Someone bumped into me, and it was like a light switch was flipped. Everyone suddenly remembered/realized I was there and had been listening. Too many people to deal with, so I ignored everyone but Kara, Setrai, and Phyna.

Kara looked horrified, and maybe a little angry. Phyna, well, I couldn't read dragon features well, but she seemed concerned, I thought. Setrai was fluttering off the ground, head raised and meeting my eyes. There was anger there, but I thought there was a little shame too.

What should I say? What do I do? "Why my fault? I promise you, I didn't attack your door." Blast it! I hadn't meant to say that.

"No, of course not. No one thinks you did," Kara tried to soothe. There was a low murmur.

"Of course you didn't. Everyone knows you don't have magic." Setrai tossed her head. "But this wouldn't be happening if you weren't here."

I bit my tongue. How does one even argue with a statement like that?

"You don't know that." Phyna tried to step between us.

"I *do* know that. You think this is normal? No, this is because the school insists on having humans here." Setrai turned back to me. "If you weren't here–"

"That's enough." The crowd parted allowing Thylica through. "I realize you are upset, but there will be no accusations tossed about without proof. As you say, everyone knows that humans do not have magic. Violet did not do anything to your door, and we will not devolve into blaming one person for the actions of another." She was looking around the crowd. More murmuring but I couldn't tell what it was about. Thylica gave Setrai a strong look.

The fairy went white, before turning to me. "I apologize for my statements." It sounded like the words had been dragged from her throat.

I tried to remember the proper form for something like this. "I accept your apology, and my condolences about your door." There, that sounded semi-appropriate.

She gave me another nod, and I moved towards my room. I had to get out of here. Too many people, and they were all staring. Kara was saying something, but I couldn't listen then. I gave her a smile, or tried to, and I think I told her I'd talk to her later. Then I locked myself in my room, and tried to pretend this never happened.

***

Ilse came out of her room that night, ready to go to dinner. Then looked at me surprised, when I showed no signs of going too. I almost always ate dinner with her. "Are you not hungry?"

"No, not–" my stomach growled, and Ilse arched an eyebrow at me. "Maybe a little, but I've got some crackers here. I think maybe I should stay in tonight."

Her other eyebrow joined the first. "Has Char been bothering you?"

"No. He's fine. It's nothing like that."

"Then what seems to be the problem?"

"It's not a big deal really. Just…" I sighed. "Just stupid people saying stupid things."

"I see." The timber of her voice lowered. "Well, there's only one way to deal with that."

"There…is?" Why did I very much not like that sound of that?

"Stand up." I didn't move. "Trust me." With a sigh, I did as I was told. Ilse shook her head inside a hand. "Not like that. Stand up straight. Shoulders back, head high. Haven't you ever had posture lessons?"

"No, not really." I did my best anyway. I held a record for being able to walk three blocks with five books on my head so I tapped into that posture.

"Good, excellent. Why didn't you have training?"

"It wasn't considered necessary." Wasn't like I went to finishing school or took dance lessons or anything.

"Everyone should have posture lessons." Ilse circled around me correcting minute flaws. "Good. Now, the first thing you must have is poise and control. No matter what they say, what they do; they cannot affect you. Understood? Head up, don't give them any satisfaction. No anger, certainly no tears. Pretend they aren't there if you have to. Not the best of plans in the long term, but it will do temporarily."

"I can't do that."

"You most certainly can. You won't be alone. Just try. You may find deep breathing to be calming."

I took a few deep breaths. "Maybe I should just stay here tonight.

"No. You cannot allow stupid people to have power over your life. You must be in control. Try."

It wouldn't be easy, but Ilse was right. Hiding in my room solved nothing. I had as much right to be here as anyone else, no matter what someone with illusion magic might say. "I'll try."

She nodded. "Good. Just stay close to me, and you'll be fine."

It was late enough that we didn't run into anyone until we got to the lobby. That made it a little easier, because I could at least pretend that the people on the other floors might not know who I was. Thylica was on duty, but she didn't say anything other than a greeting.

On the way to the cafeteria, at least twice a conversation stopped as we got close. Ilse glided past as if they were ghosts, and I tried to follow her lead. I couldn't glide like she could, but I followed, eyes straight ahead. Not looking to the right or the left.

Dinner was …bearable. Just. There were so very many people there. That made it easier and harder. I don't like being surrounded by people, I really don't. But I also knew that there was no way that everyone there had heard about, or even cared about my problems. Probably most of them didn't care about me one way or another. It was a little freeing to think of it that way.

Of course there were some who did care. Despite my best efforts, I could hear the whispers. Not the words, but the tone. No, Ilse was right. They weren't there. It didn't matter what they thought. Besides, trying to follow Ilse's instructions for how to walk took enough effort that I could work on tuning out the rest.

I made it to our table, wondering how a hundred yards transformed to five miles. Ilse was there already, waiting. "You are doing well. Now, focus on me, not the rest of the cafeteria."

"Right. Um…" I didn't have a clue what to say.

"How were your classes?" Ilse asked when it became clear that I was floundering.

Before I could answer, there was someone at our table. I looked up to see Phyna standing there, looking about as bashful as it is possible for a nine-foot long dragon to look. "May I join you?"

I looked at Ilse, who looked back at me, eyebrows raised. Hoping I was interpreting her correctly, I invited Phyna to have a seat.

"Thank you. I wanted to… I'm sorry about Setrai. I'm sure she doesn't really mean it."

I wasn't nearly as sure. "You have nothing to be sorry for. Setrai is entitled to her opinion, and I understand it was a stressful time."

Phyna didn't look happy, but she agreed.

Ilse looked like she was trying to hide her curiosity and confusion, reminding me that I hadn't actually told her what happened. "The infamous door attacker struck again."

"Ah, I see." She turned to Phyna. "My condolences."

"Thank you. They have it fixed by now, I just…" Phyna bit the end of her tail. "I don't want to say it isn't a big deal. It is. Just, in the large scheme of things…"

"It doesn't seem particularly important?" I asked. I could see her argument. No one got hurt, no permanent damage was done, why get bent out of shape? On the other hand, I had been through it, and it *did* hurt. It was a shock, realizing someone hated you that much. Reading the insults was painful, and it was scary, seeing the door attacked like that. Sure, some of that faded when I found out it was an illusion, not brute force, but not all of it.

"Yes! What do you think?" Phyna asked.

"I check the door, whenever I go out," I admitted. "I have to open it a little, standing to the side, to make sure nothing's there. I get nervous walking the hallway sometimes. I know what you're saying, but it *is* an attack. I don't blame Setrai for being mad." Blaming me, yes, that I could be upset about. Being mad, no.

"I wasn't aware you were that troubled," Ilse sounded reproachful.

"It's not so bad when I'm not alone."

"Hyde has a great counseling department," Phyna said. "I've visited them."

"Everything alright?" I asked. Phyna probably didn't want to tell me her intimate secrets, and I certainly didn't have a right to ask, but if she was going to mention seeing a counselor then it was only polite to make sure she was fine, right?

She nodded slowly. "Anyway, you make an appointment at the infirmary."

I dropped the subject. No prying. "I'll consider it."

Ilse started talking then, mentioning the classes she would have that night. We listened, letting the topic of classes and homework dominate. After dinner Ilse walked me back to our room, instead of just to the dorm. She said it was so she could grab something before class. I didn't call her on it.

"You shared quite a bit with Phyna. More than may have been wise." Ilse didn't look up from where she was stacking her books.

"I didn't share that much. I doubt she's going to go around telling people I'm traumatized. Which I'm not, by the way."

"No, you are not. As to who she will tell what, we have no way of knowing. Perhaps she will say nothing.

Even still, you spoke of personal matters in a public place. Be wary of that."

It was council training. That was what was making Ilse so paranoid. "I doubt anything she might say would be worse than the rumors that already exist."

"Perhaps. Still, be careful who you trust. Particularly when you are the scope of rumors and gossip." Ilse finally looked up at me.

"I'll be careful. But right now, I don't want to alienate any friends I may have." I gave Ilse a smile to let her know I included her in that.

Ilse smiled back and shook her head. "They would eat you alive in the vampire council."

"That, I do not doubt."

***

Two days later, there was a dorm meeting, but not before another door was vandalized, this time on the second floor. Two girls who I had seen around sometimes, but I don't think I had ever even talked to them.

The dorm meeting was similar to the floor meeting and about as successful. As if there was a single girl who didn't know, we were informed about a rash of vandalism that affected several rooms. This was touted as completely unacceptable behavior, and any information anyone had about the incidents should be reported right away. If the culprit or culprits confessed now, there would be leniency. If not, there was a high chance of expulsion when caught.

There were some whispers at that, and a lot of looking around, but nothing that couldn't be simple curiosity. The hall meeting didn't last long, and it didn't look to me like the school was making any progress.

Ilse didn't seem very impressed either. As soon as we got to our dorm, she spoke up. "I've made a list of any races capable of casting illusions."

"So have I. Switch lists? See if either of us missed any?" We did. I had missed nagas, partially because their illusions were always snake related, and leprechauns. Ilse hadn't put mermaids on her list. Other than that, our lists agreed. We scratched off the ones whose illusions were a completely different nature than ours, but that still left a good fifteen possibilities. "Okay, the school probably did this too, and it didn't help. That means we need to think of something new." I tapped my pencil eraser against the paper. "Any idea what the school has done?"

"I know they tested every magic user in the dorm. No one matched the signature," Ilse admitted.

Well, there went that then. "Then it will take something very clever or lucky to find them," I sighed. "Okay, what do all the rooms have in common?"

There was the obvious. They were all in Price Hall, there were no rumors of attacks like this in other dorms. Because it was in Price, each room had two girls living there. "In order, we have a vampire, and a human. A light elemental and a dryad. A dragon and a fairy. Do you know about the second floor girls?"

Ilse leaned back. "I believe that they were a magicus and a shifter. Lizard, I believe."

No two beings were the same race. Was that significant? "What if… No, that's stupid. Doesn't fit."

"What?" Ilse asked.

"I'm wrong. It doesn't fit. Just… I was thinking. I *am* human and you can pass. Mostly." Ilse raised an eyebrow to that, but didn't argue. "Lumina can pass. The second floor girls can pass. But Setrai and Phyna can't. It doesn't fit."

"No, they cannot. But if, as you suggest, this is a vendetta against humans or those who appear to be human, there may be other, personal reasons for targeting either Setrai or Phyna, or possibly both."

"Yeah, but that complicates things. If some are targeted for a different reason than others." I frowned. "What about a copycat? Someone did the first one, or maybe more than one, and others continued. It happens sometimes with crimes."

Ilse shook her head. "Officially, they all have the same magical signature."

"This is a nightmare." I brushed hair from my face. "Maybe they'll just lose interest."

If I had known what would happen next, I would have kept my big mouth shut.

Chapter Ten
Escalating Troubles

I came back from math class with Krystal, one of the ice elemental twins. It took time, but I could usually tell them apart now. Krystal was quieter, a little taller, and had a tiny birthmark under her right ear. Bria was a hair shorter, more outgoing, liked trying new hairstyles, and had slight white flecks in her irises. Of course, at the moment, it was easy to tell, because Krystal was in my math class and Bria wasn't. Apparently they tried not to share classes in order to cut down on confusion.

Her door was next to mine, so we walked down the hallway together, discussing the current unit on binomial coefficients. Krystal was having a little more difficulty with the concept than I was, so I suggested we study together later.

"That would be wonderful. When?"

"How about seven? We could study in the lounge." That would be about two hours before meeting Ilse for dinner.

"Perfect."

I smiled, and reached for the doorknob. The moment my fingers brushed the knob, the door was engulfed in flames. I jumped back with a shriek, continuing to back up until I hit the opposite wall. Hitting the wall apparently restarted my brain too, because that's when I realized my hand didn't hurt, I couldn't feel any heat, and there wasn't any smoke. It was another illusion.

The next thing I realized was that Krystal was still screaming. I looked over to her, standing rooted in spot, eyes wide, paler than snow. Ice elemental. Fire was probably really bad for them. She had also jumped back to the wall. Unlike me, she had jumped into it hard enough to break skin. There was a fine line of blood starting to run down her temple.

"Krystal, it's not real! It's another illusion." She wasn't screaming anymore, but I didn't think she could hear me either.

I moved between her and the fire. "It's not real. Krystal, it can't hurt you."

She was shaking, eyes locked on the flames. Vaguely I could hear doors opening. I hoped Ilse wasn't one of them. Fire is very bad for vampires too. I moved closer, lifting my hand to block her vision of the hallway.

Krystal jumped, and stared at me. Well, she wasn't looking at the fire anymore. It was something. "It's just another illusion. No fire." I pulled out a handkerchief and put it in her hand, pressing it to her cut. I might not know much about ice elemental physiology, but I knew you used pressure to stop bleeding.

"The flames… The fire…"

I could see Denise out of the corner of my vision. "Get Bria. She's…" I stopped, realizing I didn't have a clue where Bria was.

"Library." Krystal gritted out, through clenched teeth. Well, if she could feel pain, then at least the shock should be wearing off.

Denise nodded, turned into a dragonfly and flit away without a word. Arie poked her beak out a second later. "Sheesh, vandalism wasn't enough for you? Now you have to attack directly?" Then she spotted the fire and jumped back with a startled squawk.

I ignored the accusation and her fright. "Get Thylica. She needs to know." Out of the corner of my eye, I saw her move, but didn't bother to see where she went. "Krystal, you're bleeding. It's not really bad, I think; but I think you should go to the infirmary. Okay?"

"No, I want Bria first."

Fair enough. A large dragon head came around my shoulder, forcing me to stifle my jump. "Phantom Flames. Shards and scales, I've heard about it, but never seen it. Impressive," Phyna rumbled in my ear.

It was, I had to admit. "I would appreciate it more if it hadn't taken me by surprise."

"Well, there is that."

Krystal still looked shocky, and the very realistic looking and sounding fire didn't help any. So I talked her into waiting in the lounge. The door was already open so neither of us had to touch it, and she couldn't see or hear the fire from there. Well, I couldn't. Hopefully she couldn't either.

Fortunately, Bria came running up the stairs a few minutes later. I guess the elevator wasn't fast enough for her. Thylicia was only seconds behind her. Leaving the sisters some privacy, I went into the hallway to answer Thylica's questions. The hallway was actually empty, which said a lot for why Thylica was RA. The flame illusion roared on, but I ignored it to focus on the elf.

Her ears were twitching madly, a sign I had learned meant extreme agitation for elves. She had been mad about the vandalism, but now that someone was actually hurt, even if it was unintended, well, I was very glad I wasn't the one responsible. Whoever was might end up finding out the truth to the rumors that Thylica was a champion at the battle ax.

Unfortunately, there wasn't much I could tell her. From my point of view, I touched the door and flames shot up. I realized that it was fake and Krystal freaked out, probably scraping her head on the rough wall texture.

No, I didn't know what caused it, or why someone would plant it. Yes, it startled me badly. I did mention what Phyna said; mentally apologizing to her as she jumped to the short list of people Thylica would want to talk to. Hopefully she wouldn't try to talk to Krystal until she was feeling better.

The ice elementals came out a moment later, Krystal holding my now mostly red handkerchief to her temple, still looking pale and shaky. Bria was supporting her a little. "Here, let me look," Thylica said. Krystal moved the handkerchief, and the wood elf gently laid her hand, glowing blue, over the cut. "That should numb the pain, at least long enough for you to get it looked at. I'm still learning to heal scratches, so you're better off going to the infirmary. After that, I need you to come back and tell me what happened. Do you know where the infirmary is?"

Krystal was resolutely not looking down the hallway, but at least she was coherent. "No." She turned to her twin, who shook her head.

"I can show you if you like?" I offered, taking a quick glance at Thylica to make sure she didn't have any further questions for me.

Thylica nodded as the twins agreed. "Okay, it's not too far." I really hoped I'd be able to find it from this direction. Fortunately, I didn't get us lost, and found the infirmary just as Thylica's pain numbing whatever was wearing off.

When blood is smeared over half your face, they don't make you wait long for medical treatment. Krystal didn't even have time to fill out forms before she was taken back to be treated by Dr. Zyloas. Unlike me, she showed no hesitation at having a zombie doctor. Bria wasn't allowed back with her, so she stayed in the lobby, using the time to interrogate me. I understood why. If Rose had been hurt because of something weird, I'd be trying to demand answers too. Unfortunately, I simply didn't have much information, and people kept asking me the same things over and over.

Dr. Zyloas called in Nurse Persephone after a minute or two. Bria tensed up at that. "Why do they need another healer? It's just a bad scrape." Ice patterns swirled at her feet.

"Well, she was also in shock. But probably they want someone who can just close the wound so she stops bleeding. I know Nurse Persephone can dispel magic, I wouldn't be surprised if she can use magic to heal too. Pretty sure zombies can't."

"Oh, that makes sense. No, zombies don't have magic." She leaned back on the chair with a long exhale. "She seemed alright to you?"

"Krystal? She wasn't hurt badly. It just looks serious because of the blood. Head wounds always bleed a lot. She'll be fine."

Bria seemed less than reassured. "There was no actual fire? At any time?"

"No. It was just a really convincing illusion." I was starting to get the impression I was missing something. But I had no idea what. "I'm guessing that fire is really bad for ice elementals."

"Very much so," Krystal said, leaving the medical room. She was still pale, but she wasn't shaking, and the blood had been cleaned up. I couldn't even see where her scrape was, so it was probably healed already. Good.

Bria was on her feet instantly. "You're okay? Really okay?"

Krystal nodded, while taking a shaky breath. Then she looked to me. "You were on fire for a moment. Are you okay?"

Huh, I hadn't realized that. "I'm fine. It wasn't real. No burns, no smoke, nothing. Startled the living daylights out of me though."

Krystal gave me a weak smile. "No, I definitely handled it worse."

Couldn't really argue with that one. "Well, no one can blame you for not liking fire." Krystal shivered, hard. Bria stepped closer and put an arm around her. "Would you like me to change the subject?"

"Yes." I almost didn't get a chance to finish before Bria cut in.

"Okay." Unfortunately, that meant I had to actually think of something to say. "Well, do you still want to study math at seven?"

I didn't think it was that funny, but Krystal needed a moment to sit down, she was laughing that hard. Of course, it really didn't have anything to do with what I said. As she was bent over, the back of her shirt stuck up, and I was able to see something on her back. It took me a second glance to be sure of what I was seeing, but I wasn't mistaken. There was a huge burn scar, running from about an inch under her neck, from shoulder to shoulder. I couldn't see how far down it went, but the burn must have been severe. It was old, she had obviously grown since being scarred. No wonder the fire freaked her out.

Bria glared at me in a warning manner, so I took the few seconds I had to force my face into a neutral expression. "Is that a no to math?"

"No, math at seven. Thank you." Krystal wiped a little frost from her face. Then she got a little more serious. "So, what was that? With your door?"

I shrugged. "Phyna called it Phantom Flames. I haven't heard of them."

"So how did she know about them?" Bria sounded suspicious.

"If you asked me to name it, I probably would have called it something like that, too. If she had heard or read about it, I imagine it would be easy to identify. Besides, she seems to collect information." It seemed to be a dragon trait. Phyna had expressed a desire to read every book in the library before graduation. Probably didn't hurt that she was a distant relation to Ms. Graz.

The twins nodded, not seeming completely convinced, but not arguing with me either. "Ready to go back?" I changed the subject. The last thing we needed was more division on the floor.

We got back to the dorm, where they were finishing up taking down the illusion. Thankfully, Ilse didn't appear to have woken up. I can't imagine it would be pleasant to open the door into what appeared to be an inferno. Krystal went to talk to Thylica, and I decided to work on homework in the lounge until the flames were gone.

To my surprise, Bria showed up before I could finish unpacking my stuff. I would have thought she would want to stay with Krystal. Then again, it was possible Thylica wanted to talk to her alone.

"Everything alright?" I asked, when Bria just stood there.

Bria looked around the room, which was empty except for the two of us, checked the laundry room, which I assume was also empty, and then shut the door. "I wanted to thank you. For what you did for my sister."

I blinked. "I didn't do anything. Not really."

"From my understanding, you triggered the illusion. Meaning for no matter how brief a time, you thought you were threatened by fire. Yet as soon as you realized the fire wasn't real, your priority was my sister's well-being. You took charge in an emergency, and stayed when you could have left, duty done. You provided care and comfort without ever acting inconvenienced, or as if Krystal was silly for her reactions."

I shrugged. "Fire is scary. I imagine more for you than me. And I've freaked out far worse over a fire than she did." I was twelve at the time, and was never permitted to play with a chemistry set unsupervised again. Fortunately, no one got hurt.

"You saw." It wasn't a question.

"A little. Enough. If I had been burned like that, I'd probably freak out about fire too."

Bria closed her eyes, as if in pain. "I would prefer you not mention it to her. Or anyone else."

I put up my hands. "Not my, or anyone else's business. I won't ask."

"Good." Bria thumbed through my biology textbook, but I doubted she saw the words. "You never asked about your handkerchief." There was something in her voice, like I was supposed to be picking up something, but I didn't know what.

"I guess I forgot about it. Well, I certainly don't want it back."

"Good. It's probably been burned. Security reasons."

"Security? Hygiene, I could see. Or health. But security?"

"So no one uses her blood in magic. Didn't you know about that?"

I sat back in my seat. "Wait, that actually works? I mean I've heard about things like that, but I thought they were myths."

"Not in the slightest. Be careful where you leave any part of you."

I tried very hard not to make a face at that. "Yeah, I'll remember that. Ick."

Bria smiled and shook her head. "I've strayed far from my point. Thank you for your help, and if you ever need a favor that either of us can do, let us know." She left before I could figure out an answer to that.

***

The next day or two, several of the more powerful magic users on the faculty spent a lot of time and effort into incorporating anti-illusion wards into the doors and walls. From what Denise said, it would make it harder for someone to use illusions while on the floor, and there was no way to root them onto the doors, walls, ceiling, or floor itself.

Though, if my research was right, someone could use an illusion to disguise themselves on another floor and then come up. It was just harder to maintain. But both tactile illusions and true Phantom Flames could only be cast by a very powerful illusion caster anyway. It let Ilse and I cross another three ideas off our list, but we were still stumped.

It quickly became evident that more illusions might not be necessary. Arie's accusation didn't die down. No one came out and confronted me, even the harpy didn't say it again; but I heard the rumors and saw the way some of the girls were looking at me. The whispers redoubled, and more people were avoiding me. Girls who had been neutral or even friendly before. I had a lot of time to practice Ilse's tricks of walking and pretending to be calm and collected.

Nor was that the only break in friendship. The ice twins seemed to be avoiding Phyna as much as possible without being actually rude. Kara actually growled at Setrai when fairy came into the lounge, saw us there, and left. I know there were other fights but I didn't know all of them. We may not have figured out who was doing this, or why, but if it was to get us all fighting each other, it was working.

I wondered if Hyde always had this much strife, but my friends were freshmen like me, and wouldn't know. Adrian was a second year, but I wasn't sure it was a good idea to ask him. He probably wasn't an unbiased source anyway. That left Thylica and Taria to ask. Both of whom seemed surprised and furious by everything that was going on, which would seem to imply this was new. So, if this *was* new, why?

Strangely enough, I received a major hint written on my door. I came back from gym class the see Kara and the ice twins attacking my door with sponges. Rather sweet of them, really, even if it wasn't very effective. Someone had written on my door in permanent marker. No insults this time; no threats. Just one sentence. *Hyde doesn't need humans.*

Because it didn't harm the door, the wards didn't notice it. Because it wasn't magic, it couldn't be dismantled by the staff, and because it was permanent marker, well, it wasn't coming off in a hurry.

Kara froze when she saw me standing there, reading the message, with no expression on my face. "Violet...just." She dropped her sponge. "I'm sorry."

I shook my head. "You didn't do it. Does Ilse know?" She had been furious about the Phantom Flames, but I think she was also just as glad to have missed it, even if she wouldn't admit it.

"Don't think so. She hasn't come out."

Made sense. Risa said the doors were mostly soundproof and Ilse was probably asleep. Besides, writing with a marker isn't that loud. "It isn't coming off, is it?"

"Not easily. In fact, I'm not sure we've made any progress," Bria admitted, scrubbing the 'Hyde' with her sponge like it had insulted her.

I looked at the message. "How wide would you say that was? About a foot?"

Everyone looked at it. "Can you give that in metric? Or Interdimensional length?" Kara asked.

"Blast. I don't have Interdimensional standards memorized yet. In metric, that's, um, 2.54 centimeters to an inch, twelve inches to a foot, about thirty centimeters? Give or take?"

"Yeah, that looks right. Why?" Kara asked.

"Because if we can't get rid of it, the second best option is to cover it up. Doesn't the bookstore sell posters?"

"Yeah. So we should probably stop getting your door wet." Krystal collected the sponges.

"Probably. Thank you for trying to get rid of it. I really do appreciate it." It also made me wonder if there were a few other things they might have managed to get rid of before I found out about them. It wouldn't have surprised me if they tried.

Thinking deep thoughts and walking are not a good combination, I proved by once again nearly walking straight into Adrian, who gave me a funny look. "Didn't you *just* go in?"

"I did, and discovered I had to run an errand. Why are you still here? For that matter, why are you following me anyway?"

"I have my reasons. What's the errand?"

"I'm never going to get a straight answer out of you, am I?" I rolled my eyes. "Well, turnabout is fair play."

He shadowed me as I stalked to the bookstore, just as I knew he would. Foreknowledge or not, it aggravated me. I was getting tired of being followed. I was getting tired of this evasive routine, and I was getting just plain tired of all these things happening.

Even as I was growing more annoyed, I didn't know why it was bothering me so much that Adrian was acting the same way he always did. Maybe I was still reacting to the message. Why did someone want me gone this badly? Was *everything* that was going wrong because someone wanted me to leave? But why?

"Hey, Adrian. Got a question for you." I impulsively spun around. Adrian blinked in surprise and came to a quick, much more graceful stop to avoid colliding with me.

"What would that be?"

"Why do so many people on this campus hate me?" I couldn't explain why I thought this would help, but I wanted to hear his answer.

He obviously wasn't expecting a question like that. "I don't think the problem is quite as big as you think. Many know very little about you, and some believe what they hear. That's where the problem lies."

I went back to walking. "Yeah, the juiciest gossip spreads the fastest."

"Plus, you find out about the two percent who hate you, not the eighty percent who don't care one way or another."

"Eighty-two percent?"

"You have friends."

He had a point, even if he probably made up the numbers on the spot. I had been trying to resist temptation, but finally I couldn't. "How about you? Do you hate me?" I carefully didn't look at him as I waited for his answer.

I still saw his look of quickly covered surprise from the corner of my eye. "Honestly? I tried, at first."

"Why?" *Why did you want to hate me? Why not now?*

"I have my reasons." Adrian wasn't looking at me, even as he held the door to the bookstore open for me.

"You know, getting answers from you is harder than getting them from Professor Pod." Even once you got used to the clicks and whistles that seemed randomly interspersed, there was still the fact that he was lousy at simple explanations. Maybe he spent too much time teaching the upper levels, but he was constantly pulling in things that were too advanced for our class. Fortunately, I was pretty decent at math, and the book was easy to understand.

I jumped as Adrian actually laughed at that. It was the first time I had ever heard him laugh. I had seen it, back on the mainland, but I hadn't been close enough to hear him. He had a nice laugh. Rolling and easy.

"So you *do* laugh. I take it you've had Professor Pod too?" I started leafing through the posters. It would have to be something big enough to hide the message, and something neither Ilse nor I would mind.

"Two classes so far. Likely more in the future."

"My condolences." I pulled out a poster. A lighthouse on a cliff over a choppy, storm-swept sea, with some inspirational saying about light in the darkness. The saying was a little trite, but I liked the picture and hopefully Ilse wouldn't mind either. Best of all, it was wider than it was tall. Perfect.

While I was there, I also picked up a blue and purple Hyde sweatshirt. I was still having trouble with the cold, and it was only September. I paid for my purchases and we left before I spoke again. "So, are you a math major?"

"Chemistry."

"Hmm, you wouldn't know how to get rid of permanent marker, would you?"

"Get it off what?"

"Varnished wood."

I could half see Adrian shrug. "I'd try rubbing alcohol. That should get most of it."

I stopped, turned, and looked at him. "Why didn't I ask you that five minutes ago?"

He eyed at me curiously. "Because you didn't? Why?"

I ignored him and ducked back in the store to buy some rubbing alcohol. Leaving again, I was confronted by him staring at me, appearing to wonder if I had lost my mind. "Someone wrote something on my door with a marker." I shook the bag. "I came to get a poster to cover it up, but if your rubbing alcohol does the trick, that's even better. Thank you, Adrian."

"Don't mention it. What did they write?" His voice deepened, and got gruffer. Once again I wondered what animal he shifted into.

I tried to wave the whole thing off, but he wasn't willing to drop it. "Oh, something about humans not being needed at Hyde."

"They're wrong, you know." There was an odd note in his voice, making me pay attention. "Humans are necessary for Hyde. I don't know how or why, but my sister says it's true. She Knows things." I could hear the capital letter there. Ilse *had* said that some shifters were psychic.

Before I could ask him about that, I remembered something else. "Taria said that there have always been humans at Hyde, and always would be."

"Look it up, she's one of the school's founders. If anyone would know, she would."

The school was even older than I had thought when I applied, almost a thousand years old. "What exactly is Taria?" I usually tried not to ask that question. Some thought it was rude, and there were many here who didn't have counterparts I knew of. But Taria seemed to be something else entirely.

"Taria is unique. As far as anyone can tell, she is the only one of her kind. Hard to define a species with only one individual."

I nodded. Without another specimen to compare and contrast with, it was impossible to know what was a species trait and what was individual. We were back at the dorm, and I had a lot to think about. "Thanks again. I'll let you know how the alcohol works." He waved it off, but I saw him watching me until the elevator door closed.

***

The rubbing alcohol did the trick, eliminating almost all traces of ink. I did remember to show Thylica, both before and after cleaning, so we wouldn't get written up for damages to the door. The poster ended up on my door instead of the main one.

Ilse didn't mind the poster, but she was furious about the message, and I was once again told to ignore the idiots. Easier said than done. I decided to change the subject before her anger re-sparked mine. "Do you know how letters and packages can be mailed to the school? My parents want instructions."

"Instructions for your dimension should be in the student packet. Or you could make arrangements through the post office in the town on your mainland. Though I was under the impression you were communicating with your family."

"Through email. My birthday is next week, and they want to send a package."

"Oh, how quaint. I suppose you younger races would celebrate birthdays. When is it?"

I decided not to comment on the 'quaintness' of it. Made sense that someone who lived as long as Ilse wouldn't be terribly concerned about individual birthdays anymore. I wasn't sure of her exact age, but I knew she was over two hundred. Vampires mature slowly.

"September thirtieth."

"How old will you be? If it is not rude to ask."

"Some people get offended but that's usually when they're older. I'll be nineteen."

Ilse shook her head and muttered something about infants that I pretended not to hear. "The school has a postal drop in all dimensions. The school handbook should tell you what you need to know." Ilse smiled suddenly, a smile that disappeared as quickly as it came.

"Ilse? What was that look for?"

"Why, whatever do you mean?" Ilse sounded so mystified that I almost believed her. Almost.

"That look. The look as if you just came up with some idea I should probably be extremely leery of."

"I don't know to what you are referring. I shall check the door now."

I couldn't figure out a way to bring the topic back and wasn't convinced I hadn't imagined it. Wasn't convinced I had, either. I'd just have to wait and see.

It wasn't a long wait. Kara didn't have a subtle bone in her body, and apparently Tim was worse at keeping secrets than I would have imagined. When Kara started trying to figure out my favorite colors without explaining why, I figured she knew about my birthday. Tim was the one who let slip about the party. He might not have come out and said it, but we both knew I figured it out. I didn't call him on it; he looked embarrassed enough as it was.

Instead, I talked to Ilse. "Did you tell Kara about my birthday?"

"It may have come up." Ilse didn't look up from her book. Now I knew she was hiding something. Normally she wouldn't act so rude.

I tried to keep my voice level. "She thinks she's being subtle."

"Not a generally accepted strength for werewolves, I admit."

"She hasn't said she knows. That means she's planning a surprise."

Ilse shrugged.

"Tim's in on it. I think the ice twins are too."

"You've made some real friends at Hyde." Ilse turned a page. I doubted she was reading though.

"Best I've ever had." It was true. "Kara's planning a surprise party, isn't she?"

Ilse had far too much experience with politics teaching her how to control her reactions, but I did see her lick a fang quickly. "If it is a surprise party, then by definition, aren't you supposed to be unaware of it?"

I ignored it. "She's trying to make it fairly big, isn't she? Kara loves big gatherings with lots of people."

"She does."

"How many people is she trying to convince?"

Ilse finally looked up at me. "You don't sound enthusiastic."

"How often do I voluntarily join large groups?" I wasn't afraid of crowds, I just got very uneasy sometimes. It had only gotten worse at Hyde. Ilse had noticed a few times.

"Point taken. I'll talk to Kara."

"She'll be upset, won't she?" I sunk into the couch.

"Perhaps a little."

I sighed. "I hate large parties."

"I'll talk to her."

"No, let her do what she wants. It's really nice of her to organize this. No one's ever thrown me a party before." I had never had enough friends to invite. "I'll act surprised." I tried to sound calm, maybe even pleasant, but I think it came out more resigned. Evidently Ilse thought so too.

"She wants you to enjoy it. It is *your* party."

"Can you try to steer her towards keeping things low-key without letting on I know?"

"I can do that. It's probably better than inviting the whole dorm anyway, or even just the whole floor."

I winced. Half the floor wasn't even talking to each other right now. Kara was a hard person to be angry at, so almost everyone was still friends with her. As a result she didn't always see how people weren't friends with each other. I'd seen it before. She'd invite a few people over who couldn't stand each other, and be confused about why it was so awkward.

Anyway, it was nice of Kara to do this, really nice. I was not going to be the one to rain on everyone's parade. Besides, maybe it would be a distraction from the nasty cold going around. I was on the tail end of it, but Kara and Tim seemed to be picking it up. All I had to do was be determined to have a good time. Everything would be fine.

Chapter Eleven
Once in a Blue Moon

My birthday was the thirtieth of September. The twenty-eighth was a full moon. Since the first was also a full moon, this was a blue moon. I had missed August's full moon by a couple days, so this was my second full moon since coming to Hyde.

Not being a Were of any kind, and having only a passing interest in astronomy, I never paid much attention to the lunar cycle. I wouldn't have realized it was a blue moon, if Kara hadn't mentioned it at breakfast that morning. Probably wouldn't have realized it was a full moon at all if the school didn't keep track of the lunar cycle. Three public clocks tracked the moon cycle, the weekly paper kept an astronomy page, and most of the calendars listed moon phase.

Still, it wasn't something that affected me. Kara, on the other hand, was affected. Last full moon she admitted how tiring the transformation was, and how even with the zealopor to sleep through the night, she was sore, worn out, and ravenously hungry the next day. Needless to say, she wasn't a fan of blue moons, putting her through all that twice in a month.

Apparently being sick only made it worse. Kara was in the most serious stage of the cold, and her resistance was currently at its weakest. She was stuffed up enough she could barely breathe through her nose, and her sense of smell was about gone. Kara claimed that was extremely disconcerting to a Were, which I didn't doubt. I also knew that she was going through cough drops like candy. I commiserated as well as I could at breakfast, and forgot about it by lunch other than getting Kara a 'Get

Well' basket from the campus store with the intention of giving it to her tomorrow. Forgot completely about it, until that night.

About midnight, I was trying to convince myself to stop reading and go to sleep. I had music class the next morning at eight, and a morning person I was not. I had almost persuaded myself to put the book down when total chaos broke out.

It wasn't until later that I was able to separate what happened and in what order. Everything happened within seconds of each other. But looking back, the first sound was a scream that quickly transitioned into a howl. Within a second or two, there were more screams, in a different voice. Almost as soon as that started, there was a really loud buzzing sound, and some light near the ceiling started brightening and dimming rapidly.

I was already moving, even if I didn't know to where. Ilse beat me to the living room and was almost out the door. "That's an alarm. Someone is badly hurt." I followed without thinking about it.

All up and down the hallway, doors were being flung open as everyone came out to see what was the matter. No one was coming out of 612, Kara and Denise's room. Their door was pulsing with blue light. I could guess what that meant.

Before I could figure out what, if anything, I could do, Thylica arrived up the steps at a run. She made some hand motion to the door, and if flew open without her touching it.

Being directly across the hall, I had one of the best views into the room. Not that I wanted it. It was my first, and hopefully last, look at a transformed werewolf. Kara was definitely not asleep, and judging by the furious, hungry look in those golden eyes, wasn't aware either. The wolf-human leapt at the door with a vicious howl, claws extended. Claws that, like the fangs, were already dripping blood.

She was maybe halfway to the door when Phyna caught her in the air and pinned her to the ground. Were-Kara thrashed and fought, howled and tried to bite, but dragon scales are thick and Phyna, being nearly nine feet long, outweighed her by a couple hundred pounds whichever form Kara was in.

Thylica, who apparently had not panicked at nearly becoming werewolf chow, entered the room, hand glowing white, and shot a ball light directly at the snarling werewolf. Kara stiffened then went limp.

The RA stepped into the room and started snapping out orders. "Setrai!" The fairy looked up, startled. "Call the infirmary; tell them we have a badly injured student who can't be moved."

Setrai dashed to her room. A moment later she came back out. "The phones are down!" I suddenly remembered a notice we had gotten about maintenance on the phone lines.

I'm pretty sure Thylica swore. I know I wanted to, and I don't swear. Looking up from her spot next to Denise, the wood elf eyed the crowd. "Cal!" The wind elemental jumped. "Go find a healer, one with Healing Touch, and tell them the same thing. Then tell them that we have a werewolf who did not respond to the zealopor. Go now." The brunette nodded and literally flew to the lounge. "Good. Phyna, you can get off her, but stay close. That won't keep her under for more than an hour, possibly less. Krystal, Bria, if necessary, can you ice up Kara's door so she can't get out before morning? Good, be ready to do that, just in case. Everyone else, stay out of the way. Morpha, where's Felicity?"

The chimera responded quickly. "Sound asleep. Didn't even twitch when the alarm went off. I checked."

Thylica nodded, kneeling next to an unconscious and badly bleeding Denise. My first aid training was kicking in and nastily reminding me of just how fast people could bleed out. I wasn't sure what the RA was trying to do, but from the frustration on her face, it wasn't working. "Where's that healer? She won't stop bleeding." I don't think we were supposed to hear that.

Five minutes for Cal to get to the infirmary at least. Who knew how long it would take the healer to get here. Denise had already lost enough blood to be unconscious, and looked ashy. The healer couldn't be here fast enough. No, there had to be a way! I saw one of the ice twins, I think it was Bria, shiver as if cold. That's it! "What if you induced hypothermia?" I got a number of stares, and explained as quickly as I could. "Lower core temperature, so the body conserves heat by shutting down or slowing certain functions. It can slow or stop bleeding in an emergency situation. It's risky though. Frostbite is likely, and that can be deadly."

Thylica bit her lip, ears wiggling as she looked at Denise. "Not riskier than doing nothing. The healers can deal with frostbite." She turned to the ice twins. "Do one of you have enough control and are willing to try?"

"Krystal probably can," Bria volunteered, turning toward her twin. "Just sit next to her and radiate cold. You've done it before. We have to *try*."

Krystal, who had looked about to argue, swallowed hard, and took a seat next to Denise. Eyes closed in concentration, she stretched one hand out over Denise's heart. Ice crystals formed on the carpet. Slowly, almost imperceptibly at first, the bleeding slowed, then stopped. Denise's breathing did not.

Just then, two people teleported into the hallway. One was a female, about two feet tall, with skin that was inky black, dotted with shiny white spots all over. It was like looking at the night sky. She was apparently the teleporter, because she just stood there as the healer rushed over. I hadn't seen him before. He was about twice the size of the teleporter, green, feathered, with furry flippers. After a minute or so of waving his flippers around, the worst gashes were closed up, and Denise's color and breathing looked better.

"Good thinking on the cold, may have saved her life. Now, what's this about the werewolf?"

"Over there. I put her under, but it won't last long, and it's dangerous to put her under too many times." Thylica gestured.

"How do you know she took the herb?" He waved his flippers over Kara, but in a different way than he did when he was tending to Denise. It was less directed, more like he was scanning for something.

"Kara cares too much to risk hurting someone," Thylica answered stiffly. I was pretty angry at the accusation too. Though I'm sure he had to ask.

"She's not allergic and doesn't have a history of bad reactions. Where is it anyway?"

"Not here." Thylica looked around, then eyed the milling crowd who was hoping for news. I had come inside to explain hypothermia, so I got drafted. "Violet, go into her room, the one on the left, and see if you can find it. It should be in a small gray pot."

I slipped around the chaos and into Kara's room, feeling like a thief. It wasn't the first time I had been in Kara's room, by far. She was always inviting people in, and I got more than my fair share of invites. It got awkward when she invited someone anti-human as well, which still happened sometimes. Still, it was the first time I was in without her direct permission. Something that would probably matter even more to Kara than to me.

Fortunately, I didn't have to snoop. The pot was on her desk, open. I picked it up and was hit with a familiar smell. Trying to place it, I brought the zealopor into the main room. Then it hit me. "Aloe?"

Both the healer and Thylica looked up at me sharply. "What about aloe?" The healer asked suspiciously.

"That's what this smells like."

"It shouldn't." He briskly took it from my hands and gave it a cautious sniff. "It does." Talking to himself, he continued, "Aloe would–" he stopped, realizing almost everyone on the floor was still watching. "Thank you." He turned to Thylica, "The shifter is stable enough to move now. Crostyas can teleport her to the infirmary and bring some zealopor back. Or give some to the elemental to bring back, if she's still there. It won't be as effective, though, since she's already transformed. If you can seal her in her room until morning, just in case, it would be helpful."

"Already made plans."

"Good. Then all we need is space."

"Right. Krystal, Bria, you two stay here. Everyone else, to your rooms or elsewhere. This isn't a show."

The crowd slowly dispersed, with great reluctance. Arie made some comment about my recognizing the problem awfully fast, but I was too upset to pay attention to the harpy. Ilse and I went back to our room, where Ilse kept the door open a crack and stood there listening. Ilse's hearing was better than mine, so I kept quiet, trying not to distract her. After a few minutes, she nodded and shut the door completely.

"What did you hear?"

"Aloe ruins the zealopor. Because someone put aloe in it, the herbs didn't make her fall asleep."

"Someone wanted her to attack Denise? That's awful!"

Ilse was grim-faced. "It's a good thing you figured out it was sabotage. If they thought that the fault was hers, like if she hadn't taken it, then she would be expelled, probably imprisoned, possibly even executed." I gasped. "It is a serious offence. Especially in Inter-dimensional territory. Denise was nearly killed. And Kara…"

I sunk into the sofa. "Yeah. Will Denise be alright?"

"The healer said that Denise should recover completely. They can practically work miracles at the infirmary, depending on the injury."

"Um, stupid question, but she won't turn into a werewolf, will she?" My research on Weres had said it was mostly genetic but there were ways to transform a non-Were into a Were. I just hadn't found anything that said how.

Ilse gave a small smile. "No. Shifters cannot be turned into Weres, period. *You* could, but not through being bitten. If I recall correctly, it requires a special ceremony involving drinking a special herbal mixture and sharing blood with a Were. This has to be performed at least four times, at certain lunar phases. It also isn't always successful, as the human body may reject the change. That is, shall we say, less than pleasant. Personally, I don't recommend it."

"Wasn't planning on becoming a Were." I managed a small smile.

"Good. You could become a vampire instead, which is a much better choice. Though it does take longer, and if the change is rejected, the human dies. With Weres, they are simply horribly maimed."

Right, that didn't encourage me to try either. "Um, I'm fine being human, thanks. Though out of curiosity, how does one change from a human to a vampire?"

"To begin, the vampire drinks a little bit of the human's blood, directly, not stored, under the full moon for three months. Each time, a few drops of blood are placed on a silver mirror, mixed with mud, and a ground up vampire rose. These only grow in certain dimensions. The human drinks this mixture, don't make faces at me, they do. Then the third month, they drink some of the vampire's blood too. Over the next month, they become a vampire. Or they die."

Mud. Drinking mud. The idea of drinking blood bothered me too, but I could as least see how someone who wanted to become a vampire probably wouldn't be as grossed out by it. All the same, I was perfectly content with remaining human. And whether it was her intent or not, Ilse had temporarily distracted me. "What about Kara? What will happen to her?"

"There will be a hearing, where they determine Kara's level of culpability. If it is decided she was not at fault, then nothing will happen to her, discipline-wise anyway. Mentally…"

"It's not her fault!" She would still feel so guilty.

"Unless she ruined her own zealopor."

"Kara would never do that."

"I don't think so either, but it isn't impossible." I glared at her. "Fine, she's completely innocent. But the school still needs to investigate."

"When will the hearing be?" I asked. Kara would need some emotional support.

"Probably sometime tomorrow. You may be asked to testify."

"Me? Why me? Will everyone on the floor have to testify?"

"Possible, but unlikely. However, you were the one who suggested hypothermia, and the one who identified aloe in the herb."

"I recognized the smell."

"Yes, but being the one to discover the sabotage, as well as one of Kara's best friends—"

"One of fifty."

Ilse smiled but didn't comment. "They will have to be sure that you didn't add the aloe after the fact to provide an alibi for your friend."

"I didn't even know aloe was bad for her!" I insisted.

Ilse held up a hand to calm me. "It isn't. Unless it's added to their zealopor. I know you had nothing to do with it. Just as I know Kara is not to blame. But the school must investigate. That way they can find the real culprit, and when certain people make foolish comments, we can rub their noses in the truth."

"People like Arie?"

"Ignore her. You should sleep. It's after one."

"You think I can sleep after this?" I asked in disbelief.

"I think you have to try. You have class in the morning. And if you are called into the hearing, you do not wish to be sleep deprived." She had a point, even if I didn't want to admit it. "I am off to class. Make sure the doors are locked and don't let anyone in." I knew she didn't have class until three, but didn't bother to say anything. She probably wanted to gather information. I'd find out what she learned later.

***

I didn't sleep well, but I did get some. Enough to not quite fall asleep in Music. Professor Shale noticed, but was understanding. About once a week in music, someone would start to fall asleep, and she'd sneak up on them, letting her snakes tickle them or lick an ear. This time she didn't do that to anyone. I guess the faculty knew what happened.

The students certainly knew something. Something, but not everything. The rumors were everywhere, and got wilder by the hour. I tried to ignore them. Any real information would just fuel the fire.

I was not interrogated as such, but Taria was waiting for me when I finished math. It wasn't my day for history, and I guess she didn't want to wait. Adrian, my usual stalker, was there, but skedaddled quickly at a glance from her. I had to hold back a stab of jealousy as he turned the corner.

"Now, Violet, it won't be that bad. I just have to ask you a few questions. I'm not going to read your mind per se, but I will know if you lie. Is this acceptable? You are not under investigation and can refuse."

If I did, they would be investigating me next. "That's fine."

"Excellent. Would you prefer to go to my office, or stay here?"

"How long do you think this will take?"

"Hopefully not more than five or ten minutes."

"It would take almost that long to go to your office. Here is fine."

"Very well." Professor Pod was leaving, so she borrowed his classroom. Taria took a seat, wings stretched like giant ribbons, and closed her eyes for moment, saying something about scanning for eavesdroppers. "To begin, perhaps you can tell me if you noticed anything unusual about Kara yesterday? Do you believe you would be in the position to notice if she was acting strangely?"

"I eat breakfast with her and Denise most mornings and typically see her at least a couple other times a day. So, yes, I think I would notice if she was acting odd." Taria nodded. "Yesterday, she seemed pretty normal. I mean, she's had a cold for a few days, and she wasn't quite as cheerful as usual because of that and the full moon, but that was all."

"She mentioned the full moon?"

"Yeah, complained a bit about it being a blue moon so she had to go through it twice this month, once while sick. From what she tells me, it seems the change is pretty exhausting."

"Good word for it. But she gave you no clue anything might be unusual about this full moon?"

"No, after a few complaints, she didn't even mention it."

"I see. Very well, in your own words, what happened last night?"

There wasn't much to tell. It was thinking it over to explain to Taria that I was able to separate the sounds and figure out the order. Taria listened carefully, almost pouncing when I mentioned the aloe. "You recognized the scent?"

"When I picked up the pot, I knew I recognized the scent, but it took me a moment to place it. When I did, I said it out loud. That's what got Thylica and the healer interested."

"How familiar are you with the scent of aloe?"

"I have an aloe plant at home. The scent is fairly distinctive once you know it."

"What do you know of the chemical makeup of zealopor?"

"Nothing. At first I thought the aloe was part of it."

"At first?"

"Ilse told me it didn't."

"Did you add the aloe?"

"What? No!"

"I didn't think so. I simply had to ask." Her wings touched the ceiling. "I have no more questions for you. Do you have any questions?"

"Is Denise alright? Can she have visitors? Is Kara alright? She's not in trouble, is she? Who–"

Taria held up a hand as her wings joined together and came to a sharp point. "Denise has been stabilized and is expected to make a complete recovery. You will have to contact the infirmary and ask if she can have visitors. Kara's situation has not yet been fully determined, and cannot be discussed until resolution has been met."

I nodded. I wasn't happy about it, but if it was me, I wouldn't want everyone discussing me either. Taria dismissed me then, and I left, not in the slightest bit surprised to see Adrian waiting around the corner. "She'll be okay." He didn't look away from the window.

I looked at him, a little surprised he was talking to me at all, and even more surprised that he was trying to comfort me. I must have looked miserable.

"The werewolf. If she didn't sabotage her own zealopor than they can't punish her. The question is who hates her that badly. Or her roommate." He started to walk as I did.

"But *everyone* likes Kara. I don't think Denise has any enemies either." As far as I could tell, that wasn't an exaggeration. Even Arie was polite to Kara, and she wasn't friends with anyone but Tatiana, the pixie at the other end of the hall.

"Don't know what to tell you."

I shivered. "Things just keep getting worse. The illusions were bad enough, but this could have been deadly. Why would anyone do this?"

Adrian shrugged.

"Are things like this happening all over campus? Or is it just Price?"

"It looks like your dorm."

"My floor?" Other than that one illusion on the second floor, I hadn't heard of problems anywhere else.

Adrian nodded reluctantly.

"Were things like this last year?"

"No."

"So what changed? What makes this year so much different than last year? It can't all be because of me. Can it?"

"No," Adrian said, immediately.

"You know something." I didn't know why I thought that, but I was sure. His reaction only confirmed my suspicions. "You know something. Adrian, if you are hiding important information, then so help me–"

"I don't."

"I don't believe you."

"I don't know much. Just what my sister said. Last year, I almost gave up on Hyde, but she stopped me. She told me…" He paused, as if stumbling over words. "I can't tell you exactly what she said, and I don't think you'd believe me if I told you. But she told me that things were going to get bad here. Worse than last year. But I'd be needed. She mentioned you, too."

"Me?"

"Something about purple. I realized the first time I met you, and I knew. I tried fighting it, denying it, but things kept happening. You kept nearly getting hurt in front of me, and I couldn't ignore it anymore. She said it was important that you stayed here, stayed safe."

"That's why you keep following me? To keep me safe?" I shook my head. "And you couldn't have just told me? 'Hey, Violet, I've been told by a Seer that you might be in danger. Mind if I follow you around? Maybe ask some of your friends to do the same?' I would have listened. I might not have believed you, but maybe I would have. Heck, I was willing to believe just about anything those first few weeks."

"I figured you had heard the rumors by then. You had no reason to believe me or trust me, and every reason to tell me to get lost."

"So you tried stalking me, which is so much more socially acceptable." I'm not usually this sarcastic, but I didn't usually have this much emotional overflow either.

Adrian shrugged. "I made sure to always have an excuse the first few days. When you never bothered to ask, I stopped coming up with them. Besides, by thinking of me as a possible threat, you were more alert and careful of other possible threats. I was trying to keep you safe, not make sure you liked me."

"You have a very cynical worldview, don't you? By the way, I didn't find out anything about you until after you started following me."

"Must have miscalculated there," He muttered.

"Why me, anyway? I'm no one special."

"Neither am I. But you don't have to be special to play a role in destiny."

"You sound like a fortune cookie," I complained.

"I just know what she told me. I don't think she knows any more than that either."

"When you say you can't tell me what your sister said, you mean that literally, don't you?" Something in his face suggested it.

"Unfortunately, yes. It's a long complicated story, but basically I'm sworn to secrecy of a type. She could tell you, but I can't. I'd rather not test it too far. I've seen someone whose tongue literally tied itself into knots when they tried to break something like that. It was every bit as painful as it sounds."

I shuddered. "Yeah, I'd pass on that too."

"Then make sure you don't discuss Hyde too closely with anyone who isn't in the know. The consequences are similar or worse."

"Thanks for the warning. I have to go now." I waved goodbye and went in my dorm.

The first thing I did was call the infirmary. They said Denise couldn't have visitors, but she might be able tomorrow. Next I knocked on Kara's door to check on her and give her whatever support I could. She didn't answer. When she didn't answer after the third knock I decided maybe she wasn't in. I'd try again later.

So I couldn't do anything for Denise or Kara, and I didn't want to think about what Adrian said just yet. Well, one thing about college, it didn't matter what kinds of crises were going on; there was still homework to be done. Not that it was always easy to focus on that homework.

I spent about an hour trying to make sense of my history text before deciding to take a break. It was giving me a headache, and I was starting to get hungry. Maybe after a snack.

I kept packages of microwave popcorn in my room, so I grabbed one and headed out to the lounge where the microwave was. I stopped at Kara's door first. "Hey, Kara? It's Violet. Are you there?" Nothing. "I'm making some popcorn. Do you want some?" Still no answer. With a sigh, I left.

There was a fifteen-foot snake sunning herself on the couch in the lounge, who I nodded to, before heading to the microwave. I had seen the snake often enough to know she was one of the girls on the floor, but hadn't figured out which one. She hung around the lounge in snake form a lot, so I had finally gotten used to it. The first time I saw the huge snake, it was quite a surprise. I didn't scream, but I did jump back and look around to see if someone was playing a trick on me. That was how I learned that snakes can give a pretty good impression of laughter. The things I learned in this school. Most of it had nothing to do with classes. "Want some popcorn?" I asked.

"Yes, please." Since shifters can't talk in animal form, unless their animal can talk, she must have switched back. I turned around to see who I was talking to.

It wasn't completely helpful. I didn't know her name, but I recognized her as the blonde who lived on the other end of the hall, with Celeste, the other vampire, I thought. I had seen her around, and was pretty sure she was in my history class.

"Sure, popcorn will be ready in a couple minutes." She was watching me, unblinking. "I'm sorry, but for the life of me, I can't remember your name."

"Sylvia. Sylvia Rhodes." There was a smile-smirk.

"Sylvia. Right. I'll try to remember that. I'm Violet."

"I know."

"I'm sure you do." I muttered. She raised her eyebrows. "I think most people on the floor know my name."

"I think most of the dorm, possibly the campus, may know your name."

I shrugged. "Not much I can do about it. Oh, popcorn's done." I opened the bag, shook it, and offered her some.

Sylvia took a handful, thanked me, and ate it, kernel by kernel, still watching me. Perhaps it was my imagination, or maybe it was a carry-over from her snake form, but she didn't seem to blink often. It was unnerving.

I was about to ask if she wanted something, but she spoke first. "You recognized the scent of aloe pretty quickly." It was not quite a question, not quite an observation. I decided to answer it like the casual comment it probably wasn't.

"Despite the name, I'm actually a bit of a black thumb." She snickered at that. "Aloe is one of the few plants I don't kill off in the first couple weeks. I've got an aloe plant at home that I've kept alive for two, three years. Plus, the goop inside the leaves is practically a miracle cure for burns and sunburn."

"Really?" Now she seemed interested.

I looked her over. Blonde, almost as fair as Ilse. "Burn easily?"

"Unfortunately."

"Well, they're nice and hardy. Just don't over-water them; they're succulents, like cacti. You can find them in supermarkets sometimes. Um, are there supermarkets where you live?"

Sylvia gave me a slightly exasperated look. "I *am* from 13A, same as you."

"Not every place, even in our dimension, has supermarkets. I don't know where you are from."

"Fair enough. I'm from Ireland actually. Yes, you can laugh. There is at least one snake in Ireland. And there are supermarkets."

I nodded. After a moment of hesitation, I asked a question that had been bothering me. "Can I ask a semi-stupid question?"

"What kind of snake am I?" Evidently she got that a lot.

"Yeah. I'm pretty sure you're a boa or a python of some sort, but I'm not up on snakes enough to tell which."

"You're further than some. I'm a reticulated python."

"Oh, okay." I tried to think of everything I knew about reticulated pythons. It wasn't much, just that they could get very, very big, and sometimes there were albino ones. Thylica walked by then, and I quickly flagged her down. "Thylica, is the floor doing something for Denise? A card, flowers, anything?"

"That's a good idea," Sylvia agreed.

"It is. I hadn't thought that far ahead, but it would be a thoughtful thing to do. Sylvia, I've seen you draw, you're very good. Would you be willing to make a card? We can get everyone to sign it. Violet, no offence, but it might be best if we didn't publicize this was your idea."

"Fine with me."

"Good. I can start with collection for flowers now."

For the most part, money was dealt with electronically, with our student IDs doubling as a bank card. But we also had slips of paper that we wrote our ID numbers on, the amount we wanted to spend, and our signature, for times like this; when we owed another person money, when the electricity was down, etc. The papers were enchanted and turned black if anyone wrote the wrong ID number, or an amount higher than they had. Both of us filled out a slip, and Thylica left several other slips, and a box to put them in, enchanted so only she could open it.

"Sylvia, when you are done with the card, just leave it here, and I'll put up signs telling people to sign it." Thylica was about to leave, but I wasn't finished yet.

"What about Kara? Is she alright?"

"Physically, yes. I checked on her this morning."

"And everything else?"

"I truly couldn't tell you."

"Is she in her room?"

"I couldn't tell you." I left it at that, even as I wondered if that meant she didn't know, or wouldn't tell.

Kara didn't respond when I tried again to talk to her, and offer her popcorn, on my way back to my room. So either she wasn't there, or she really didn't want to talk to me, or possibly anyone.

My attempts to do homework worked a little better this time, and I finished my history assignment and worked on a paper for Professor Argus until Ilse was up.

We signed the card before dinner, being close to the last people to sign it. Probably for the best. After dinner, I tried one more time to talk to Kara, failed again, and finished my paper while Ilse went intelligence gathering. She came back just as I was proofreading my draft.

"Official version is that her zealopor was sabotaged by person or persons unknown. Kara is in no disciplinary trouble, but for the rest of the semester, Thylica will have to monitor her transformation, ensuring she takes the zealopor and falls asleep."

"Well, that's not too bad."

Ilse disagreed. "To a non-Were. To a Were, it's downright insulting. All Weres are drilled from childhood in taking personal responsibility for their transformations. This says the school doesn't trust her to be responsible. What if they insisted you have a rubber mattress protector because they didn't trust you not to urinate in your sleep?"

I blushed. "Okay, put that way…" I thought about it awhile. "On the other hand, considering what happened…"

"I don't deny that they did their best with a bad situation, but Kara is bound to be mortified. Or will be once she gets over her fear of it happening again. No one's seen her since she talked to Taria. Some say she hasn't left her room at all."

"Shouldn't she be really hungry, having transformed and all?"

"Yes, she should. Hopefully she has food in her room."

Kara often had something to pass around to those who visited her in her room, but I couldn't remember ever seeing something substantial enough to count as a meal. I really hoped I was wrong. She hadn't responded when I offered popcorn, so hopefully she had something.

"This wouldn't have happened if she didn't have a cold," I muttered. If I could smell the aloe, then under normal circumstances, Kara certainly could.

"Maybe, maybe not. To be most effective, zealopor has to be taken within minutes of transformation time. Unless she made it a point to check beforehand, then even if she figured it out, it might have been too late. She might have been able to warn Denise, she might not."

I wasn't sure how to answer that one. My eyes fell on the computer screen, but it didn't have any answers for me, either.

"Are you finished with your paper?" Ilse and I had an arrangement. I was a faster typist, so I would type up her papers, and in exchange, she proofread mine. Since she was better at catching spelling and grammar mistakes, it worked well. It might not have worked if Ilse didn't actually know English, even without the translation spell, but she did.

It was a distraction ploy, and I knew it, but I certainly didn't have any more ideas. Besides I really did need the paper proofed. Professor Argus was extremely strict. "Yeah, I think so." I relinquished the computer.

Ilse took the seat. "Are you certain that's how you spell 'Chaucer'?"

I was tempted to answer that I was very sure that was how *I* spelled 'Chaucer' but refrained. "I looked it up. Twice."

Ilse gave a half-shrug and continued. I made some hot chocolate. I was chilly and never could stand watching people read what I wrote. "Is there anything we can do?"

"About your paper? I'd reword this sentence, but other than that–"

"Not the paper, and you know it. Kara. Denise. One or both of them."

"If I think of anything, I'll let you know. I am sorry about this ruining your birthday."

I almost laughed. "I completely forgot."

***

My birthday wasn't completely forgotten, but it was much lower key than Kara had probably planned. She still wasn't responding to anyone knocking on her door. There was no party, which I was now doubly glad about. It would have felt so callous, considering the circumstances.

Ilse had given me a necklace the night before, an amethyst pendent. I made a point of wearing it the next day. Tim, the ice twins, and even Adrian made a point of giving me small gifts at various points in the day. A few others wished me a happy birthday. My package from home hadn't arrived yet, but probably would soon.

Denise was up to having visitors, so I made sure to see her. She said she was healing nicely, seemed to be in fairly good spirits, for her, and clearly didn't blame Kara for what happened. That was good.

I mentioned trying to talk to Kara but she wouldn't respond. "Keep trying? Wolves shouldn't be confined too long," She said as I was leaving.

"I'll do what I can." Though I suspected it wouldn't be much.

On my way back, I tried again, but it was as successful as all my previous attempts. Eventually, I gave up. I was expecting a phone call from home.

My parents did call me, and we had a fairly decent conversation, if you ignored the fact that I had to sound like an idiot because there was no way to explain even the basics of the school. I decided against telling them anything about Kara's transformation gone wrong. Even if I could find a way to sanitize it enough to tell them, it would probably make them very uncomfortable with my choice of schools. They were already concerned enough with the way I was so vague about everything. I had just gotten off the phone, reassuring my sister once again that I'd be home for Christmas when there was a knock on the door.

Ilse was still asleep, so I carefully opened the door to find… no one. Looking around, I spotted something on the floor. A package wrapped in sky blue paper with an elaborate multi-colored bow. After everything that happened, I probably wouldn't have touched the box if I hadn't recognized the handwriting. It had been a surprise at first to discover that Kara had beautiful copperplate handwriting.

Opening the box, I found a beautiful journal with an etched leather cover, and a handmade card. Obviously this had been planned days ago, as the card was signed 'From Kara and Denise'. "Oh, Kara."

Chapter Twelve
The Wolf in Her Den

It had been two days since full moon. Two days that Kara had hidden herself in her room, not even leaving for classes as far as anyone could tell. I knew it wasn't my place to interfere but I couldn't ignore it anymore. Putting the card down, I walked across the hall, and started knocking on the door. No response. I waited a moment before knocking again, louder.

Phyna left her room about then, probably going to class. "She isn't answering."

"I know."

"I tried too, couldn't get a response."

"She'll respond eventually. Even if it's just to yell at me to stop and leave her alone." I knocked again. "Kara, it's Violet! Can we talk?" No answer. Phyna twisted her head in a way that seemed a bit like a shrug, wished me luck, and went off to class. I knocked again. "I really need to talk to you. It's important." Still nothing. "I'm not leaving until I get a chance to talk to you."

"What do you want?" Asked an empty sounding voice behind the door. Oh, Kara. This couldn't continue.

"I'm not shouting through the door. Can I come in?"

"It's not safe."

"It's completely safe. I trust you." After a pause, the door opened a crack. I had to open it the rest of the way, and by the time I was inside, Kara was practically hiding behind the couch.

"You know I'm not going to hurt you, right?" I took a seat not far from the couch.

"I'm not worried about you hurting me," Kara sounded exasperated. Well, it was better than depressed. "I'm worried about hurting you."

"Do you want to hurt me?"

"Of course not!" She pulled away from the couch in horror.

I shrugged. "Then don't. Why would you?"

"I hurt Denise."

"That was because someone sabotaged your zealopor and you ended up shifting to Were form. It isn't full moon, and you're not in Were form."

"I know all that." I had never heard her sound so irritated. Maybe I was going about things the wrong way, but I didn't have any other ideas.

"Are you sure? Because you aren't acting like it." Kara sputtered, but I continued. "Are you more dangerous after attacking someone? Get a taste for blood or something?" I doubted it. Ilse would have mentioned something like. Besides, Kara might not be human, but she certainly wasn't an animal either.

"No, not really."

"Then what?"

"I attacked Denise! I nearly killed her! Don't you get that?" Well, she was out from behind the couch. Kara was now pacing furiously as she raved, making me dizzy.

I had an idea. It could make things better, or make things worse. But I figured this was one time where doing nothing might be worse than doing the wrong thing. "Did you do it on purpose?" Kara stopped as if I slapped her. It hurt, but I continued. "If Denise walked in right now, would you attack her?"

"NO! Of course not!"

"Did you sabotage your own zealopor? Because the Kara I know wouldn't do that. And the Kara I know needs to stop blaming herself for something that wasn't her fault." She looked ready to argue. "I visited Denise today."

Kara deflated and stared at the carpet. "How is she?"

"Getting better. She says she'll probably be released in a day or two."

"Good." She hesitated. "Does she want a new roommate?"

I hadn't thought of that. I could see why it might be a possibility though. "No, I don't think so. She didn't say anything about it. In fact, she's worried about you."

Kara's eyes flew to mine. "Me? Why? She–"

"She's worried because no one has seen you since full moon, except for the administrators. She's worried because she knows you don't have much food here. She's worried because she knows it wasn't your fault and you're blaming yourself."

Kara went back to studying the carpet. "I wish it hadn't happened."

"So do we all. But it did. Now what?"

"What if I leave, and something happens? What if someone gets hurt? What if–"

"I don't know what will happen if you go out. But I have pretty good idea what will happen if you don't leave."

"What?" Kara asked.

"You'll stay here, depressed. Not eating, probably not sleeping," Her eyes had deep dark circles around them, and her hair was lanky and greasy. Probably hadn't taken a shower either, "until you collapse." Or worse. "Probably giving whoever sabotaged your zealopor exactly what they want. Someone very wise told me not to let bigoted idiots win. I know this is different. I know this is harder. But you won't be alone."

Kara nibbled at her lip. "Do you think…? Is it too late for Denise to have visitors today?"

"I doubt it." I smiled.

"Will you come with me?"

"Sure. Then we're going to dinner, because you have to be starved. Just let me leave a note for Ilse. Maybe she'll meet us there."

"Thanks. Oh, and Violet? Happy birthday."

***

It was not too late to visit Denise, thankfully; and it seemed to do Kara a lot of good. Both girls were more concerned about the other than they were about themselves. Denise apparently hadn't had many visitors and I was the only one willing or tactless enough to talk about Kara. Since I had been worried, Denise had been worried too. Or maybe she had been worried before that. It was hard to tell her emotions sometimes.

Afterwards, Kara was more cheerful, but still seemed frail. But she was trying, working on being more like her usual social self, and less hide-in-her-room-under-the-covers. So after I took a trip to town to pick up my birthday package, I invited her to visit with Ilse and me. She didn't seem up to inviting people to her room yet. Which wasn't surprising when I realized that it would have had to have been someone who she invited over who sabotaged her zealopor. I decided not to mention that one to Kara just yet. Even if she already had figured that out, it could only hurt her to think about.

Kara, always attracted to shiny objects, spotted the box with stickers on it quickly. "So, what's this?" She sounded almost like her usual self while drugged on cold medicine, like she had been for most of last week. Kara wasn't still on cold medicine, but you couldn't tell from her attitude.

"Package from home. It just got here today."

"For your birthday? Aw, it was late."

"Not too bad. Mom says they'll try to mail it sooner next time."

"You have not yet opened it?" Ilse observed.

"I didn't want to until I got back."

"So open it now," Kara suggested, bouncing slightly on the couch.

I smiled. "Well, if you insist…"

"We insist. We simply insist." Ilse smile-smirked. Kara didn't say anything, but bounced a little more.

"Okay, okay." I felt a little self-conscious opening gifts in front of them, but they seemed interested. Besides, Kara got packages from home every other week or so, and even Ilse had gotten a package or two. "Hm, microwave popcorn, good. Ooh, cookies. Anyone want some?" I passed around the bag. Kara took one, Ilse declined. I took one myself, and went back to the box. "A card, I'll read that in a bit. New gloves, excellent. Oh, it's cute." Rose had sent me a purple plush bear with a fancy pen rubber banded to his hand. The pen was also purple, with a small pressed violet inside a clear tube, while the purple part of the barrel said what the violets meant in the language of flowers.

"That is cute," Kara agreed, admiring the bear. "And soft."

"A new scarf, a bit more food, vitamin C, and some CDs. Pretty nice this year."

"Indeed, though you might have trouble getting your bear back from Kara." Kara dropped the bear as if burned. Ilse winced. "I was being humorous. Attempting so, anyway."

"Sorry, I'm a bit oversensitive."

"No, your nerves are just a bit raw. It will get better." I took the pen off the bear, then made it hug her arm.

"Are your parents worried about you being cold?" Ilse asked, lifting up the gloves and scarf. Probably more to give Kara time to recover than because she was curious.

"Yeah, this is a lot colder than I'm used to, and I'm having trouble adjusting. I'm going to ask for a new coat for Christmas. It's September, no, sorry, October, and its freezing. Hey, maybe you would know. I've noticed that it actually seems to be colder on the mainland than it is here at Hyde. Do you know if they do something to regulate temperatures here?"

"To an extent. Part of it is the number of buildings and people in close proximity, which is greater than that of the town, in most dimensions at least. That generates heat. In addition, the school has protections against extreme temperature shifts and fronts. Storms are also mitigated. In the middle of winter, Hyde may be up to five degrees centigrade warmer than the mainland."

"Nice to know. Thanks, Ilse."

"What's this?" Kara asked, pulling a paper from the card.

"I don't know, let me see." I took it and rolled my eyes. "My horoscope. I don't know why they sent that. They know I don't believe that. None of them really believe it either."

"Horoscope?" Ilse asked.

"Some people believe that the position of the stars at the time of your birth affects your personality and things in your life. They look up the positions of the stars and planets to predict things."

"Stars. Burning gas objects millions of miles away. These are supposed to control your life?" Ilse asked, voice dripping with skepticism.

Personally, I didn't think it any more outlandish than Ilse's fortune stones, which I had seen her consult a couple times; but I had enough sense not to tell her so. "Some people believe it. I never put much stock in it. Anyway, depending on when you're born, it's supposed to be associated with a certain constellation. I'm a Libra. Anyway, it doesn't matter."

"Okay, now we need cake," Kara decided, setting up the bear so it looked like he was reading my birthday card. "Do you have any cake?" I was pretty sure she was just trying to change the subject before things got tense, but I was fine with that.

"I do actually. Adrian gave me a cake yesterday, from the mainland. It was his present to me. Before you ask, I got Dr. Gronk to check it out. He said it's fine as long as I'm not diabetic or have serious food allergies." I didn't think Adrian would try poisoning me, not after our talk the other day, but Ilse would have been furious if I hadn't checked it out first.

Reassured, Kara accepted a piece. Ilse didn't, but I'm not sure she actually eats anyway, so I wasn't bothered by that. We didn't have candles, but I did make a wish. I wished Denise would recover, Kara would get back to normal, and everything would settle down at school.

***

Denise got out of the infirmary a day later, and things did seem a little quieter for a while. Wednesday night I was in the lounge trying to do my literature homework. Trying was the operative word. Kara was there too, trying to help, but we weren't in the same class and weren't covering the same material. It was making things difficult.

While she was trying to help me figure out how Trwzqletz the Grave influenced Rocyhgh the Bold, Arie came in to heat up some kind of soup. "You're still working on this? Honestly, it's completely obvious."

I was pretty sure I heard a low growl from Kara, but ignored it. Much as it pained me to do so, I swallowed my pride. "Then perhaps you can help me. I'm a little lost. These are completely new to me."

"Sorry, I have better things to do with my time than tutor wormbrains." Interesting insult. She may have been too busy to help me, but she apparently wasn't too busy to stand there scoffing as I struggled with the concepts and terms.

I was about ready to give up, or at least move to another room when Celeste, the other vampire on the floor, came in. She was carrying a book, and seemed to be looking for someplace to read. "Oh, I didn't realize this room was occupied."

"That's a book by Trwzqletz the Grave, isn't it?" I asked, recognizing the title.

"You've heard of him? He's one of my favorites."

Kara and I smiled. "May I ask a favor?"

Celeste was more willing to help than Arie was, and was even patient enough to ignore the harpy's comments. We generally pretended Arie wasn't there, even as she leaned over the table to sneer at my handwriting. At last, she got bored and left. Several other girls stopped in for various reasons, but no one else stayed long.

Finally I was finished. "Thanks, Celeste. I was having a lot of trouble with that."

"It is not a problem," Celeste said, starting to stand.

My homework done, I gathered everything. "I'm done, if you want the lounge. It looked like you wanted some quiet."

"Yes, Sylvia is shedding. It makes her irritable."

"Oh, is it painful?" I asked, concerned.

"No, it may be a little uncomfortable, but it doesn't hurt. She's simply cranky."

Kara had left to meet Denise about twenty minutes ago, and Ilse would probably wake up soon. I checked my stuff to make sure I had everything. "Wait a second, where's my pen?"

"Pen? I thought you were using a pencil."

"Yeah, I started with math and never switched over. But I brought a pen, too. A special one that my sister gave me for my birthday." It wasn't on the table, or under. Celeste helped me check under furniture, occasionally lifting furniture so I could look, but we didn't find it anywhere.

"Are you certain you brought it? Perhaps you left it in your room?"

I gave the room one last scan. "I was sure I brought it, but maybe you're right." It wouldn't be the first time I misplaced things. It took me five minutes to find my hairbrush this afternoon and I tried to always keep that in the same place.

"I hope you find it."

"Me too."

***

I had music class the next morning, and once again proved that morning were not my forte, this time to the tune of being ten minutes late to class. While I was usually cutting it close, I had never been this late before, and felt bad about it. According to class rules, if we miss roll call, we are supposed to check in with the teacher after class, so I did, making sure to apologize.

Professor Shale, normally easy-going, was in an exceptionally good mood for some reason, which made things a lot easier. "Don't worry about it. I don't always like dragging myself out of bed either. Sometimes the snakes even try to latch on to the pillow." The tiny serpents wriggled and hissed as if agreeing.

I giggled at the mental image. At least I didn't have that problem. "I have my homework."

"Good. Thank you. Here, let me change you from absent to late. I assigned the class to read chapter eight in the book and answer review questions one through five, that's due next class. Have you been listening to your CD?"

"Yes, I like this section." It was dimension 6A at the moment, so the music was really different, but I found it interesting. At least it was melodic. The previous section was 5C, and that was very discordant.

"Good. You'll be fine then. Now, shoo. I have another class to teach." She was smiling, and the snakes looked like they were waving.

Adrian waiting in the hallway wasn't a surprise. Tim trying to stare him down, was. At the moment, it looked like a draw, but tempers were clearly fraying.

"Hey, Tim. I didn't know you had this class." I moved closer to them, deliberately interrupting the contest.

"Hello, Violet. You are correct; I do not normally have this section. I take music in the afternoon, but today I wished to partake in the special lecture at three."

"The one on poetry and war?"

"The same. When I inquired, Professor Shale agreed to let me substitute this one instead."

"Good. I'll not keep you then." I moved further from the doorway. Sylvia and Arie passed by just then. I waved. Sylvia waved back, Arie ignored me.

"Yes, I need to go. I shall see you later then." Tim smiled at me, shot another look at Adrian, and went in the classroom.

I turned to Adrian. "I don't want to know, do I?"

"He's protective of you." Adrian shrugged, moving out of Felicity's way as she pushed past me into the room. There wasn't tons of room, but I'm pretty sure the werecat could have gotten by without pushing me.

"He's a good friend. Is this an exceptionally popular class or what?" I moved even further away so not to get caught up in a group of students heading in.

"It's a required class, and Professor Shale is a popular teacher. Besides, most diurnal students would probably prefer a nine o'clock class to an eight o'clock. That said, the yeti probably isn't the only one taking an earlier class to attend the lecture."

"You could be right. I'm off to breakfast." I was about to leave when the strangest expression came over Adrian's face. Before I could say anything, or even do more than register that something was wrong, Adrian tackled me to the ground, covering me with his body. Chaos broke out a second later.

Chapter Thirteen
Fire and Rock

I distinctly remember that my first thought was 'earthquake' followed quickly by 'snow'. Then there was something about it being far too loud. I was wrong about the first two, but I'll stand by the too loud one until the day I die.

The ground may have shook, and the building wobbled, dumping a ton of plaster dust on us, my 'snow', but it wasn't tectonic plates shifting. It was a classroom. Professor Shale's classroom. There weren't any other classes nearby.

"Was that an explosion?" I asked Adrian. The shifter was already starting to stand. Once upright, he brushed dust from his hands before offering me help up.

"Looks like it. Are you hurt? Violet, we can't go in there!" He called after me, even as I reached the glowing blue door. I had to force back flashbacks from full moon.

"People are hurt!" I stopped at the doorway despite myself. "Oh, no," I breathed. Two bookcases had fallen, desks and personal items had gone flying. People were bleeding, trapped, some even turned to stone. "What do we do?"

I felt Adrian behind me even before he spoke. "*We* wait for the professionals. I promise you that they're on their way, or will be within seconds."

I ignored him, carefully entering the disaster. Professor Shale was trapped under her desk, unconscious and bleeding badly. It looked like she had a head injury. A quick scan of the room told me she was probably the most seriously injured. "Help me move the desk," I said to Adrian, who had followed me in. As long as we didn't drop it on her, it wouldn't aggravate her injuries.

He helped me without a word. Her spine looked alright, but her head looked pretty bad. Kneeling carefully to avoid the broken glass, (*her glasses, her glasses broke, stone, stone, stone* Stop it!) I checked her head, obviously her worst injury. There was a small concave part of her head, where she was hit by something. Okay, I couldn't put pressure there, it might damage her brain. (*If it wasn't damaged already.*) The snakes in that area were partially crushed but 'alive'. That was probably a good sign. I wasn't sure just how interdependent the snakes and Professor Shale were.

"Leave it for the healers," Adrian tried again. This time I listened, sort of. Students in the classroom who weren't badly hurt or trapped started to come out of shock and help too. One, a pink feathery-flippered girl, said she could heal and came over to take a look. Probably the same type of being as the healer who helped Denise.

That out of my hands, I moved to the side of the room, where one of the bookcases had fallen, trapping Arie, Felicity, and a guy I didn't know. Adrian followed my cue, and I didn't even have to ask for help lifting the bookcase. Arie was closest to me, and didn't seem too badly hurt, so I offered her a hand up. She looked at me, liberally powdered with plaster dust, sniffed disdainfully, and carefully got to her feet without my help. Obviously she didn't realize she was covered in more dust than I was.

"How's your arm?" I asked.

It was bleeding, and she was cradling it protectively. "I don't need your help." She scowled at me. I hadn't even realized a beak could scowl, but she clearly was.

"Suit yourself." I turned to the guy. Wood elf, it looked like. He hadn't done more than sit up and was holding his ribs. "Are you alright?"

"Cracked ribs, I think. I'll be fine. Check on the others."

I nodded. The healers had finally arrived, and they could probably handle things better without my interfering. No one was trapped anymore. Adrian was, I suppose 'fending off' might be the best term, Felicity who was giving him full credit for saving her. I didn't care. I was more preoccupied with the middle of the room.

Now that I didn't have anything I needed to be doing, I couldn't hold back the cold waves of panic anymore. The middle of the room wouldn't be ignored any longer. Professor Shale had been facing that direction when the explosion went off. In the almost exact center of the room were four students turned to stone. Some guy I didn't know, the orange cat/mole/plant guy from orientation, Sylvia, and Tim. A curtain seemed to go through my mind, and that was the last thing I noticed for hours.

***

Kara told me, much later, that Adrian dragged me away from the room, found her and Denise, got Kara to stop yelling at him long enough to explain, and handed me over to them. She says that Adrian claimed I stared at the stone students for more than ten minutes before they were taken away by the healers, then continued to stare at that spot without reacting to anything going on around me until he dragged me away. I have no reason not to believe her, and I doubt Adrian was lying, but I don't remember any of that.

The next thing I *do* remember was finding myself sitting in the cafeteria with Kara, Denise, even Ilse who was draped with cloth and wearing sunglasses I'm pretty sure she borrowed from Denise. Not too many people wore purple sunglasses with yellow palm trees on them. Somehow it had gotten to noon, and I had an omelet in front of me. The cafeteria stopped serving omelets after ten-thirty, so we must have been there awhile. There were a few bites missing, so I evidently ate some. Or someone else took some while I was... 'out'. Not that I cared. "Ilse? What are you doing here? You should be asleep."

"I awoke when the school-wide alarm went off. Denise sought me out when it was obvious you were in shock. Normally, you would have been admitted to the infirmary, however..." She trailed off delicately, probably not wanting to remind me of what happened.

"But it's daylight."

"Which is why we are sitting in the shadows."

I nodded, both grateful and embarrassed that everyone was so concerned. "Thanks, guys. Do we know what happened?"

"Current tally, as of an hour ago, is eight seriously injured and four stone. No deaths. Yet," Adrian answered from the next table. I looked at him curiously, wondering how I missed noticing him before. On the other hand, at the moment I wasn't even sure how I got from the music room to the cafeteria. I just figured either Adrian or Kara was probably responsible. "Wolf Girl and I agreed to a temporary truce. Though your roommate is still threatening to bite me."

I decided there were more important things to worry about than whether or not everyone liked each other. They had obviously decided the same, so I'd leave it alone. "There is a way to reverse being turned to stone, right? I remember sh… she said that at the beginning of the semester."

"There is," Ilse answered hesitantly enough for my throat to seize up. "However, it requires the willing participation of the medusa responsible in the first place."

I swallowed hard. "How's Professor Shale?"

"Not good. Brain injuries are difficult even for magic to heal. They aren't sure if she'll wake up," Kara said, tearing up a little.

"The best way. The fastest, safest, easiest way to cure people turned to stone requires the willing participation of the medusa. But there are other methods. Once the immediate crisis is settled, the school will look into those options," Adrian said into a cup of water.

Well, that was something, but I really hoped Professor Shale recovered. "This is awful. I can't believe this happened."

"Classes and all extra-curricular events have been canceled until further notice. Classes are expected to resume Monday. It is recommended that students remain in the dorms or the cafeteria while the campus is being searched. The library is closed while the investigation is ongoing," Ilse told me.

The music room was in the basement of the library. "Yeah, Ms. Graz is furious. The library is her life," Denise said. She mused a moment. "I wonder if she bleeds ink."

I wasn't sure how to respond to that, so I didn't try. "Okay, I know Tim and Sylvia, but does anyone know who the other two students are? Who were…?"

"The freshman's name is Coltier, I think. He's a Tryver from dimension 3C," Adrian said. I'd have to look up Tryvers. I hadn't learned about them yet. "The other, Restlo, he's my roommate. He was last year, too." He stumbled a bit over the sentence, voice thick.

"Oh, I'm so sorry," I said, hearing my sentiments echoed a couple times. Even Ilse looked sympathetic.

He waved it off. "Being turned to stone saved them from worse injuries. As long as they can be restored."

"Does anyone know what happened, or why?" I asked.

"All that is known so far is that it was an explosion and the injury count. They make general announcements occasionally, telling which buildings are safe, etc. Everything else is conjecture," Ilse said.

"Rumors say everything under the sun, but in general, everyone agrees it was probably deliberate," Denise continued. At our questioning looks, she explained, "You'd be surprised how easy it is to overlook a dragonfly, especially when she doesn't want to be seen."

"They're going to want to talk to all the students who were there, probably later today or tomorrow," Adrian warned. "Including us. *Especially* us."

I nodded, not worried about it yet. I usually get nervous talking to authority figures, but right now I was too numb. "It was pretty well contained, the blast, wasn't it? It wrecked the music room, and shifted tiles for about six, seven feet in the hallway outside, right?"

"More or less. You better eat something," Adrian said. "You do like mushrooms, right?"

Oh yeah, still hadn't touched the omelet. "Yeah, mushrooms. Good. Um, I'm not really hungry." I do like mushrooms, but I wasn't sure I could eat at the moment.

"Unsurprising. Cold eggs are not particularly appealing," Ilse said, completely ignoring the fact that I don't think she eats food in the first place. "You need something light. Some soup, perhaps."

I could tell a losing battle when I saw one. "Okay, I'll see what they have." Maybe stretching my legs would help. Clear the cold numbness that seemed to have settled into my bones. I started to stand up, but my legs, somehow replaced by noodles, gave out under me. Fortunately, I landed on my chair instead of the floor.

"I'll get it." Kara dashed off, not even checking to see what I might want.

Ilse shook her head. "Weres." She liked Kara fine, but I got the impression that Ilse really wasn't fond of Weres in general. Kara ignored it, if she even noticed, and I didn't know what to say, so I ignored it too. Ilse turned back to me. "Are you well?"

"A little dizzy, but mostly just numb. I feel like I might start screaming soon, though."

"You wouldn't be the only one. I can show you the scream zones if you like," Denise offered.

I'm sure I gave her the strangest look, but I couldn't pull myself together enough to stop staring. "Most Weres, some shifters, and a few other beings are especially prone to scream therapy. The school has dedicated zones where they can do that and not bother anyone," Denise explained in a blasé tone.

I was saved from trying to think of a response when Kara came back, putting some cream of something soup in front of me. With everyone watching, I forced myself to take a bite. Chicken. It was cream of chicken.

"That's alright, isn't it? Not too heavy? You like?" Kara asked anxiously.

"It's fine. Yes, I like cream of chicken." I glanced at my watch. One o'clock, and I was the only one with dishes in front of me, other than a few cups. "You know, you guys can eat too." Maybe then they'd stop staring at me.

"Good idea. Ilse, I can fetch you some lunch if you tell me what you want," Kara offered. The vampire section was near the windows.

Ilse tactfully whispered her suggestion to Kara, knowing some of us, like me, weren't completely comfortable thinking much about her diet. Kara and Denise went to get food. Adrian didn't move. Ilse gave him a raised eyebrow. "I'll wait a bit. I ate breakfast, about eight-thirty."

I giggled the, gathering their attention. "Sorry. So you eat while I'm in class. I wondered." They were still watching me, and even I could tell my voice sounded strange. "I'm still in shock, aren't I?"

"A bit," Ilse confirmed. "Do not be alarmed. You will be fine."

"Oh, I know. It's a little embarrassing, really. I mean, I wasn't even hurt. I was outside. I've even had some training for emergency situations. Not a whole lot, but some. I was fine until I saw Tim. And the others, of course."

"Tim is one of your good friends, so of course it would upset you to see him like that. You barely know Sylvia, and I do not believe you know the others at all. It is only logical that Tim's predicament will affect you the most," Ilse quietly gave me permission to be biased. "As for your training, you told me yourself that it was not an area you wished to excel in. Have you ever needed it in an emergency situation where more than one person was injured? I thought not."

"Actually, I was pretty impressed." Adrian caught our attention. "Your training must have helped. You kept your head and went about helping those you could instead of being overwhelmed by what you couldn't change. The healers said you correctly prioritized the injured and knew what was and wasn't beyond your abilities. It wasn't until you couldn't do anything to help that you allowed yourself to slip into shock."

"There was no 'allowed', it just happened."

"I'm not so sure. I watched you. You saw the stone students at the start and deliberately ignored them in favor of the actively injured. Then everything came on at once."

"You reacted even better. How did you know about the explosion?"

Adrian shrugged. "I didn't. Not until just before. Then I just knew there was danger. Something must have tipped me off, but I don't know what. And I wouldn't have gone in if you hadn't. Remember how I said to wait?"

"You didn't go into shock."

"Not yet."

Kara and Denise came back then, and the conversation was dropped. Kara said that she had gotten some food for Celeste too. I looked around until I spotted the vampire staring into the air, looking preoccupied. Sylvia was her roommate. She must be worried. I made a mental note to check on Celeste later.

"Oh good, you're eating." Denise looked at my empty bowl. I blinked at it. When had I finished my soup?

"Yeah, I guess." I thought for a moment. "You know, now I *am* hungry." I stood up, successfully this time. "Do I have to re-swipe my card? I mean, we came in for breakfast and it's lunch now."

"Oh, you didn't hear. They don't want students going into potentially unsafe areas, so after they checked the cafeteria, they said it would be free today. For the first hour, we weren't in here either." Kara shook her head. "Poor Ilse had to wait under a tree until they opened."

"I'm sorry. I don't mean to be–"

"You did nothing wrong," Ilse said firmly. "Just as Denise was right in informing me. I had already found out about the explosion in the library, and knew you were likely to be there or nearby. If nothing else, she stopped me from worrying. Now, get your lunch."

I don't think anyone was surprised that Adrian decided to get his lunch then too. Other than Ilse threatening him with her eyes, no one reacted. True to our normal patterns, Adrian didn't say a word, though he was clearly keeping a closer than normal eye on me. Probably to make sure my legs didn't give out under me again. Since it would almost take fainting in public to top my embarrassment of going into such deep shock, I was very glad nothing of the sort happened.

We stayed in the cafeteria until very late, just like most of the school. There was no point in going anywhere else. Every once in a while, an announcement would be made that this building or that was now safe to enter. Caution was urged, but we were told not to panic. Classes would resume Monday.

Denise and Kara went about gathering information occasionally. Denise was the one who told us when they put up a list of students they wanted to talk to, and what time they were to see Taria. I was one-fifteen tomorrow. Adrian was twelve-forty-five.

***

The next day, I was still more numb than nervous. Until I saw Adrian leave Taria's office, pale and almost shaking. "Adr–"

He quickly covered my mouth and pulled me further down the corridor, looking around wildly. When he decided we were far enough away, he let go and backed off. I had never seen him look so scared. "What? What's going on? Are you alright?"

"Be careful; just, be careful. They're looking for blood this time." He hesitated, as if debating something. "Be really, really careful. Remember how to guard your mind?" I nodded, trying not to shiver. "Good. Now, go. You don't want to be late. Remember: You. Are. Innocent."

"I *know* that."

"*They* don't. Prove it to them. I'll wait in the lobby. The one on this floor."

I nodded again, and, with a great deal more trepidation, walked over to Taria's office and knocked on the door.

"Enter."

When I did, it was obvious that the office was definitely bigger than it had been last time. It had to be. Not only were Taria and I there, but so was Ms. Graz and a jet black unicorn. "Ms. Peters, thank you for being so prompt. This is Dean Clixot, the dean of the school, and you already know Ms. Grazletz."

"Yes, hello."

"Please sit down, we need to ask you a few questions. This shouldn't take long."

I sat down and took a deep breath. Despite Adrian's warning, I was pretty sure that keeping Taria out of my head would just make them think I was hiding something. So, I was only mildly guarded.

"You have Professor Shale's Music of the Dimensions at eight o'clock Tuesdays and Thursdays, correct?" The Dean started out.

"That's right."

"Yet you were still around almost fifteen minutes after class ended. Is that typical for you?" Taria asked.

"No. I was late yesterday, so I stayed behind, like we're supposed to. Then I saw…" I choked but forced myself to continue. "A friend and said hi to him. That got me talking to someone else…"

"Who was your friend, the first one?" Ms. Graz asked.

"I don't know his full name. But his name is Tim. He's a yeti." I swallowed hard. "He was turned to stone. It wasn't even his normal class."

"He told you that?" Taria asked.

"Yes. He said that he normally had music in the afternoon, but wanted to attend that special lecture." Which had gotten canceled, or postponed.

"Did you attempt to persuade him not to attend class at that time?" Dean Clixot asked.

"No," I answered, surprised. "Why would I?" It wasn't like I knew what would happen.

"Can you recount your movements? Starting with Wednesday about four in the afternoon, until the explosion?" Ms. Graz asked.

It was a pretty typical day. I had gym, did some homework at the dorm, did my studying with Kara and later Celeste, met Ilse for dinner, and took a quick trip to the library to return some books. I looked around the library, but didn't check out anything new. Then I went back and went to bed. Even while I was telling them, I realized how weak it was. I had large portions of time where there was no one to verify I was where I said, and I even admitted to being near the scene of the crime. But it was the truth, and there was no way I wanted to lie to a mind reader.

Then I said what I did on Thursday. That was much shorter. I overslept, and ran to class. They didn't interrupt my story, but I kept feeling like they were waiting for something.

"When did you leave?" Ms. Graz wanted to know.

"I'm not sure. Apparently I slipped into shock. The next thing I remember is sitting in the cafeteria hours later."

"I see. Well, Ms. Peters, we appreciate your help. There's just one more question I have for you. Is this yours?" Onto her desk, Taria dropped a pen. A purple pen. A very familiar purple pen.

There was only one reason she would be asking me about it right here and now. It must have been found in the music room, probably somewhere incriminating. Telling them I lost it the night before wasn't going to cut it.

I swallowed hard and looked them all in the eye. "Yes, it is."

Chapter Fourteen
Guilty Innocence

"How did it go?" Adrian asked, within a heartbeat of my closing the door.

"I thought you were going to wait in the lobby." I stalled, not sure what to tell him.

"Changed my mind. It was your pen, wasn't it?" So he did know. No point in trying to lie then. Good, I was lousy at it.

"Yes."

"What did you tell them?"

"The truth. It's my pen, and I lost Wednesday night in my dorm. I have no idea how it got to the music room."

Adrian winced. "Not good, at all."

"Worse than lying to a telepath?"

"Point. Definite point. So, now what?"

"They're discussing the situation. Deciding what to do."

"Your pen isn't enough proof. They'll want to read your mind," Adrian warned me.

"I figured as much." I wondered if he was worried for me or himse- Stop! Don't think about that. Just think about the last few days, then everything would be fine. Before I could figure out what, if anything, I should say, I was called back in.

"Good luck," Adrian muttered, backing off again.

I nodded and went in. The three faculty members looked even grimmer than before. Taria began. "Ms. Peters, because of the circumstances, we'd like to see your memories of the past two days before making our decision. This is not a request we make lightly, and you have the right to refuse. However, such a refusal will make it much harder to prove your innocence."

"You would only look at the past two days?" I didn't want my mind read at all, but it was better than being suspected of this.

"Wednesday afternoon until Thursday afternoon. Anything I see that is not directly against the school rules will be completely confidential."

I sat up straighter, inhaling deeply. "What do I do?"

"Concentrate on your memories of Wednesday afternoon. Lunchtime will do. Once you have those memories, drop your shields."

Exhaling, I closed my eyes and tried to remember Wednesday's lunch. Tim was there, and I had a hamburger? Yes. We talked about Denise's recovery, and how Kara was doing better. Slowly, I tried to relax my defenses, the flimsy shields I had learned to build through a telepathy workshop. When I thought I had gotten it, I opened my eyes and nodded.

Taria looked at me, first calmly, then with her brow slowly furrowed, followed by putting her hands and wing tips to my temples. Finally, she backed off, shaking her head. "I can't read her. She's a closed mind."

"What?" Everyone but Taria asked. Including me.

"I cannot feel her mind. Not a single thought or emotion. That means an empath probably won't be able to read her either. I've read her before. This is new."

"How did this happen?" I asked, very confused.

"There are a few possibilities. The rare few are born that way, but you aren't one of them. Occasionally when a telepath suffers from serious illness, they may be a closed mind upon recovery, but you were never a telepath. Certain magical items can render their wearer invisible to telepathic reading." She cast a quick look at Dean Clixot, who trotted forward and waved his horn around in front of me. After a moment, he shook his head and backed off.

"No magical items. So the most likely possibility is a spell. There are rituals, generally needing some part of you. Hair, blood, or fingernail clipping are the most common, especially if the intended is unaware or unwilling. The average human sheds about eighty to a hundred hairs a day. If you sold some blood, or broke a nail, those are possibilities too. Those rituals are quite complex, but a successful casting would render you completely immune to telepathic and empathic readings. Possibly aura readings as well. It is however, a spell that physically effects the enspelled, taking a heavy toll on them. It would probably have been a factor in your 'shock' yesterday."

The faculty looked at each other. "We need a few more minutes to discuss this latest development. Sit here, please." Taria crossed behind her desk, and that whole area got dark and quiet, leaving me alone with my thoughts.

I knew I was innocent, but they didn't. I didn't know all the details, so I wasn't sure just how incriminating my pen being on the scene seemed. Now they couldn't even read my thoughts to prove I was innocent. How dependent was Taria on telepathy anyway? Why was I now telepath-proof? Was it reversible? Would they kick me out of school if they couldn't read my mind? They couldn't do that, could they? Would they think I was guilty because they couldn't prove me innocent? Innocent until proven guilty might be the law in the United States, and probably

Canada, but Hyde was a much older institution, that
followed different laws.

Would they be able to tell if I lied, if they couldn't
read my mind? I'm not good at lying, but maybe they
don't know human tells. Besides, I had never tried lying
to any of them, how would they know I couldn't lie?

Finally they were done talking. From the looks of
it, they still didn't agree with each other. Was that good
or bad?

Taria spoke first. "Your pen was found near a
small homemade bomb. Do you know how to make such
an explosive?"

"No. I know it isn't hard to find out, but I've
never been interested. Did you check it for fingerprints?"

They exchanged glances. "We cannot share our
investigative methods. Miss Peters, the faculty has
decided that there is insufficient evidence to declare you
guilty, or even put you on disciplinary probation. We
will, however, be keeping a close eye on you. Do keep
that in mind," Dean Clixot announced with a slight
whinny in his voice. I nodded. "Very well. You are
dismissed."

I left, unwilling to ask about being a closed mind
then. Maybe I could ask Taria some questions later, when
she was alone. Sometime after this had been resolved and
the real culprit was caught.

"So? What happened?"

I jumped, but managed not to shriek in Adrian's
face.

He backed off a step or two. "I wasn't trying to
scare you." The 'sorry' was in his tone, if not his words.

"Sorry, forgot you were here. Let's go before the
next appointment shows up. Besides, you aren't the only
one who will want to hear this." I didn't want to explain

multiple times, and at very least Adrian, Ilse, Kara, and Denise needed an explanation.

"Good idea. Where?"

That was a good question. Adrian couldn't come into the girls' dorms, Ilse was asleep, and I didn't want to be overheard. I mentioned this.

"I know just the place. Can you call someone? Good. Tell them to meet you in room 18 Price Hall. It's in the second underground level below the dorm. Just take the elevator to basement 2."

I had never been in any of the underground levels, and still wasn't sure how Adrian was going to get there, but I did what he said. I used one of the inter-campus phones to call Ilse. She could get Kara and Denise easily. I did feel bad about waking her up, but she had made me promise to talk to her after my interview. "Okay, they'll be there soon."

"Good. Now, follow me."

Adrian bypassed the elevator, leading the way to the stairs instead. When we reached first floor, he walked around the stairs to a locked door. He unlocked it, revealing more stairs.

"Are we allowed to do this?" I asked, backing up a bit. The school would be keeping a close watch on me. The last thing I needed or wanted was to get in trouble, especially now.

"Yes, students are allowed to use the underground levels. Any student key will unlock the entrances. But with the exception of earth elementals, trolls, and some light sensitive beings, most generally don't want to. Except in lousy weather. Restlo, my roommate, is an earth elemental. He got me started." Adrian wouldn't look at me.

"Then why lock it?" I asked, partly to change the subject, and partly because it seemed odd.

"Just in case someone gets here who shouldn't."

"How often does that happen?" The school was on an island in every single dimension, and there was lots of security to get past the dock.

"It's only happened a few times, but the consequences were pretty severe. One time was the first Great Fire." The school might be about a thousand years old, but it had to rebuild several times. Fortunately, security measures, including fire safety, got better with each rebuild.

The first sub-level looked much like the above ground levels, down to the ubiquitous gray carpet with black and white flecks. The second one, on the other hand, looked like a cave with tunnels, and the occasional torch to light the way.

"There's a level below this one, in most places, with no provided light at all. That's for those who don't need light. I've used it, but I prefer this one." Adrian led the way, no sign of hesitation. I had to keep up, because he vanished easily in the semi-darkness.

"Do you use these often?" I was already lost. This place was a worse maze than the rest of the school.

"It comes in handy sometimes. Most people don't think about the tunnels, especially the lower two."

"So you can get from one spot to another without anyone seeing you." I knew there would be times I would be tempted to do that. I could only imagine what it was like for him.

"Not necessarily. Others do use this tunnel. Oh, and sound often echoes."

"Good to know." The tunnels, while dim and labyrinthine, were at least clear and clean, no signs of animals, insects, or fungus. "Could this be how…?"

"Possible. Almost every entrance is opened by key, not card swipe. There's no way to know who came down here, when, or where they went."

"Oh, lovely." I started searching the shadows.

"Or maybe they flew, or swam. After all, the library isn't far from the water. Maybe they walked through the walls. Happy now?"

"Not really, but I see your point." I still scanned the tunnels intently and nearly had a heart attack when a large purple troll turned the corner. I calmed quickly and just waved. Adrian nodded. The troll, a relative of Klocka's, I believe, nodded back and continued on his way.

"You are far too jumpy." Adrian sounded almost amused.

"It's been a long couple of days."

"Fair enough. The library is that way." He pointed to the right. "Price Hall is this way." He led me down a different tunnel.

"How did you learn all this? I'd be afraid of getting lost here forever."

Adrian ducked his head. "I've got a decent sense of direction. Besides, there are maps in the library and a few other places. Though a lot of the official maps only show the main paths. There are tons of secret hideaways and paths those maps don't show. I think I've found most of them."

"Wow, that's cool. Where can I get a map?"

"I've been making my own maps; I can lend you an old one. It made an interesting summer project." So he had taken summer classes? Made sense, considering he was here when I got here for orientation.

I almost asked about that, but we reached Price Hall. "Room 18 is three doors down, right here."

Sure enough, Kara, Denise, Ilse, and to my surprise, the ice twins, were waiting. "Hope you don't mind. We saw them leaving, and figured it had something to do with yesterday," Krystal said.

"If you're meeting down here, then something really bad or weird is going on. We wanted to help. If you don't want us here, we'll leave, but if there is anything we can do to help…" Bria continued.

I looked around at everyone gathered. It was a good question. I really didn't want this spread about the school, and while I considered everyone in the room a friend, well, sort of, in Adrian's case; did I really trust them? Yes. Maybe I was being naïve, but I trusted them.

"Get comfortable. This may be quite a story. Actually, is there some way to make sure no one can overhear us? I don't want this being more grist for the rumor mill."

"It should not be a concern. Most of the doors are eighty percent or more soundproof. Unless we started shouting, it would take someone literally putting their ear to the door to even hear voices. Only the sharpest of hearing would discern words, and only a word or two at random intervals at that," Ilse tried to reassure me.

"Do you know how many problems are caused by people picking out words of a conversation?" Adrian snorted. "I'll watch the door." He positioned himself so his eyes were on the bottom of the door.

"Okay then." I started to tell my story. There was some surprise that the explosion was a normal bomb, I guess instead of a magical blast or something. There was more surprise when I said my pen was found at the scene, though some had already known I had lost it. The biggest shock, however, was when I said I was now telepath-proof.

Adrian actually had the most interesting reaction, perhaps because this was the first piece of totally new information to him. "That's what happened yesterday! That's why it took so long for you to come out of shock. You were probably starting to slip anyway, and then this came and threw you headlong into it. Just like…" He trailed off then.

"Just like *what*?" Ilse asked, her words suspicious icicles.

Adrian looked around before answering. "Just like what happened to Charles Morris, while they were investigating him last year."

I frowned at that. "But I heard they read his mind, and he didn't remember."

"His memories were blocked, yes." Adrian leaned back on his chair, lifting the front legs. "Then, while they were trying to break the block, he slipped into a deep shock. Nothing reached him. When he came out of it, he was a closed mind. I think they tried to do the same to me, but were only partially successful. Taria admitted that she can read my surface emotions and a bit of surface thoughts, but not deeper than that." He jumped to his feet, causing the chair to slam back down. "They can't expel you, Taria wouldn't dare. What are they doing?"

Kara, who had been pacing since I mentioned my pen, paused. "What do you mean, she wouldn't dare? Don't you mean they won't because she's innocent?"

Adrian started pacing on the other side of the room. The rest of us watched them pace, like spectators at a race. "It's more complicated than that. I don't know all the details, but I know that Taria is totally and completely devoted to the school." There were some nods and verbal agreements. This was not new information. "She said something last year. Something I don't think I was supposed to hear. She said that they needed a human. Preferably more than one. A safety net, she called it."

"Wait a second; am I here to fulfill some kind of inter-dimensional quota or something? They just need *a* human, and I would do?" Is that why they offered me a full scholarship? Not because of my academic records, my potential, or anything, just because I was human?

Adrian shrugged. "I don't know. Maybe. I mean, they have screening tests." He didn't have to mention that there might be a temptation to lower the requirements if no one fit. After all, Morris slipped in somehow.

"Why must there be a human at Hyde?" Ilse mused. "This seems important. I shall look into it."

"So will we." Bria volunteered herself and her sister. "We'll try the library."

"Well, if they didn't expel you, or subject you to the never-ending glare of doom, what did they do?" Denise asked.

"They didn't have enough evidence one way or another, so they warned me to behave because they'd be watching."

"Did they give you your pen back?" Kara asked.

"No. Maybe after they catch the real culprit."

"You had your pen Wednesday night, while doing your homework. I saw it." Kara took a seat. "Who else was in the lobby that night?"

"So I did have it. I thought so. Let's see, there was you, me, Arie, Celeste. Um, Morpha, Felicity, Cal, and Gradune all stopped by at various points. I think Lumina might have, too." Gradune was a gargoyle who roomed with Cal. I didn't see her often, and she wasn't exactly friendly, but she was more aloof than rude. Morpha was a chimera who roomed with Felicity. I had never exchanged more than three sentences with her at any one time. "That's only if it was taken while I was in the room. If it rolled to the ground somewhere, anyone could have found it."

"But you said you looked for it," Krystal said. "You looked and didn't find it."

"True, but I didn't pull out a metal detector or anything. It could have been there and I missed it. Besides, it would take a lot of nerve for someone to take it while I was sitting there."

I didn't want to believe that someone I knew would be capable of something so malicious. People had been badly hurt in the blast, and they still didn't know if Professor Shale and two of the students would make it. Apparently the infirmary was very good about healing surface wounds, burns, broken bones, frost damage, restoring missing blood, and removing most magical effects. They weren't nearly as good when it came to organ damage, spinal damage, and some of the more serious magical effects.

"There are twenty-one girls who live on our floor, and six of them are here," Denise pointed out.

"It doesn't even have to be someone from our floor. Any girl in the dorm can get to any floor. If you can skip the usual security measures by taking the tunnels, then anyone could get in." I defended.

"Not quite. I could get on the elevator with you, but my key won't call the elevator or let me in the staircases," Adrian said. "So, either someone in your dorm, likely your floor, planted the bomb, or conspired with the bomber."

"Or took my pen, either stealing or finding it, and then lost it herself."

"Now we are stretching credibility. Start with the simplest explanations, and work from there," Ilse suggested.

"Arie was there for a long time. Just laughing at you." Each word seemed to be dragged from Kara's mouth, kicking and screaming.

"Yeah, but she also had that class. She was hurt in the explosion," I said.

"It could be an attempt at an alibi," Bria said. I think Bria disliked Arie even more than I did. All I knew about it was that something had brought Krystal to tears and Bria still hadn't forgiven the harpy.

"Maybe, but does she hate me enough to risk an injury to make me look bad?"

"She was near the back of the room, to the side," Adrian said. "It's a possibility. Unfortunately, there are a lot of possibilities." He stopped pacing and sat down. "Worth keeping an eye on her, but anybody who was in that room when you had that pen could be considered a suspect. That includes you, Wolf Girl."

Kara flinched. Total, full body flinch. "I–"

"Yes, yes, we all know you didn't do it. Just like Violet didn't do it. But we don't know who did. Or why." Adrian somehow did *not* combust under the glare of everyone in the room, and directed the next part to me. "All we know is that for some reason, whoever planted that bomb wanted you to take the blame."

Chapter Fifteen
News: Good, Bad, and Weird

Contrary to most peoples' expectations, the faculty did not find the culprit inside a couple days. A nebulous cloud of worry hovered over the campus. Students went to class in small groups, and avoided non-essential activities. Since most extra-curricular activities were still on hiatus, that made sense. As day after day passed with nothing happening, the worry lessened, but it wasn't gone.

The school counselors ran extra hours. Everyone who had been close enough to have seen the explosion results were required to go at least once. My counselor was an empath, like most of the counselors the school had hired, and she was clearly uncomfortable with someone she couldn't sense. I didn't go back.

Somehow, and all my friends denied discussing it, the rumor mill had caught hold of the fact that I had been, or maybe was, a major suspect. Though, as far as I could tell, none of the rumors had the real reason why I was a suspect. Not one person mentioned anything of mine being found on the scene.

It was possible that no one knew anything, and I just made a convenient scapegoat. It wouldn't have surprised me. Several of my teachers were keeping a closer eye on me than they used to. I wasn't sure if they had been told to do that, if they were following, or maybe part of the inspiration for the rumors. Ms. Graz was the worst. I couldn't step foot in the library without her eyes on me, watching my every move.

Taria was acting oddly, too. I made sure to pay close attention in her class now, because she often seemed to be watching me. It was ironic. She taught seminars on how to keep telepaths out of your mind, and was probably one of the driving forces in making sure I wasn't expelled, but she didn't trust me because she couldn't read my mind. Which was understandable, if really annoying. We were still trying to figure out why she wanted a human in the school.

Professor Argus had never seemed to like me, and he clearly had less patience than before. I couldn't tell with Professor Pod.

Fortunately, not all my teachers seemed to dislike me now. Coach O'Rater hadn't changed at all. Sure, he still scolded me for messing up and moving my shoulders while river dancing, but he did that with everyone. Dr. Gronk actually kept me after class once to tell me that he didn't think I had anything to do with the explosion, and if I needed to talk, I could come to his office. He was also kind enough to ignore me tearing up then.

Student reactions were not as kind, though not all my friendships seemed to be damaged. I also had a talk with Slate, Tim's gargoyle roommate. They had finally rescheduled the poetry lecture Tim had wanted to go to, and we both decided, independently, to attend and take notes for Tim for when he woke up. It seemed to reassure Slate to know that he wasn't the only one worried.

Unfortunately, that was a minority. I was really tempted to start using the tunnels to get around, especially after Adrian gave me a very thorough map of the school. But as he pointed out, disappear too often, and people became sure you were up to something. Besides, if whoever planted the bomb was also using the tunnels, running into them, alone, where there would be few to no witnesses, could be extremely dangerous.

On the good side, it was less than a week after the interrogation when one of the more severely injured students regained consciousness, and while Professor Shale, and the other students hadn't yet, the healers were now confidently proclaiming they would. Though there were some whispered rumors that even when she woke up, Professor Shale might not be able to reverse the stone process, due to the nature of her injuries. The school was being very close-mouthed about that.

I wanted to visit Tim, and even Sylvia, but I was also afraid to. They had looked so horrible in the music room. So I wasn't sure if I was relieved or disappointed that they were off limits to visitors. I don't know why the school had them quarantined. They couldn't be hurt, well, not easily; and they weren't contagious. Maybe it was to preserve privacy.

My family was getting worried about me. I wasn't writing often and was giving less and less information. Some of it was Hyde in general, but it was also getting harder and harder to explain what was going on in the school. They finally called me and asked me if I was okay, and what was going on. After frantically trying to figure out a way to sanitize the story, I told them that there had been an incident in one of the classrooms, and that some of my friends had gotten badly hurt. I left out that it was deliberate, that I had been framed for it, and that I was close enough to get hurt too, even if I hadn't been. I did mention that I was close enough to be on the scene before the medical crew got there; thanking Mom for making me take those first aid classes.

Dad claimed that I probably had a mild case of Post Traumatic Stress Syndrome and should see a counselor. He sounded relieved when I said I had, so I didn't tell him it hadn't helped. Mom suggested I consider changing schools. I stretched the truth a little, claiming that this could have happened at any school, which was mostly true, though I was still implying it was an accident.

If I told them there was a bomb involved, they would have had plane tickets sent to me the next day. And to be completely honest, I wasn't sure right then if I would have taken them or not. No one had been able to figure out yet why the school was so determined to have humans, so we didn't know how important it might be. Things were getting far too dangerous, and I really wasn't sure if I should, or even wanted to stay. It was during this time that I finally met the mysterious Allison.

***

I was on my way back to the dorm after class, Adrian shadowing me, as usual, when suddenly this streak dove at him. Adrian ducked; waving his arms at what I could now tell was a bird. After a few dives, the bird rather contentedly landed on his arm, letting me get a good look at it. I was pretty sure it was a raptor of some sort, though a small one, only about the size of a pigeon. Pretty markings. I might have seen that type before, but I couldn't swear to it. With a resigned sigh, Adrian straightened up.

"Allison, what are you doing here? You graduated two years ago."

I wasn't surprised when the bird leapt off Adrian's arm and turned into a woman. Slightly shorter than Kara, I'd guess, with brownish hair and golden eyes. But the faces were similar enough to shout that they were related. This must be the older sister he had mentioned.

"I've joined the alumni association. I'm now on the celebration committee."

"So you'll be around sometimes," Adrian said dryly.

"Are you kidding? I'm staying in alumni quarters. We'll be seeing lots of each other." She stood on her toes and ruffled his hair.

"Swell." He backed away, straightening the slight mess. Despite his sarcasm, he seemed happy to see her. Then his emotions shifted. "Dad put you up to this, didn't he?"

"Adrian Percival Char, you do not take that tack with me. I am not here to spy on you, and I am not here on orders." For such a short woman, she could be intimidating when she wanted to.

"Right, sorry." Adrian rubbed the back of his head. "But still, Dad–"

"Is worried about you, apparently for good reason."

"And…"

"And he considered ordering you home. That's why I volunteered to join the alumni committee," Allison admitted.

"To spy on me."

"To keep you out of trouble, tall order that it is. And because the celebration committee exists to plan parties and other fun events. Now, be a gentleman and introduce me to your lady friend."

Adrian seemed almost lost. "Right. Allison, this is Violet. Violet, my sister, Allison."

"Oh, *you're* purple. I wondered. Here, let me shake your hand." She darted towards me. Confused, I held out my hand on automatic. Allison took it, and froze, her eyes glowing white. "Destiny has some things in store for you. Your path is a difficult one, but as long you stay right, you will never be truly alone. Friendship is your biggest strength, and even some of your foes will crumple to it. There are forces at work beyond anything you are ready to comprehend and you are caught in their web. Do not try to extricate yourself, or they will win. You must twist the web to your own ends. Only then can you turn your biggest failure into your most powerful triumph."

Her eyes dimmed back to normal, and she shook herself out of her almost trance, letting go of my hand. "Well, that was… intriguing." I stared at her in bewilderment. "Don't bother asking. I really can't explain. I saw things while I was speaking, but I don't remember them now, and won't until they happen, if then. All I remember is the words I said."

I made a concentrated effort to force my eyebrows back into place. "O…kay. Does that happen every time you shake hands?"

"No, but physical touch does make 'flashes' more likely. Especially if it's the first time I've met someone. As you can imagine, some refuse physical contact with me because of it."

"Maybe, but I imagine some would be especially eager." Next on my research list, psychics and their predictions.

"True, some are. But that's neither here nor there. I hope I didn't spook you with my prediction, and I'm sorry I can't help you interpret it. Also, I hope you don't mind, but I just got here, and need to settle in." She turned to Adrian with a grin. "So I need my strong baby brother to help me."

"I'm not a baby," Adrian muttered. Then, louder, "Where's your stuff?"

"Over by the ferry."

"Do you need more help?" I offered.

"That's kind of you, but I think we can handle it. Besides, I haven't seen Adrian since Christmas. I need to catch up on big sister tormenting, I mean, sibling bonding." She smiled.

"Right, just let me walk Violet back to her dorm. Things have been crazy around here." Well, Adrian didn't sound upset by the idea of helping.

"Sure, Price Hall is on the way to the ferry anyway. It is Price, isn't it?"

"Yeah, how did you… Oh, right. Freshmen girls' dorm."

"Exactly. So, Violet, what do you think of Hyde so far?"

"Well, it's been quite an adjustment. Even without the added chaos."

"You didn't know anything going in?"

"Not a thing. My first warning was my roommate making an off-hand comment about being a vampire."

"That's odd. The RA should have talked to you almost as soon as you got to your dorm."

"She was busy."

Allison winced. "You slipped through the cracks, didn't you?"

"A little bit, at first."

We were at Price Hall now. "Well, it was good to meet you. I'm sure we'll be seeing much more of each other."

"Bye. Oh, if I can ask, what kind of bird are you?" Different dimensions had variations in animals, but shifters generally came from my dimension or the one on either side of it, so they almost exclusively turned into animals that I could recognize or find in an encyclopedia.

"American Kestrel."

"Oh, okay." I glanced at Adrian, wondering if he shifted into a bird too, but I wasn't sure if it would be polite to ask.

"No, Adrian isn't a bird. I have no doubt that you'll find out his form sooner or later, though."

"Alright, bye then."

Allison waved, then smacked Adrian's arm so he said 'goodbye' too. He sent her a not very serious glare and waited until I went inside before leaving.

***

Professor Shale woke up a few days later, but her injuries were severe enough that she couldn't restore Tim and the others for at least a week. That was the official version, anyway. There were rumors that she might not be able to restore them at all. I was trying to ignore those. It would work, it had to.

Adrian wasn't around quite as often as before, though he still lurked on the edges. Probably he was spending time with his sister. Allison was interesting. After the first day, I had little direct interaction with her, but I could see the changes she was making. For one, there were signs and decorations proclaiming the upcoming Halloween dance (held more than a week before Halloween), popping up in various places. I saw Allison placing or directing the placement for some of them. Adrian said it was her pet project. Allison said it was a morale booster.

Whatever it was, it seemed to be working. Things were happier on campus. While Tim and the others were still stone, the other students had woken up and were recovering. Soon the word was out that Professor Shale would be able to restore the stone students in a couple days. It couldn't happen soon enough.

Another development that left me pleased, and Adrian baffled, was my friends' changing reaction to him. It started about two days after Professor Shale woke up. He had followed me to breakfast, got his food, waited to see where I would sit, then sat down two tables away, like usual.

Unlike usual, as soon as he sat down, Kara and Denise walked over to him, picked up his food and brought it back to our table.

"It's a shame to waste tables when they're in such high demand. Besides, now I'll have more dishes to play with," Denise said.

Adrian stared at them, so Kara grabbed his arm and all but dragged him to our table, with Denise moving the chairs. "Did you put them up to this?" Adrian asked me as he carefully took a seat.

"Didn't have a clue."

After one more attempt to sit at a separate table, where he again got dragged over to join the group, he came to our table first, but he always hesitated, as if gauging his welcome before sitting down. Allison joined us sometimes too. I wasn't there when Allison met Kara, but they became friends with almost alarming speed. That was probably a factor in why Kara tolerated Adrian so much better now.

Allison joined us today for lunch, and cheered with the rest of us when they made the announcement about the students due to be restored in a few days. "Great, they should be in shape by the dance. Speaking of which, I need some volunteers to help with the dance. Who wants to be involved?"

"Allison, you can't just sit here and force people into agreeing to help you. That's not fair," Adrian objected.

"Sure I can. Captive audience. People are much more likely to say yes when I ask face to face. Besides, don't you want the help?"

"Don't you mean, don't I want *to* help?" He didn't sound like he was holding out much hope.

"Nope, you're already signed up to help decorate the gym."

"I'm not even going to the dance! You can't–"

"Whether you chose to go or stay home and sulk is up to you. But you are going to help with the decorating."

Kara, Denise, and I exchanged looks, wondering if we should leave so the siblings had some privacy. Fortunately the squabble ended quickly.

"I'm not going to argue with you in public, but we will talk later," Adrian warned.

"Of course, kiddo," Allison answered serenely.

***

Things continued like that until Tim and the others were revived. That day, the night and evening classes were canceled and there was a party in the cafeteria. I managed to say hi to Sylvia, but spent most of my time catching up with Tim. When I could talk to him, that is. Everyone wanted to ask questions about what was it like being stone. Poor Tim told at least ten people, while I was there, that he didn't remember anything between seeing Professor Shale's eyes, which he claimed were pink and silver, and waking up in the infirmary. I'm sure he told several people before I got there, too.

Fortunately, that answered most of their questions then and there. I was glad he didn't remember. I could think of few things more maddening than being awake and aware but unable to move or do anything for a couple weeks.

Unfortunately, that led to one complication I hadn't anticipated. To Tim and the others, the blast happened yesterday, or earlier today. Teachers were allowing them to catch up, and their absences weren't counted against them, which was good. But there were other problems.

Adrian wasn't around for a change, probably so he could catch up with his roommate. Kara was with me, while Denise visited Sylvia. The werewolf started it by mentioning Allison. Tim was understandably confused.

"Who's Allison?"

"Oh, right. You haven't met her. She's Adrian's sister," I said.

Tim's face grew serious. "Why would she be here?"

"She's part of the alumni association. She and Kara are practically kindred spirits." I tried to gauge Tim's reaction, before dropping the big news. "Adrian hangs out with us more too."

"He shouldn't." Tim's fur bristled. "He's always causing trouble. He may well have been the one to plant the bomb in the first place."

"Tim…" Kara put a hand on his arm.

Tim didn't shake her off, but he looked like he considered it. "No, he's a menace. I am not even sure why the school permits him to stay."

Just then, I spotted Adrian. He was standing nearby, probably planning to come over, but stopped when he heard Tim. I opened my mouth to say something, but he shook his head and sauntered off.

I glared at Tim. "He saved me. He covered me to protect me from the blast, helped me rescue trapped students, and got me to Kara and Denise when I slipped into shock." My words were quiet, clipped, and precise. Kara looked at me in surprise, but the yeti didn't hear the warning.

"How did he know there was a bomb?"

"Instinct. In addition, he just heard you accusing him, without a shred of evidence. There's more proof that points to *me* than to him. Keep that in mind. Excuse me, please." I ignored the look on Tim's face and got up to find Adrian.

It didn't do any good. The cafeteria was too crowded for me to walk easily, let alone look around for someone. He might have even left the building. I finally got to the door, but couldn't see him anywhere.

A large, white furred hand landed on my shoulder. I didn't look back at him. "I apologize. Kara explained a bit further. I still don't trust him, but I understand why you do. I will not be rude to him again, to his face or behind his back, but I cannot give him my trust. Not yet. Will you rejoin us?"

I sighed, took another look around, and agreed.

***

That night, I woke suddenly and found someone standing over me. I shrieked involuntarily, only to relax when I realized it was Ilse.

"You scared me. Why didn't you knock?" I turned on the bedside light, looking up again when there wasn't a response. "Ilse?"

Now that the light was on, I could see her face. Ilse was very good at hiding her emotions, but I had never seen her look so blank. Her eyes were glowing red and unfocused. "Ilse? What's going on? Why are your eyes red?"

I stood quickly and backed away instinctively. This was wrong, this was so very wrong. Her eyes followed my movements. She couldn't hear me. She didn't recognize me. And if I couldn't get through to her soon, she was going to kill me.

Chapter Sixteen
Tense Alliances

I automatically started looking around for something, *anything*, I could use to defend myself, preferably without hurting Ilse. A valuable area had been left out of my education. No one had taught me how to deal with vampires trying to kill me! "Come on, Ilse; snap out of it! I really don't want to fight you." Especially since I'd probably lose.

At first there was no reaction as the vampire stood statue still. Then Ilse dove at me. I responded by throwing the first thing I got my hands on. Only after it was in the air did I realize it was my cup of water. The water splashed her in the face, while the cup flew over her shoulder. I reached for my blanket, hoping I could toss it over her head. Maybe that would slow her down enough that I could run to the RA.

The blanket snagged on something. Before I could yank it free, Ilse stumbled back, wiping water from her eyes. "What? Violet? What are you doing in my room? Why did you do that?"

"Ilse? You're back?" I asked, pulling the blanket closer. Just in case.

Her eyes, now their normal brown, met mine. "Whatever do you mean 'back'?" Then she looked around. "This is not my room."

She was back. With a sigh of relief, I sat back down on the bed, not sure my legs would hold me much longer. "Yeah, I woke up to find you here."

I might have been calming down, but Ilse was beginning to panic. "You didn't invite me in. You've never invited me into your room."

"That's true." Ordinarily I wouldn't mind Ilse coming in, provided she knocked first, but for whatever reason, neither of us had ever been in each other's room. I opened my mouth to say something.

Ilse cut me off quickly. "No, don't invite me now! Do not even say tonight is alright! What was I doing? What happened?"

I explained in a hurry. She seemed especially worried when I mentioned the red eyes. "Then I threw my cup of water at you. Sorry, it was instinct."

"No, no, you were right. It is very lucky you had that. Did I tell you about water's effect on vampires? Oh, I thought I had. It is one of our negative elements. Like sunlight, it is uncomfortable. Being splashed with water will pause a vampire in the throes of bloodlust." Ilse licked at her fangs. "But I shouldn't have been in bloodlust. I ate tonight. You aren't even bleeding, nor were you earlier."

"Nope, no blood. Ilse, what happened? That just wasn't you." I mentally filed the water trick away. Maybe that was where the legends of vulnerability to holy water and the inability to cross moving water came from.

"You are correct. Somehow I was being controlled. I need to talk to Wilhelm." She scanned the room. "Bar your windows, they have that option. Lock your door and light a candle at every entrance. Perhaps get some more water. I will be out, so do not hesitate to go into the sitting room, but do not leave the suite without an escort." She swept off before I could ask her anymore questions. Perhaps it was just as well, I'm not sure I could have kept my panic back much longer.

I barely managed to bar the window, draw the blinds, and lock the deadbolt on the suite door, before dashing to the bathroom. After being violently ill for a few minutes, I huddled on the floor, shaking. That had been… there were no words for it. I had nearly died. Ilse had almost killed me and wouldn't even have known it until later. I hugged my legs. That would have killed me literally and Ilse figuratively.

I might have stayed there the rest of the night if more paranoia hadn't crept in and whispered in my ear that I was still vulnerable. Lurching up, I managed to steady myself and fulfill the rest of Ilse's instructions. We weren't supposed to have lit candles in the dorm except in emergencies, but I decided this counted. The rooms were warded against fire anyway. Besides, even if I did get in trouble for this, it was a small price to pay for peace of mind.

My meager vampire studies had taught me that vampires truly shouldn't be able to enter where they hadn't been invited, and they couldn't or wouldn't cross an open flame. Pretty sure there was something about crossing moving water without a bridge, but there was no way I could put a river in front of my door. Crosses weren't very effective except against the most superstitious of vampires, and I didn't think Ilse counted. Blessed salt was a universal deterrent against evil or malice, but Ilse wasn't either, and I didn't have any. It might help shake whatever was controlling her, though, so I made a note to look into it. Ilse didn't like garlic, but other than the odd distasteful face when I ate it, it didn't seem to bother her. I had my water glass, and after filling every cup in the cupboard with water, there were six cups of water sitting around.

Truth was, I was woefully unprepared for a vampire attack. If that wasn't a thought to send shivers down one's spine, I didn't know what was. After that first night, it honestly hadn't occurred to me to worry about Ilse being a vampire.

My thoughts whirled around like a kaleidoscope. Was Ilse alright? How did this happen? Would she have really killed me if I hadn't hit her with the water? She said that water was uncomfortable, did I hurt her? How could we stop this from happening again? What if we couldn't? Ilse was my best friend here. It would wreak havoc on our friendship if I was scared of her. No, I wasn't scared of her. I trusted her. Didn't I?

Suddenly I felt a jolt of sympathy and admiration for Denise. As far as I could tell, she had never had the slightest hesitation around Kara after being attacked, and she had been badly hurt. I was huddled in a cocoon of blankets on the couch, shivering like a worm, and Ilse hadn't laid so much as a finger, or fang, on me. Good thing, if I started bleeding, it would have been a lot harder to snap her out of whatever trance state she had been in.

Terror, for all its' overwhelming intensity, is a temporary emotion. No matter how scared you are, you can't remain terrified for very long. As my terror receded, practicality started to take over. It was the practical side that was glaring at the clock for being three-forty-five in the morning. Late enough I couldn't calm down enough to sleep, early enough that morning was going to take forever to get here.

Sitting on the couch, spooking myself, wasn't helping anything, and it would only make each minute an eternity. I had already turned on every light in the suite, barring Ilse's room, so I might as well try to do something other than jump at noises. I ruled out homework right away. I couldn't concentrate. I tried reading, but the words just swirled around in my skull without penetrating. I was tired, jumpy, nervous, and bored. Not a fun combination. I finally got on the computer and played chess until morning came. It helped. Sure, I lost almost every game, but I wasn't great anyway, and focusing on the game was distracting enough that I forgot about the time, a little.

Sunrise came and went, but no Ilse. I was concerned, but not excessively. If she was trying to contact her brother, it was possible it was taking a long time to sort things out. Or maybe the school, or someone, was running tests to try to figure out what happened.

Ilse said not to leave the room without an escort, but I wasn't sure how to get an escort without leaving the room. Once it got to a reasonable hour, I called Kara, but there was no answer. That's right, she had a glee club meeting this morning. That girl was in more clubs than the rest of the floor combined. Denise was considering going with her. She must have agreed. I didn't have any other phone numbers.

I could call security to escort me between buildings, but I was pretty sure they didn't come all the way up to your door unless it was an emergency. Before I could come up with extravagant and possibly stupid ideas to contact someone, there was a knock on the door. "Violet? Are you awake? It's Krystal."

Perfect. Good thing I got dressed hours ago. I opened the door. "Morning, Krystal. Glad to see you."

"Tim's outside, waiting for you. He said that Ilse asked him to escort you, but he can't get in the dorm."

"Thanks, I appreciate it." I wondered when Ilse found time to do that, but figured I'd ask Tim. I should have known Ilse would have planned something. "I'll be right down."

"Okay. Is everything alright? You look… tired." I could practically see the ice elemental running through adjectives in her head before she could find one that didn't sound too insulting. I couldn't blame her, I probably looked worse than Dr. Zyloas. Though to be fair, she didn't look too bad for a zombie.

"Bad night." I might have said more, but Arie left her room then, reminding me that the hall was not a good place to talk. "Everything will be fine. Ilse's a little worried about something, but it should be under control soon."

"Okay, just let me know if there's anything I can do to help." Judging from the way her eyes flickered briefly to Arie, she came to the same conclusion I had.

"This is so pathetic. Your roommate has to arrange someone to escort you around campus? Are you afraid of another bomb? Or of going into a meltdown again?" Arie scoffed, evidently finding us more interesting then wherever she had planned on going.

Krystal and I met eyes. "Do you think there will be more trouble?" Krystal asked Arie.

"Probably, until certain problem elements are eliminated," Arie said, leaving little question of what she considered 'problem elements'. It wasn't a confession, but it was certainly interesting.

"See you in math, Krystal. Thank you for telling me. I don't want to keep Tim waiting." I grabbed my book bag. Krystal might have better luck with me gone.

"Not a problem. See you later."

"You're enjoying this, aren't you? How soon until your boyfriends get into a big fight? Of course, cheating on the yeti while he was stone was stupid. They're known for their jealousy. You don't deserve him."

I couldn't help it. "Wow, is that what things are like in Arie-world? I don't think I'd like it there. You have no clue at all, do you? And I have better things to do than waste my time explaining things to... wormbrains. That is how you put it, wasn't it? Have fun misreading the obvious." It wasn't very like me, but just for once, I was glad to have a retort. The look on her face as I used her own words against her was one I was going to treasure.

Krystal looked like she was trying very hard not laugh as she waved. I waved back as I strode past the sputtering harpy. Within five minutes, she'd be back to believing her nonsense, and there was a chance she'd be even more vicious now, but for once, I wasn't a doormat.

Tim was outside the main door, brushing down various patches of fur. He was such a neat freak, especially when agitated. I didn't know what Ilse told him, but he clearly knew enough to be worried.

"Hi, Tim. Thanks for the escort." I had decided on the elevator that I wasn't going to talk about this more than necessary. Ilse deserved better than to have this bandied about, and the last thing I needed was to be the center of yet another rumor.

"Not at all. Ilse said it would be prudent." There was a question in his voice.

"When did she call you?" I stalled.

"About six this morning."

I winced. "Sorry. I didn't know she would do that."

"It is of no consequence. I usually awaken early. Though I do find it curious that she should be so... distraught."

"What did she tell you?"

"Simply that it would be wise for you not to be alone."

"True enough, but this isn't the place to discuss it. So, breakfast?"

Before Tim could answer, Adrian showed up at a run. He physically blocked the path and gave me a quick onceover. "Are you hurt? What happened?"

Tim moved to intercept him. "She is fine. As to what occurred, I fail to see how it is any concern of yours."

"It's as much my 'concern' as it is yours. Possibly more." There weren't many who would stand toe to toe with an angry yeti. Adrian was not short, though I doubt he was quite six foot, but Tim was eight and half, maybe three-quarters, feet tall. Tim's white fur and cool anger contrasted with Adrian, wearing black nearly head to toe, looking like he was ready to boil over at any second.

"How did you arrive at that conclusion?" Tim actually growled.

I forced myself between the two, probably succeeding only because neither of them expected it. "Knock it off, both of you! You're both concerned, and you both have every right to be. But it isn't necessary. I'm fine. Tim, we're going to breakfast. Adrian, would you care to join us?"

They both stared at me. At least they didn't look ready to strangle each other anymore. "I'm sure Mr. Char has better things to do." Tim verbally backpedaled.

Adrian, who I would swear had been about to refuse, took one look at Tim, and answered with more charm than I thought he had. "It would be my pleasure." He gave me a half bow and offered me his arm.

I took it, and then Tim's, which was offered a second later. We weren't able to walk on the path like this, but I didn't see a better alternative. I wasn't going to pick sides or let them kill each other.

Breakfast was predictably strained. Neither Tim nor Adrian spoke to each other, though both were willing to talk to me. At least they weren't playing the 'Tell him that...' game, but they did keep slipping little snarks at each other when talking to me. I was beginning to regret not letting them fight it out on the green. At least then I wouldn't be dealing with both of them at the same time.

I tried ignoring them, but it wasn't easy. They both had such presence. "Tim, when's your first class today?"

"College algebra at eleven. In the Victor science building."

"Hm, I have history at eleven, but that's in Stevenson." The only building further from Victor was McQueen gymnasium.

"I can walk you," Adrian offered.

"What about your classes?" I had been wondering about that for ages.

"Mostly in the evening."

"I have no problem with escorting you to your class before heading to mine." Tim ignored Adrian completely.

"That would be... inefficient." Adrian let the last word roll off his tongue.

"I can think of worse outcomes."

I tried to discretely massage my temples. "I am way too tired to deal with this. Will you two please stop fighting?" They opened their mouths in unison. "Don't even think of trying to tell me it's his fault. It's both of you. I didn't get anywhere near enough sleep to listen to it. Now, knock it off!" I grabbed my cup for a refill and stormed off before I snapped at them some more. This had better not become a habit.

Water gotten, I was heading back when I spotted Tim and Adrian in an intense discussion. Fearing the worst, I hurried over. Adrian looked at us both. "I'll leave. For now. But you need to know that common understanding is that the only way to brainwash a queen vampire is with a stronger queen vampire, or a king vampire. Think of that when you do your research." He slinked off, giving me an unreadable look.

"Tim, what happened while I was gone?" I asked in a quiet voice.

"We came to an understanding."

"Did you? Because it looks like he feels unwelcome, and do not say 'good'. What happened?"

"We agreed that our mutual goal was more important than our mutual dislike. Unfortunately, when we are in the same place, we distract each other. Therefore, we shall trade off. He shall be your escort this afternoon, after lunch. I have informed him, in excruciating detail, what shall happen should you come to harm under his watch."

I took a deep breath. "And he said?"

"The splitting up of duties was his idea. As for the warning, he promised similar should I be lax in my guarding."

"Ah, lovely." Well, it was progress. Sort of. "How long will this escort thing last?"

"I truly do not know. It is my deepest hope that it will not be necessary for long."

"Right." I looked at him as an idea came. "How much did you tell Adrian about what was happening?" I wasn't sure even Tim knew what happened to Ilse.

"Only that Ilse had contacted me and asked for my help. Oh, indeed. He does display a suspicious amount of knowledge."

I took a sip of water. "He always has. Maybe he's psychic. His sister is."

Tim raised an eyebrow at that. Or would if he had eyebrows. "A distinct possibility. Psychic talent does normally congregate in families, though if I understand correctly, females are more prone than their male counterparts."

A sex-linked gene perhaps? Maybe recessive on the X chromosome? No, that would mean more common in males. Perhaps I should look into it. "I'll ask him." I doubted he'd give me a straight answer, but it was worth a try. If that failed, I could ask Allison. She was a lot more forthcoming about her brother than Adrian himself was.

"You can but try. Do you wish to go anywhere before class?"

***

The instant I walked into Inter-Dimensional History, Taria shot me a look so intense that I didn't even try to leave when class dismissed. As soon as I was in front of her and the room was empty, she spoke. "This shouldn't have happened."

"So I'm told. Do you know how to make sure it doesn't happen again?" The words may have sounded flippant, but I was truly and desperately sincere.

"Short term; continue what you are doing. I'm giving you official permission to use candles, and can give you some blessed salt if you come by after my six o'clock class. It might not be enough though. After all, if the normal rules were in effect, this wouldn't have happened. Until we find out who managed to control her and how, it is difficult to say how to prevent this." Her wings shifted to looking like upside-down bat wings. "Keep your door locked when you go to bed. Perhaps move your dresser or a chair in front."

How reassuring. "Why is this happening? So much chaos this term, is this normal?"

Taria gave an almost hysterical laugh. "There is no such thing as normal for this school. But no, even for here, this is strange." She gave me a measuring look. "You and your friends are trying to look into why there are humans in Hyde, aren't you?"

I didn't see a reason to try denying it. "Yes. How did you know? Can you…?"

"I cannot read your mind, probably will never be able to again. However the books you check out from the library is a matter of public record. The answers you seek aren't in there." She paused for a long time. "I truly hope I don't regret this. Bring your friends tonight, those you trust. With everything. I will explain a few things after my six o'clock class. Perhaps then you will understand."

I wanted to ask more, but Taria was obviously done talking for the moment. "Okay. About seven?"

"Seven-thirty. That class tends to get out late." She told me what classroom to find her.

"Fine. I'll be back then." Even expecting it, it was a surprise to see Tim waiting instead of Adrian.

"Are you ready for lunch?" Tim asked, offering his arm. It was earlier than our usual time, but not by much. Taria had kept me pretty late. Though I thought Tim had a class now. Perhaps I was mistaken.

"Yes. Say, are you busy tonight?"

"I do not have plans, why?"

Casting a quick glance around, it didn't appear anyone was listening. Still, I spoke in a low voice. "I need to be at Poe around seven-thirty. We may get some answers. I don't want to say more now."

"Very well, I shall be discrete."

Tim and I had an almost normal lunch, never bringing up last night, at my insistence. I was sick of this worried confusion. Talking it over wouldn't solve anything until we knew more, anyway.

After lunch, Tim very formally handed me over to Adrian's care. It felt like the changing of the guard. Both of them were so serious it was all I could do not to break into a fit of giggles. They might not have forgiven me for it.

"You don't have biology until two, and it's only one now. What do you want to do in the meantime?"

"Library. I can get a little homework done. Then I can concentrate on research." He knew what kind I meant. He nodded, and we started towards the library. "So, how long is your shift?"

"Kara said that she'd be available from after six until you went to bed." He smirked at the look of exasperation on my face.

"Do you have anywhere you need to be before then? Or at seven-thirty?"

Adrian held the library door open for me. "Nothing before six. As for seven-thirty, it depends on how important it is."

"I'm not sure. It could be big. Taria is agitated."

"I'll be there. Just say where."

Ms. Graz gave us a harsh look. "Let's find a study room," I whispered. Talking in front of librarians always felt weird. Once we found a quiet room, I shut the door so we couldn't be overheard. All the same, I spoke under my breath. "Seven-thirty, classroom 113 in Poe." Adrian gave a subtle nod.

We worked in silence for a half-hour. I answered the review questions in history while he read; actually read, I think, a book on the periodic table of elements. Well, he had said he was a chemistry major. After I finished, I was deciding if I should pack up, or if I could research for a few minutes when he spoke up.

"Are you dating the yeti?" His eyes never left the book.

"You asked me that a few weeks ago."

"Things change."

"That didn't."

"You were awfully upset when he was stone. Not to mention, he's very worried about you."

"He's a good friend. It's what friends do. You were worried about your roommate."

"It's not the same."

"I don't see why not."

"Retslo and I aren't close. We're still rooming together because we get along alright, but 'friends' is a bit of a stretch."

"I'm–"

"Don't apologize," He snapped. "We should go or you'll be late."

Chapter Seventeen
Choices and Consequences

I was edgy all day, just waiting for something to go wrong. A chance for actual answers to our speculations? Why should that go smoothly? Nor was I the only one tense. Adrian was practically giving off electricity, he was so wound up. When we ran into Tim again, I was mildly surprised nothing burst into flames between the two of them.

When classes ended, I went back to the library to do some more research on vampires. There would have to be some clues about what happened last night. Besides, Adrian was supposed to be guarding me and he wasn't allowed in the dorm, at least not any further than the lobby.

My research was having mixed success. The sources couldn't agree if water was painful to a vampire or not. I could ask Ilse, but she might not tell me right now. Especially if it was. Celeste might, if I could come up with an excuse on why I needed to know. It was clear that vampires didn't like water at all. I knew Ilse used waterless gels for hygiene and cleaning, but I hadn't realized why. I might have, in blind panic, stumbled across the one thing in my room that might have actually helped without seriously hurting either of us.

I moved on to other vampire topics. Two things seemed especially interesting. One, certain metals such as silver, iron, or steel had a weird effect. A vampire could use, handle, or touch one of those metals if given permission, or if they purchased the item; common use items also counted. But something made of one of those items that they didn't have a right to would be painful to touch. Weird. Secondly…

"There's no mention of wooden stakes," I muttered aloud.

Adrian looked up from his book. A vampire history book. "Wooden stakes? Oh, that's right. You would be familiar with variants of the Stoker legend."

"Yeah, and that's kind of intrinsically in them."

Adrian shrugged. "A famous vampire, who called himself Dracula, was killed that way. Not *the* Count Dracula, but one trying to capitalize on the legend. It does work, but there are more effective ways."

"It's not in the books."

"You'd be killed if someone shoved a wooden stake through your heart. So would I. Off the top of my head, I can't think of more than a handful of beings on campus who would be likely to survive it."

"Point. Definite point." Putting the book away, I saw Adrian turn and tense. I spun around. Taria was watching us. She didn't look happy. Briefly, I wondered how much she had heard and how she interpreted it.

"There you are. I've been looking for you. I'm afraid something has come up and I can't meet with you tonight." She gave us a measuring look before turning to me. "Here's the salt I mentioned, and take this. It's a protection charm. Have it on you at all times. It will help. Hopefully more than a wooden stake." She continued before I could explain. "I recommend not straying far from your room at night and certainly not alone. Ilse will be back tonight, so remember what I said."

The protection charm was a small burlap pouch tied with blue ribbon. I could tell something was in it, but not what, and opening the bag might interfere with the effectiveness.

"Alright, thank you. Um, when would be a good time—"

"I don't know. I'll let you know." Taria answered quickly before rushing off.

"Well, that was odd," I muttered.

"She told you to stay in your room. That's where you were attacked."

"I noticed. It doesn't make sense."

"She's changed her mind," Adrian said. "Something or someone convinced her not to talk to you. If you push it, she won't trust you and will resist telling you. If you say nothing, then she won't tell you."

"Great. I love catch-22s. Don't you?"

I'm pretty sure he snickered a bit at that. "It doesn't matter. There are other ways."

I nodded. Yes, Ilse would do everything in her power to find out what happened and how to prevent it from happening again. On the other hand, she had been using her contacts for a while, and we were still confused. "Well, at least you won't have to skip classes or anything now. Though I do have to let Tim know."

Adrian stared at his book without a word.

"It's only polite. You wouldn't like it if we left you to wait, would you?"

No answer.

"It's almost six. I'm ready to go back to my dorm. I'm sure you have other things to do," I said, irritated.

"Fine." He matched my tone, put the book back, and led the way to my dorm without ever glancing at me.

Denise was in the hallway, and quickly agreed to find Tim to let him know the meeting tonight was canceled. Kara invited me over to watch movies with them, but I politely declined. Stress, worry, and lack of sleep were taking its toll. Maybe I'd be lucky and be able to get some rest. I did promise Kara I'd let her know before leaving the dorm.

Any thoughts of sleeping fled when I saw the paper on the desk. Figuring Ilse had left a note; I dropped my book bag and went to take a look. It was an envelope with my name on it. Odd. It wasn't sealed, so I opened it and pulled out the note and another slip of thick paper. It couldn't be. I ignored it and read the note.

Violet,

Apologies will never be sufficient for my actions. I have no words or explanation for what occurred. For your own safety and the sake of the friendship we have (had?), I beg of you to take these tickets. Flee, Violet. There is no safety for you here. Forget Hyde, forget me. Save yourself.

Ilse.

There were plane tickets in the envelope. A special flight from Wollaston Lake, leaving tonight at ten. I'd be flying through the night, and get to Newport News early tomorrow. I could be home in time for breakfast.

Home. Safe. Away from beings I didn't understand who hated me for being human. Somewhere where I wouldn't wake up with a bloodthirsty vampire over me. Where illusions wouldn't trick me into walking into rooms that could kill me. My friends wouldn't be turned to stone, for being in the wrong place at the wrong time, because someone wanted me gone.

Ilse clearly didn't want me here anymore. Did anyone really want me here? Yes, Taria, for some reason. She wanted a human in the school. Well, so what? Why should I care what she wanted? Why should I risk my life? What was here that was so worth the risk?

It was six-thirty. I might not have time to pack up everything, but I could pack up the necessities. Maybe someone would mail me the rest. The ferry ran until nine. Or I could call Paul, I still had his number. He said he had a boat. The lake hadn't frozen yet.

It was the smart thing to do. Leave. Leave and never look back. My eyes roamed over the sitting room. What was mine? What was essential?

A picture caught my eye. Ilse, Kara, and I, from the day I got my birthday package. I was wearing a Hyde sweatshirt. The one I had bought when I found that message on my door. That Hyde didn't need humans. Adrian said it did.

I closed my eyes and sunk into the couch. Who was right? Why was I here? I still didn't know, and every time I tried to find out I ran into dead ends. But what if it was important? I guess when it came down to it, it was a question of who was I going to listen to? Some anonymous voice writing on my door, or Adrian and Allison?

But Ilse had given me the tickets. Suddenly I laughed at my own stupidity. It was a ragged, hysterical laugh, but it was a laugh. The tickets weren't because Ilse didn't want me around anymore; it was because she was worried about me. But what if I was wrong? What if she did want me gone? There was only one way to find out. I'd have to talk to her.

I slumped on the couch and tried to reign in my thoughts as they scurried around like hyper gerbils. Maybe I should do some packing, just in case. No, I should wait. Find out some more before I made any major decisions. But what if I waited until it was too late? Too late for what? Tickets could be canceled, rescheduled.

Too late for me. Things kept being more and more dangerous. No one had died, and I hadn't even been badly hurt, but that was as much luck as anything. Luck runs out sooner or later. I had been trying to avoid the thought for ages, but I couldn't hide from it anymore. Despite the help of my friends, I was risking my life here. Possibly risking theirs, as well. What was I risking it for? Was it worth it?

Finally I heard movements behind Ilse's door. Good, I was going to go crazy if I thought like this much longer. "Ilse? We need to talk."

For a moment, I thought she would ignore me. Finally, she opened the door a crack. "Didn't you see my note?"

"I saw it."

"Why are you here?" So she did want me to leave. That hurt, but I pushed it away.

"Because we need to talk."

"It's too dangerous. I still don't know what happened, and I don't know how to prevent it from happening again."

"Ilse—"

"No, just, have dinner with Kara or someone, maybe spend the night with them. Thylica can help you find a new room tomorrow."

Frowning, I looked at the tickets. As I thought, they were for tonight. "Ilse, what was in your note?"

"You said you saw it?" She answered back, puzzled. "I said to have dinner with Kara or someone, and talk to Thylica about a new room assignment."

I looked around for another note. "Then where did the plane tickets come from?"

"Plane tickets?" Ilse finally left her room. She looked awful. Instead of her usual pale complexion, she looked gray, her eyes were dark and bloodshot, and her fingers wouldn't stop twitching. I had to avert my eyes to keep from staring. "What plane tickets?"

I handed over the note and the tickets, continuing to look for another note. No note. Ilse gasped behind me. "I did not write this. That is my handwriting, but I swear by the bloodlines, I did not write this. Nor buy tickets. Where did you find this?"

"Computer desk. It was in an envelope when I came in." Our eyes met with a growing horror. Someone had been in the room.

* * *

Thylica was able to tell us that there was no magic on the note, the tickets, or the door. While not an expert, I didn't think the lock looked like it was picked. The RA denied that anyone had gotten access to her key, which was a skeleton key to any room in the dorm. Not today anyway. The other RAs also had keys that could let them in, as did the RD; but they all had been pretty busy today, with the meetings to prevent something like last night from happening again.

The wood elf was the one to suggest that maybe whatever had taken control of Ilse to try to get her to attack me might have controlled her long enough to write this note instead of the one she thought she had. Getting the tickets might have been a bit harder, unless whoever controlled her gave them to her. It was a theory. The only one we really had at the moment. However, Ilse had acquired an amulet last night that was supposed to prevent her from being controlled again. Which meant that either the theory was wrong, or the amulet didn't work. I wasn't sure which was worse.

"Sorry, I can't help you. Violet, I've been meaning to ask. Do you want new rooming arrangements? I've been authorized to expedite it if you want." Thylica asked.

Ilse's face lost all animation, reminding me spookily of last night. But her eyes were brown, and worried.

"No, I believe I'll be fine. Taria gave me a protection charm and told me some precautions to take," I answered, trying hard not to betray any unease.

"Are you certain? I promise, I will not be offended," Ilse said.

"I trust you. Come on, I'm starving. Let's get dinner." I left Thylica's room with Ilse following slowly after me.

"You really trust me?"

"I'm still here, aren't I? Oh, I promised Kara I'd let her know if I left the dorm."

"Maybe we should invite them to join us." Seeing it would make Ilse more comfortable, I didn't argue.

Kara and Denise were quick to join us, and we found Tim on the way. He thanked me for making sure he was informed the meeting was canceled, but didn't mention it anymore. I had forgotten about it in all the confusion. By mutual agreement, Ilse and I didn't mention the note in the room. Not yet. Not in such a public place.

Still, I couldn't help noticing that we left the cafeteria at ten-fifteen. The same time the first plane was supposed to leave. I shivered.

"Cold?" Tim asked.

"Some," I answered, not lying. It was below freezing. We hadn't had any snow yet, and the lake hadn't frozen, but the creek on the island was slushy in the mornings. My new gloves and scarf were coming in very handy, and a new coat was definitely top of my Christmas list. Then something distracted me from the cold. "Hey, what's that?" I pointed to a strange light in one of the more forested areas of the island.

"I don't know," Kara said. "I've been there, several times, but I've never seen that."

We exchanged looks. "We should just leave it alone," Ilse said, even as we all started to walk closer.

"We don't have to get close, just take a look. Doesn't that look like the 'someone's hurt' signal?" I asked.

Tim cocked his head. "The color is quite similar but I do not believe it is an exact match. The frequency sounds different." We entered the tree line.

A shriek pierced the air. Without thinking, I started running towards the blue light. That seemed to be the right direction. "Violet, wait!" Someone called in a loud whisper, but I couldn't tell who. I could sense the others running after me, but they couldn't catch up. It didn't even occur to me, then, that they were all faster than me.

I got to the light and stopped. The light wasn't coming from anything and there was no one there. My friends were still trying to catch up, but hadn't managed it when I heard it. A harsh, disguised voice echoed in the clearing. "YOU SHOULD HAVE TAKEN MY GIFT!"

Covering my ears, I fell back, trying to get the ringing to stop. I only opened my eyes because there was something bright coming at me. A fireball, aimed straight at my face.

I didn't have time to panic, scream, or even move when something large and black knocked me to the ground, fire impacting with it instead. On the ground, trying to gulp air back into my lungs, I managed to turn slightly. A black panther. That's what hit me. A black panther, with a badly burnt shoulder.

My friends were running up to me, but I barely noticed. I was locked in the gaze of pained green eyes. Looking at the eyes, I wasn't surprised when the panther shifted into Adrian a moment later. His hand automatically clutched at his shoulder, face drawn together in pain.

"What is he doing here?" Tim demanded.

"Playing human shield," Denise said.

"Either he has really wonderful timing, or really terrible," Ilse added.

"Hey, there's no need–"

"Enough! He's in pain. Let's get him to the infirmary." I interrupted Kara. For a second no one moved. I stood up, trying not to show how sore I was, then tried to help Adrian up. "Whatever you may think, whatever his motives might be, if he hadn't pounced on me, that fireball would have hit me. Also, it might not be a bad idea to leave before whoever threw that tries again." Adrian was significantly heavier than I was, and in just enough pain to make helping him difficult.

Before I could manage, Tim scooped him up, as Adrian let out an embarrassed squawk. "You are correct. Ladies, you should get back inside. I will see Mr. Char to the infirmary." He started walking briskly away.

I didn't doubt Tim. I really didn't. I had no reason to, and he seemed to be feeling bad about doubting Adrian. I was sure he would take care of Adrian, and probably get him back to his dorm. All the same, "I'll go with you."

"We all will," Ilse said.

"I can walk," Adrian grumbled. No one paid him any attention. I did notice that he wasn't actually trying to get Tim to put him down. Well, he tried once, spasmed in pain, then held still.

"That trap, how did they know *I* would be the one to trigger it?" I asked.

"You were meant to find it. From the smell of it and the results, it seemed to be a compulsion spell, a selective targeting spell, and a selective hampering spell. Get you there, and slow down anyone else. If I hadn't been so close to begin with, I wouldn't have been in time to help either."

"Smell? You can identify spells by scent?" I didn't know that was possible.

"Some of them. Only in panther form. Though really strong magic I can sometimes smell without it."

"You do have the strangest habit of being in the right place at the right time. In the right form, too." Ilse's voice was carefully neutral.

Adrian tried to move, but stilled quickly. "Oh, the heck with it. You'll figure it out eventually, anyway. I'm a defender psychic."

"I see," Tim said slowly. "This explains much."

"Not to me. What's a defender psychic?" I asked.

"There are several different forms of clairvoyance which psychics can specialize in. This is a natural specialty, not a trained one. Retro-cognizants see glimpses of the past, pre-cognizants, the future. Some only see things that affect certain areas, such as family or friends. I know one who can predict the weather perfectly up to two weeks in advance, but nothing else," Ilse explained. "If I understand correctly, Allison is a mix of tangible psychic and important events psychic. She reads people by touching them, which gives her an impression of things that will happen. A defender psychic usually has one or a select number of people that he has a bond with. I say 'he' because rarely is there a female defender psychic. This bond allows the psychic to know when that person is or is about to be in danger. The bond usually forms on first meeting, without either side trying to form it. Adrian likely knew the moment he saw you, that he would have to protect you.

"Tried ignoring it," Adrian ground out through clenched teeth. "But you kept getting into trouble. Easier to just go along, try to head it off."

We were almost there, fortunately not passing too many curious students. Tim offered to let Adrian shift into panther form if he found it less embarrassing.

"Jaguars weigh about four hundred pounds. Besides, shifting when injured *hurts*. Higher chance of getting stuck, too. I only changed this time because I had to." His voice was getting stronger. I hoped that meant he was in less pain.

"Jaguar? I thought you were a panther?" Denise asked.

"Black panthers aren't their own species. It's a term for the black phase of jaguars, leopards, and cougars. I'm a jaguar."

We got to the infirmary and signed Adrian in. Now, Tim put him down, but still kept near his good shoulder. The infirmary was pretty empty, so Adrian barely had a chance to sit down before he was called back.

"How come I've never heard of…?" I trailed off as Ilse tried to signal me to be quiet.

Leaning closer, she explained in a low voice. "They are quite rare. In the past, there were attempts to force them to bond to royalty and other important persons. A bonded psychic of this type can be the ultimate bodyguard. Unfortunately, forcing the bond can drive the psychic to insanity, occasionally causing them to attack the one they were meant to protect. There are still many misconceptions about them. If he truly is what he says, he has taken quite a risk telling us."

"Do you think he's lying?" I asked.

"No, I believe he was truthful," Tim said. "Therefore, we owe it to him not to spread his secret."

There was general agreement, before we settled into silence to wait. Adrian came out about ten minutes later, surprised we were still there.

"How's the shoulder?" I asked.

"Mostly second degree burn. First in some places. Should be mostly healed in a week. Shifters heal fast, and between the healers here and the salve they gave me, I have an extra head start on healing." He looked at his coat. "Good thing the coat's got some fire protection woven in. Gonna have to get that reinforced."

Very nice. I hadn't realized his signature coat had magical protection. No wonder he always wore it.

"Good, you can do that tomorrow. Now you need rest. It's after eleven." Kara nodded as if to give the statement weight.

"Right, I can–"

"You can go straight home. The five of us can manage without your escort. In fact, maybe we should walk you home." I smiled.

Adrian snorted. "Actually, they called Allison. She should be here right about…now." The door opened and a kestrel swooped in, scolding us all soundly before landing as Allison in front of Adrian.

"What did you do? You…you…" She punched his good arm before giving him a hug he slowly returned. "Don't scare me like that."

"Sorry, Alli, it was necessary."

The rest of us slipped off to give them some privacy. Tim offered to walk us to our dorm, while we offered to walk him to his. We compromised. The freshmen dorms were on opposite sides of the dock, forty yards apart. We walked to the middle, then went our separate ways, looking back frequently. It was kind of stupid, but it worked.

It was past eleven-thirty and I had been up since before four. I was more than ready to crash. However, as soon as we got to our rooms, Ilse started getting nervous again.

"Ilse."

"Someone is trying to kill you. Have you not noticed? They want you gone. When is your luck going to run out?"

"I'm not the only one in danger, and so far I haven't gotten hurt." That wasn't entirely true. I was pretty sure I had picked up some nasty bruises tonight, but no one had thought of that yet, and I wasn't going to remind them. It was definitely better than the fireball to the face I would have gotten if Adrian hadn't tackled me out of the way. If he had second degree burns through a magical coat, I didn't want to know what it would do to my unprotected face. "Taria told me a few precautions, and gave me a protection charm and some blessed salt." Ilse seemed a little reassured. "We'll figure this out."

"I certainly hope so."

267

Chapter Eighteen
Pieces in Motion

The next morning I had music with Professor Shale. She had just come back to teaching the day before. Like Ilse, she was a lot more skittish. Her sunglasses handle had been replaced with a strap, making them more like goggles. Even with that, she seemed to be avoiding looking directly at anybody. The snakes didn't move much, though the ones that had been crushed seemed to be recovering.

It was two weeks to the day of the explosion, and it was obvious that everyone was thinking about it. Nervous energy ran through the class, almost visibly. When someone dropped a book, somewhere in the back, most of the class jumped, and there were a few screams.

Other than the book, class was almost anti-climactic. The worst thing to happen was when the CD player wouldn't play the disc, so she had to find a different player. It was Bach, as we were currently on notable composers from 13A. Though there were some rumors that Bach may have originally been from another dimension and slipped through the barriers. I didn't buy it, but it wasn't worth arguing over.

Professor Shale was less friendly, in general and to me in particular. She had been in such a good mood on That Day, easily forgiving me for being late. Today, she was distant, suspicious, and I suspected she was watching me through those tinted goggles. I was glad I wasn't late today. I guess someone told her about my pen.

They had finally given me my pen back, saying they couldn't get any more evidence from it. On one hand, I was glad to get it back, since it was a present from

Rose. However, I couldn't even look at it without thinking about the explosion, seeing Tim and Sylvia as stone, and everything else. I ended up sticking it in a drawer and trying not to think about it.

The 'Halloween' dance would be tomorrow. I really didn't care much about it. I had never been to a dance in high school, and no particular inclination towards attending this one. A fact that didn't save me from being roped into helping with set up. I'm still not quite sure how that happened, but I do know there should be laws against Kara and Allison conspiring together.

I was painting signs because Allison obviously had no idea of my complete lack of artistic ability. Most of my friends were helping in various ways. Kara and Denise were painting signs with me. Adrian was constantly climbing a ladder to place decorations at Allison's orders, in between muttering that he wasn't even going to the stupid dance. Slate was helping him, proving that stone gargoyles really could fly. I had wondered about that. Tim had been put to work moving heavier items, like tables. Felicity was twining streamers. Celeste had wandered over and was working on the lighting. Allison and Ilse were doing sound checks.

I took a break from mangling signs to grab a slice of the pizza Allison was providing for her 'volunteers'. Tim came over a moment later for a drink. "The hall is coming along nicely, is it not?" He asked.

"Mostly." I sighed, eyeing my signs. Allison really should have assigned me something else.

"Are you looking forward to the dance?" Tim offered me a water bottle.

"Oh, I'm not going. Are you?"

"Not going? Why ever not?"

"Why should I?" I shrugged.

"No one has requested for you to partner them?" I might have been imagining things, but I thought his eyes flickered briefly to Slate and Adrian.

"Not exactly winning any popularity contests here. How about you? Do you have a date?" I tried to remember whether or not there were any female yetis on campus. Or anyone else Tim seemed interested in.

"I do not. That being the case, may I serve as your escort? As friends." He continued quickly. "Should you receive a legitimate date, I will, of course, back off."

Perhaps I shouldn't have been terribly surprised by that, but I was. "Are you sure? I mean…"

"I am most certain."

"Then I will be happy to go with you. As friends. And if someone else asks, then I'll tell him he shouldn't have waited so long." The dance was in less than thirty hours.

Tim laughed. "I will warn you, I won't be wearing a suit." His eyes twinkled.

I laughed back. "I'll manage. How fancy is it?"

"Semi-formal." Allison swept by. "Glad you're coming. Here are your tickets." Tickets came out to one Hydeonian or close to five US dollars, but Allison promised a free ticket to every volunteer who helped for more than two hours.

The kestrel shifter was passing out tickets to everyone now, putting one near people who couldn't take it; like Celeste, Ilse, Adrian, and Slate. I probably wouldn't have paid attention, except that I was close enough to hear when she passed a ticket to Felicity. Their hands touched as the ticket was handed over. It was only the briefest of contacts, but evidently it was enough.

"Tonight. It will happen tonight. Something you don't expect, can't prepare for, and it will change everything. Be careful, you are in danger." She snapped out of it. "I'm dreadfully sorry. I–"

"How dare you?" Felicity snarled. "Don't try that fake 'psychic' trick with me. You don't know anything about me. Just leave me alone!" With that she flounced off, slamming the door in her wake.

For a moment no one moved or spoke. "I'd better go after her. Make sure she's alright," Celeste volunteered from the tech cage. "If she is in danger, then she'd better not be alone."

A few people offered to go with her. I didn't because I doubted the werecat would want my company in the best of times, and definitely not now. Celeste waved off all offers. "No point in making her feel ganged up on."

"Right. Good luck," I offered, before going back to ruining the signs. I had come to help, so I'd better get back to it. Such as I could.

There was an awkward silence broken only by low, muttered voices. Poor Allison looked almost ready to cry. I wished I knew how to cheer her up. Fortunately, even if I didn't, someone else did. After hanging up his current poster, Adrian jumped off the ladder from a height that made me wince and walked over to his sister. I couldn't hear what they said, but she did look more cheerful when he went back to the ladder. Kara was smiling, so I suspect she could hear them.

"Signs are looking good." Allison came by, checking on us. "Um, Violet, why don't you work on lights for a while? Celeste left and…"

"And my painting skills could fit in a nucleotide. Got it."

"I didn't say that."

"You didn't have to." I smiled. That was fine. I didn't really like painting anyway. Lighting I could do. I had tried the drama club in high school. I wasn't good at acting, but I was pretty decent as tech crew. Better than painting any day.

Both the light controls and the sound block were in the tech cage, about a floor up. Ilse was almost finished there. "So, Tim asked you to the dance." It wasn't a question.

"Did you know he was going to? Because I don't think your hearing is quite that good."

"Actually, I can read lips."

I laughed, experimenting with different lighting combinations. "Why am I even the slightest bit surprised at that?"

"No idea. Don't you think some people might be upset by that?"

"Your reading lips?"

"No. You going to the dance with Tim."

I tried to think if anyone might have a crush on him. "Was someone else hoping to go to the dance with Tim?"

"Not to my knowledge."

"I'm pretty sure there isn't a stigma against inter-species dating at the school."

"None in the slightest."

"Then what's the problem? Oh, I see. Yes, I'm sure there are a great many who would prefer I not go to the dance at all. Too bad for them." That may have come out a little more bitter then I meant it to, but there was only so much pretending I didn't exist I could do before getting fed up entirely.

"While you are indubitably correct, that wasn't my concern."

"My mind reading skills aren't up to par. What are you thinking?"

"I was thinking of who might ask you." Ilse finally looked up from the sound board.

"Ilse, I count an entire three guys in the whole school as something more than passing acquaintances. Tim, Slate, and Adrian. I barely know Slate. Adrian isn't going to the dance and hasn't asked me. Tim did."

"And if he had?"

"Who? Slate or Adrian."

Ilse could tell I was being deliberately obtuse now. "Slate, of course. I have it on good authority he plans to propose. Adrian."

"Slate plans to propose to Adrian? Wow, who'd have guessed? Think we'll get invites?"

"Violet," Ilse said, sounding wearily resigned.

"I don't know that Adrian thinks of me that way. Even if he does, I'm not sure how I feel about him. And even if I did, there's still the slight fact that the dance is *tomorrow* and Adrian didn't ask me. Tim did."

We stopped talking as the ladder approached, not wanting to be overheard. Allison said we had sound and lights done a few seconds later.

Ilse performed an unfairly graceful leap from the tech cage to the floor below. Having no desire to break my leg or neck, I decided it would be very much in my best interest to take the stairs. After taking one last look to make sure neither of us were forgetting anything, I started to leave. Adrian's voice stopped me dead.

"So you are dating the yeti." He didn't look at me as he hung the streamer end, but his voice accused me of lying.

"He asked me to the dance. As friends. Since I'm not exactly being deluged with offers, and he's a good friend, I agreed. Is that a problem?" Seriously, what right did he have to be upset?

"Are you using him?" The words were bitter, edged in anger. That anger inflamed my own.

"Using Tim? For a date? He suggested we go as friends." I was turning red, I knew it. How dare he accuse me of using a friend like that? "Look, I fail to see how it's any business of yours. If you truly cared about who I went to the dance with, you should have–" I stopped. "Never mind. Just, never mind. Leave me alone." I left the cage, letting the door slam behind me. I didn't even want to think about this.

I tried pushing it to the back of my mind but I was only partially successful. By the time I was on the main floor, I was pretty confident that I could talk to almost anyone there without snapping, as long as I didn't so much as look at Adrian. If I did, I'd probably explode or something. "What do you need now?" I asked Allison, in what I thought to be a very reasonable voice.

"I think we're done for the day. I can't do anything else until tomorrow." She switched to addressing everyone. "Good job, everybody. Thank you so much for your help. I hope to see you all at the dance."

I tried to fade into the background. I didn't want to talk. I was still on edge, and wanted to lash out. I needed someplace quiet, where I'd be left alone. Denise said something about going to class, one that met in the library.

"Mind if I tag along?" I asked.

"No, not at all." Denise answered. To my relief, no one else came with us. Not that it was a quiet trip.

"The computer mouse, is the plural mice or mouses?" Denise asked when we were halfway there.

Confusion overpowered irritation. "You know, I'm not sure. Why?"

"Because the library needs to get new ones. These ones are on their last tiny, little paws."

That one took me a moment. Mice, paws, legs. "They're about to die?"

"Yup, soon they'll be dead as tiny little dormice."

That one took me even longer. "I think it's supposed to be 'dead as a door nail'."

"That's silly. Door nails aren't alive, so they can't die."

"You have a point. But that's still the saying."

Denise shook her head. "I have to get to class. If you decide to go back before I leave, call security?"

"I'll wait," I promised. We split up then. Nodding to the suspicious librarian, I went to the top floor, intending to do a little more research. Taria said that we wouldn't find the answers in the library, but it was always possible that she was mistaken. Or just trying to get us to stop.

It was about thirty minutes later that Celeste found me. "Violet, thank the bloodlines I found you! I need your help. Felicity is hurt."

Immediately I dropped my book, dashing after her. "Where is she? What happened? Wait, why my help?" I couldn't imagine Felicity would want my help, but if she needed me, I couldn't ignore it.

"Downstairs, I'm not sure, and she asked for you." Celeste led me to an elevator, hidden in a corner. I really wished I had found that months ago. Then I wouldn't have had to navigate the evil steps all the time.

"That doesn't make sense. She hates me."

"She's jealous. She doesn't hate you," Celeste assured me, as the elevator swiftly carried us to the first underground level. As soon as the doors opened, the vampire took off at a run.

"Shouldn't we be calling a healer? Or getting her to the infirmary?" I darted after her.

We turned a corner, and there was Felicity crumpled on the floor. "Oh, no. What happened?" I whispered. I started to move closer, but stopped. My mind was screaming at me that something was wrong. "You aren't explaining anything. Celeste, what's going–" I never had time to finish my sentence as something hit me in the back and everything went dark.

Chapter Nineteen
Revelations and Realizations

Books and movies make it look easy. You're knocked out, so when you come to, you fake being unconscious to gather information. It's not that easy. For one thing, there is a lot of disorientation in waking up. I certainly didn't know what was happening at first. I remembered quickly, but I definitely would have blown it in those first few seconds if I wasn't magically restrained and silenced. Not that being restrained and silenced is a good thing, but it did mean that I could fake unconsciousness a little longer.

"What's keeping her? She should be here by now," An unfamiliar male voice was complaining. "We have to be quick."

"We have time. The girl was alone for once. No one knows she's missing yet." Celeste. So, I had been tricked and kidnapped. Was Felicity in on it? Even if she was, considering what Allison said, she was probably in over her head.

I hadn't opened my eyes yet, but as I became more aware, I realized I could feel body heat next to me. Very warm body heat. Weres usually ran hot, so there was a good chance Felicity was next to me, probably restrained as well.

"I wish she'd hurry up," The male voice said. Okay, judging from sound, and I was pretty bad at that, he was in the same room, about ten or fifteen feet away. Must be a big room.

"Patience, Morris. Patience," Celeste chastised, from about the same location. "After all, our 'guests' aren't even awake yet."

I had never heard the word 'guests' sound so much like 'slugs' before. Morris, could that be Charles Morris? Last year's human, now expelled? How did he get here? Also, how did Celeste get involved? She was a freshman, like me.

More than that, I thought she was at least somewhat a friend. We weren't close, but she never seemed to be part of the 'anti-human' crowd. I trusted her.

This wasn't the time. I could feel betrayed later. Now, I had to find out what kind of mess I was in, and how to get out. I risked cracking an eyelid. Felicity was next to me, apparently unconscious. Celeste and Morris were on the other side of the room, about twenty feet away. In between us were candles, strategically placed, and a few other elements that suggested a ritual spell, probably a very powerful one. I was most worried about the very sharp knife that the ritual evidently included.

Spells, rituals, what did I know about them? Not much, I wasn't due to take Magic for Non-magic Users until next semester. I did know they were very particular. If you made the slightest little mistake, it could fall apart, probably back-lashing on the caster. The more powerful the ritual, the more finicky they usually were.

I also knew that only magic users could use a ritual of any significant power. Vampires can't use magic, and if Morris was Charles Morris, then neither could he. So, the mysterious 'she' they were waiting for was probably the caster, then. No wonder they were waiting.

"You're sure this will work? Your bomb didn't," Morris said.

"It served its purpose. The faculty doesn't trust her anymore, and she'll be removed for sure when they find her here. Especially with the Were dead."

I had thought Celeste and Felicity were friends. Really friends. Guess not. Even with the magical restraints, I could feel Felicity shiver. So she was awake. I couldn't blame her for being afraid, I was ready to shiver myself.

Celeste said no one knew where I was. That was probably true, but maybe not. Denise knew I was in the library and would likely investigate when she didn't find me there after class. How much time had passed? Did she know I was missing yet? For that matter, there was Adrian. If he was a defender psychic, and bonded to me, wouldn't he know I was in trouble? Yeah, we had a fight just a little while ago, but he'd still help, wouldn't he? Of course, I wasn't sure he'd be able to find me. Even I didn't know where I was.

Fine, I could hope help was on the way, but I couldn't count on it. I'd have to figure a way out for myself. Taking stock, I tried to figure out exactly what I could do. The answer was simple and found quickly. Not much. My mouth would not open at all, and none of my limbs could move independently. I did seem to be able to force all my weight in a direction, but couldn't experiment too much without being noticed. Being on the floor, I could roll, and if someone stood me up, I could probably fall in the direction of my choice. At the moment, that didn't seem like a lot of help.

On the other hand, if rituals were as tricky as I had been led to believe, perhaps something as simple as my being in the wrong place at the wrong time would be enough. Or even just not being in the right place at a crucial time.

Having even an inkling of a plan made me feel a little better, but not much. For one thing, what about Felicity? From what I could tell, they were planning on leaving me alive, at least for now, but Celeste had flat out said Felicity would be dead. Apparently Celeste wasn't big on the whole 'friends' thing.

No time for that now. So, how could Felicity and I get out of this mess, especially if we couldn't talk to each other to plan? In fact, any obvious movement from either of us would give away the only current advantage we seemed to have.

"You're both awake. Good. We'll be starting shortly," Celeste said from directly above us. I always forget just how silent vampires can be. Well, there went that advantage. Oh well, wasn't that great anyway.

"This is taking forever," Morris complained, still across the room.

"Can you perform the spell? No? Then be silent!" Celeste snapped. "She'll be here soon."

I think Felicity tried to ask who would be here. I know I wanted to know. Celeste ignored us. "I suppose it wouldn't hurt to prepare everything." With one hand, she hauled Felicity up and dragged her to the center of the circle, careful not to smudge any lines, before dropping her unceremoniously. "Just stay still." She smirked.

Then she came back and dragged me over to the circle, but not inside. Could I smudge the lines? Would that help? I couldn't do anything with her watching me.

Walking to one side, she picked up a small tub. "This is a special ritual, to aid in a major goal. It requires the hide of either a werecat or a large cat shifter. They must be alive and conscious as the hide is removed, kept alive until the removal of the heart. Needless to say, it is a forbidden ritual in every dimension. It failed last year, and I'm not sure where you got the details to try it this year, Violet. Perhaps Char told you enough to research it. I should mention that performing the spell comes with a severe penalty. You may well be put to death for this, after you confess." I tried to shake my head. It didn't work, but she understood anyway. "Oh, yes. You'll confess. In detail, explaining to the last degree just how you did it and why. That's one of the last steps. And since no one can read your mind anymore, they will have no choice but to take your word for it. That was a stroke of brilliance."

"Since when can magici do that?" Morris asked.

"She didn't. Our benefactor did."

"How come we don't know who this benefactor is?" He whined.

"Perhaps they don't trust you not to go blabbing it everywhere." Celeste barked back. With a shake of her head, she turned back to us, opening the tub, and putting it next to Felicity.

"Do you recognize this? You told me about it. A most intriguing salve that can force a Were into their animal form," this was said in a sneer, "regardless of the lunar phase. I learned so much of Weres from you. Enough to sabotage the wolf's herb. I had to test it, you know. Find out if you were telling the truth. I kept expecting you to figure out that it was me, but you never did. Not very bright, are you?" Felicity stared at the smirking vampire in growing horror.

While they weren't looking at me, I rolled over the lines closest to me, smudging them, and nudged the nearest candle out of place. It wasn't enough though. I couldn't just disrupt the ceremony; I had to stop them from skinning Felicity alive!

"Why aren't we starting?" Morris said. That man had less patience than my sister did when she was five.

Celeste seemed to think something similar. "Because timing is essential. We cannot afford to get this wrong. If you are so impatient, guard the door."

"I'm not supposed to be here, remember?" Morris complained.

"I certainly do," Another male voice rumbled. Adrian! Taking advantage of his moment of surprise, he shifted into panther form and tackled Morris, growling in his face, and ready to bite.

"Get away from him!" Celeste demanded, dragging me upright and holding the knife to my throat before anyone saw her move. Adrian growled but didn't move. Trying to breathe without being cut by the knife, I wondered if that was a good thing or bad. "I mean it." Cold metal pressed hard into my skin. I couldn't even swallow. Black edged into my vision. Now was not the time to faint! "I have no need to remind you that this could get messy should she start to bleed."

Reluctantly, Adrian moved away from Morris. Celeste moved the knife a fraction of an inch away from my neck. Then, before anyone could say anything, he leapt to Felicity, grabbed her arm with his teeth and tossed her to the side. She hit the wall and went limp.

"Fangless leech!" Celeste swore. Adrian tensed, but she adjusted the knife so it covered more of my throat and pressed down. I only knew that it didn't break skin because Celeste didn't react to my blood. Adrian forcibly relaxed a degree. "So, you knocked the Were unconscious. Not a bad idea, but you forgot something. A shifter is actually a much better match. There's a reason you were the intended target last year. I believe someone wanted a fur coat out of the deal."

Adrian tensed. Celeste continued. "Oh, do you remember that part? Tell me, how much do you care for the zero? Would you die for her?" Adrian didn't move, even as Morris got up and kicked him. I winced internally as I noticed it was his burned shoulder. "Grab a rope," Celeste ordered Morris.

No, no, no! I didn't want Adrian, or anyone, to die for me! This was wrong. I couldn't speak. I couldn't shake my head, even if I wasn't restrained, I'd probably slit my throat. All I could do was beg him with my eyes. Run and get help! She wouldn't kill me, and she couldn't do the ceremony with Felicity unconscious.

It wasn't working. He stayed statue sill, staring into my eyes as Morris tied his paws up. When he was almost finished, Celeste relaxed her grip on me and moved the knife. Finally, something I could do. Momentum is not a difficult force to gather, and by quickly rocking backwards when she wasn't expecting it, I was able to knock us both off our feet. Immediately, I rolled away from her. It was a temporary solution, but it was something.

Apparently Morris wasn't a boy scout, because Adrian was able to slip out of the rope, change to human and deck him before Celeste regained her balance. "Give it up, Celeste. You've lost."

"Lost? Hardly. You aren't fast enough to stop me before I kill your little girlfriend, and my associate will be here momentarily. You are outgunned, Adrian Char." Celeste had gotten to me, but wasn't touching me yet.

"Who's your associate?" Adrian asked, not trying to move closer.

"You'll find out. If you live long enough." Celeste grabbed me, dragging me up by my hair. "I don't *need* either of you alive. Felicity will work for the ritual, and the human dead works as well as expelled. Surrender and I'll let her, at least, live." She smirked. "Give it up, Char. You've lost."

To my astonishment, Adrian smirked. "Lost? Hardly. You see, I didn't come alone." Suddenly the upper wall behind him went clear revealing some kind of control room. Inside were Tim, Ilse, Kara, Denise, Allison, the Ice Twins, and Taria. "Didn't you know? They put cameras in the training rooms to avoid another event like last year."

Taria picked up a microphone. "Celeste Travoz, put her down, move to the far wall and put your hands on your head. Refusal will be met with extreme consequences."

The door opened again, revealing several security officers, at least two poised to deliver a magical blast. It wasn't easy to turn my head to look at Celeste, but I managed. She was panicking. So far she hadn't moved, but it could go either way. I couldn't even use my last trick, because she was holding my hair.

Two thoughts hit me at once. One, Celeste was not going to calmly surrender as long as she thought she had any sort of edge, like a hostage. Two, someone, presumably one of the security guards, had undone my restraints and I could move again. With a deeply heartfelt prayer, I moved.

One hand went to my hair, pressing it to my head, while the other pushed her arm away. At the same time, one leg swept her feet out from under her. It worked, knocking her down again. Of course, I fell too, but I was expecting that. So I was moving first, so I was no longer between Celeste and the door.

Adrian moved faster than anyone had the right to, and grabbed me away. This time Celeste didn't try to get up. Security swarmed over Celeste and Morris as Adrian drew me away. "You aren't hurt?"

"I think I'm fine. Felicity!" The Were was starting to shift a little.

"She should be alright. Weres and shifters heal fast. I didn't throw her that hard. I just needed…" Adrian followed me.

"I know. Celeste said she had to be conscious." More security took over, pushing us out of the way. After a few minutes, they assured us she'd be fine.

It took ten minutes or more for enough people to clear out that Adrian and I could leave without getting in the way. Adrian filled in the time by muttering explanations to me. As far as we could tell, he felt uneasy when Celeste came to me, definitely felt it when I was knocked out, but had to wait until they moved me to where ever they were going. Apparently defender psychics can latch on to the location of their bonded protectorate. Unfortunately, the warning they get when their protectorate is about to be in danger, is usually only a few seconds. So he didn't know there was a problem fast enough to intercept it this time. That explained why he had been following me around for months.

"I would have been nearly ten minutes faster, but Allison had warned me recently about not rushing in alone on something big. So I had to call her, and your friends, and come up with a plan." He sounded impatient with the whole process, so I carefully didn't mention that had he come alone, we might both be dead by now. "Allison got Taria, who mentioned the cameras."

"Um…" If there were cameras, then what about my last foray into the training rooms? That's obviously where I was. I probably would have known earlier if I had seen it with the lights on the first time.

"They only check if they know something went wrong. It will have been overwritten by now," He muttered under his breath.

The room was almost completely cleared by now, Felicity had been taken to the infirmary, and the group from the control room was waiting for us in the hall. Before we could join them, we both had to have a cursory medical exam, which as far as I could tell, consisted of a medic waving a crystal over us. When I asked, he said it would light up if held over an injury. The verdict was that we both had minor aches and pains, but nothing worth going to the infirmary over.

Taria waved a hand to keep the others back. "You are both uninjured? Good. I think we should adjourn to my office."

After we all relocated, Taria had me fill in what happened, to the best of my ability. I knew she'd be watching the video too, but I suppose she considered it necessary to hear my perspective too. Maybe she figured I'd feel better talking about it, too. I did, a little, but I was also glad that everyone who would need to know was here so I wouldn't have to tell it again.

When I finished, Taria was quiet for a long time, possibly having a telepathic conversation with someone. "Alright. Violet, do you remember when I told you that I would give you more information? It's time." She looked at each of us in turn. "If anyone wants to leave, now is the time. I completely understand. Knowledge can be dangerous."

No one moved. "With all due respect, I think we're already involved," I said after a moment.

She sighed, wings folding themselves into a box. "I know. That is why I'm telling you now. This story begins a long time ago. Millennia ago, in fact. The dimensions were more closely connected then, and it wasn't uncommon for dimensions to war with each other, or beings to war with other races from their own dimension. The Inter-Dimensional Council hadn't been formed yet, and there was little or nothing to regulate or prevent this fighting." Taria paused and pulled a scroll out of a drawer.

"Many were troubled by this, and various plans were made to try unifying the dimensions and preventing open warfare. The idea for a school was not mine, I admit, but I quickly fell in love with it. Of course, the idea was only sound as long as it worked for everyone. So an oath was made. An oath between myself, a human, a vampire, a Were, and an elemental. We would have a school, open and fair to all. We negotiated for the land, and it's ours as long as the oath is upheld. One of the main conditions of the oath is that there must always be at least one representative of each of the beings who made the oath. As the only one of my kind, I must remain at the school. Not a decision I've ever regretted." She unrolled the scroll, showing an old drawing of Taria and four others making an oath.

"While humans were, and are, one of the most numerous of the different races, fewer and fewer humans are still suitable for the school. It is becoming quite a challenge. Were you brought in to fulfill a quota? Yes and no. We need humans. However, even if we had a hundred, you are a suitable match."

"So, is this an attempt to close the school? Is that why I was targeted? Why would anyone want to close the school?"

"I do not know. Hopefully further interrogation of Charles Morris and Celeste Travoz should reveal more." She turned to Adrian. "I wish you had managed to get the name of the third accomplice," he started to bristle, "but I understand why you revealed our presence when you did. The risk was no longer acceptable. Unfortunately, Mr. Morris is a closed mind, and Ms. Travoz likely is too by now."

"What will happen to them?" I asked. I still didn't know much about inter-dimensional law.

"That has yet to be decided, but your part is done. We have it under control."

I'm not sure any of us bought that, but no one said anything.

"One thing. Because there are at least two major players still out there, we cannot share too much about what happened tonight."

"To catch who knows too much," Ilse said.

"Precisely. While the official story has yet to be decided, it will be announced tomorrow. Ms. Travoz will be officially announced as responsible for the bomb, possibly some other incidents as well. Because it is an ongoing investigation, I must ask you not to inform anyone of details, or discuss it where you might be overheard. Are there any further questions? No? Very well. Ms. Teps, Mr. Char, I believe you both have classes tonight. I give you permission to not attend. I'll speak with your instructors. Goodnight."

Chapter Twenty
Aftermath

Leaving the office, we got to the stairs before agreeing that we needed to talk this over. It wasn't hard to decide that the best place to do that would be where we met last time. Though we hadn't considered that there might be a few difficulties for those who hadn't been before.

Tim was a little too tall for the tunnels. He didn't have to duck, in most places, but it was close, and he seemed to be feeling a bit claustrophobic. Allison wasn't happy either. Probably a bird thing. Adrian walked next to her, holding her arm, trying to distract her. Must have worked, because soon she was scolding him about all the risks he took. I hadn't realized how nerve-wracking watching had been.

Once we were set up in the room, Adrian took a seat watching the door and began. "They were pawns."

"Agreed. In all likelihood, the magicus somehow got wind that they would be discovered and decided to cut her losses," Ilse agreed with him, possibly for the first time.

"You are probably correct. So, if they were pawns, what is the magicus? The queen? The valuable piece for the benefactor to move?" Tim asked. I thought the analogy strange until I remembered that Tim was part of the chess club.

"No, probably just a bishop or knight," Allison said. "Probably thinks she's higher, but she's only slightly more valuable. This goes deeper than anyone has guessed. We haven't seen even the tip of the iceberg."

Everyone got quiet. "Well, we know a few things," I said, startling a few people. "One, there's a female magicus involved, second year or up. Two, someone wants the school closed. That seems like a bad thing."

"It is. Very bad. It must not be allowed," Allison said, eyes glowing a bit. Then she shook herself out of it. "Sorry."

"Nothing to be sorry for." I sighed. "That means I need to stay. Doesn't it? No matter what happens, as long as I'm the only human, I need to be here." We still didn't know who else was involved, or what they would do to try to get rid of me, one way or another. I didn't particularly want to leave, but I did like having the option if things got untenable here.

"Hey, you aren't alone," Adrian said, catching my eye. "We don't want the school closing either. Or anything to happen to you." The last part he said while carefully not looking at me.

"He's right," Ilse said. She pulled out her fortune stones. Seeing us looking at her, she actually looked a bit self-conscious. "It could not possibly hurt." The major stone was blood, the second balance. She frowned at it. "Expand and find a new balance?"

Kara looked at them. "Hey, Violet, that one looks like your horrorscope thingy." She said, pointing at the scales.

I snickered. "Horoscope. And yes, I'm a Libra, that's represented by a set a scales. It's the only one that isn't after something alive."

Ilse looked thunderstruck. "For three months, *three months*, every question I asked involving school brought the balance stone, and you never told me it meant you?"

"It doesn't mean me. Libra is one of twelve star signs that the year is divided into. There are millions of Libras, probably over a hundred in this school. It's a coincidence," I said, leaning away from the irate vampire.

She muttered a bit but sat down when she realized I wasn't deliberately hiding information from her. "Believe that if you like."

I didn't try to argue with her, knowing neither of us could convince the other. "So what do we do?"

"Ooh, we could form our own oath?" Kara suggested.

"Those aren't to be taken lightly." Denise cautioned.

"One we can all hold to. Like to be tolerant of others, and not to betray each other or the school." Kara insisted. "Oaths have power and the more people involved, the more power."

"That's true. They can be a great blessing or great destruction," Allison said.

"The wording would be crucial. It would have to be something we could all agree on," I said.

"How about this? 'I solemnly swear to uphold the standards of justice, friendship, and tolerance. I will not betray the principles this school was founded on, or my fellow oath-takers.' Would that be sufficient for all?" Tim spoke up.

"Alright, if anyone doesn't want to do this–" I was cut off.

"I'm in. An oath of that sort should prevent my being controlled to act in a way that would break it. An extra layer cannot hurt," Ilse said.

"So in. Weres love being in a pack," Kara said. Denise nodded along.

"We're in. We owe you a debt," Bria said, Krystal agreeing quickly.

"This is about the school, not me." I protested.

"It is and it isn't. But I'm not surprised you don't accept that. Adrian and I are in." Allison smiled.

"I'm in. I always wanted to be a knight." Tim joked.

I was almost speechless. "Well, then I guess I have to agree too. Do we swear individually or as a group?"

"As a group," Allison said. We practiced a few times until we had it down, wrote it out so we wouldn't forget anything, then Allison put her hand in front of her. It took some shifting for us all to get a hand in, but we did. "On three. One, two, three."

As we started to swear, our hands began to glow with a blue light. My hand tingled, like when it fell asleep, only instead of hurting, it felt good. When we finished, there was a bright flash making everyone blink a lot.

"That's a strong oath." Adrian warned. "The consequences might be more than we were expecting."

"They are. But it will be for the best." Allison said. "Our enemy has weaved a web of deceit and treachery. We are weaving one of friendship and loyalty. We are connected now, and only with those connections will we succeed." She shook her head. "Sorry, fortune cookie again."

"It's fine. Now, I don't know about anyone else, but it's nearly one, and I'm going on exhausted. We can worry about Morgana or whoever tomorrow." I said. Fortunately, everyone caught the reference to Morgana Le Fay.

"Right. Dance tomorrow, well, later today. Remember that." Allison said, tugging on Adrian's arm. "C'mon, Pink Panther."

Kara couldn't let that drop. "Pink panther?"

Allison's grin was just short of evil, while Adrian winced. "Oh, he never mentioned it? Well, shifters tend to first change into their animal very early on, like three or four. Adrian was a late bloomer, not shifting by the time he was five. Unusual, but not unheard of, especially for larger animals. Well, one day, we're watching old Pink Panther cartoons. I'm about to change the channel, but he gets mad, and shifts into the cutest little baby black panther. I've got pictures, and videos, somewhere. I've been calling him Pink Panther and giving him Pink Panther stuff ever since. Fair's fair. He does the same to me with Tweety."

Judging from the amount of smirks, Adrian would probably regret Allison sharing that. "Interesting," Ilse said, sounding carefully neutral.

"Swell. Allison, did you have to tell them that?" He started ushering her away.

"Of course, why shouldn't I have?" We could hear them bickering down the tunnel.

"I had better catch up, or I fear I'll become too disoriented." Tim said.

We said goodnight, and the rest of us took the elevator to our floor. After going to our respective rooms, I was ready to drop. My hand was on my door handle when Ilse stopped me.

"I am very glad you are alright."

"Thanks, me too."

"I'm sorry. I was wrong about Adrian."

"I think he wanted it that way. Anyway, if you feel the need to apologize, it should probably be to him."

She waved a hand that could mean she'd talk to him or not. "You said earlier that you weren't sure how you felt about him."

I sighed. I was too tired to do this. "He's attractive, yes. He's… intriguing. He can be a nice guy when he doesn't think people are around to notice. Not to mention, he's saved my life, a few times now. Is there something else I'm supposed to say here?"

"If he had asked you to the dance?"

"He didn't. He's not going."

"But if he had?"

"Don't go telling the resident matchmaker?" I nodded at Kara's door. "I'd probably have said yes."

"I see. Goodnight."

"Ilse, why are you asking?"

"Simply curious." If I hadn't been so tired, I probably wouldn't have fallen for it.

***

The next day school was abuzz. Celeste was expelled and being held on criminal charges for the bomb. No mention of the ritual or of Charles Morris. Even as we read the report, we knew we had barely scratched the surface. There were still too many questions. Ilse admitted that there was tension between her family and Celeste's, which was normal for politics, but she was positive that Celeste was neither stronger than her, nor a king vampire. We still had to find Morgana, yes, the name stuck; and hadn't a clue as to who the benefactor was or what they wanted. But we were confident we'd find out.

Ilse spent a good portion of the day awake and out of the room. She said it was in preparation of the dance. It seemed a little odd, but I didn't ask. I had plenty to do myself.

First, I made it a point to find Sylvia. Not having any better ideas, I brought over a bag of microwave popcorn. Maybe that would, not cheer her up, but help a little. She was reluctant to open the door, but did eventually. She looked pretty shaken. Even thanking me for the popcorn, she sounded out of it.

"Are you alright?" I asked, then winced at what a dumb question that was.

The pretty blonde gave a ragged laugh. "I'm fine. I just discovered my roommate was responsible for a bomb that turned me to stone. Why shouldn't I be fine?"

"I'm sorry."

"For what? You had nothing to do with it."

"She tried to frame me for it. The night before, she stole a special pen of mine, and left it on the scene, so it would look like I did it." I confessed.

Sylvia stared into space a while. "So she really didn't care at all, did she? Didn't care who got hurt, who suffered. Do you think she would have cared if I had been killed?" Her eyes held mine.

My instinctive response was 'Probably not', but I stifled it. "I don't know. I apparently didn't know her at all."

Another bitter laugh. "That makes two of us."

"Is there anything I can do?"

The snake shifter looked surprised, then smiled. "No. Thank you for telling me, for checking on me, but no. It isn't your fault, what happened. It isn't mine either. I just need a little time to get over it. You better get ready for the dance."

She was right, but still. "Alright, but if there's anything I can do…"

"I'll be fine." She walked me to her door.

That settled, I now had a problem. Small, compared to everything else, but a problem none the less. I hadn't brought any fancy dresses from home. I didn't even own a formal dress. Both Ilse and Kara offered to let me borrow something, but I wasn't close enough in size or body type to either of them to pull that off. Just as I was about to try to convince myself that a blouse and skirt would work, Krystal knocked on my door. Denise had told her my problem, and the twins were almost exactly my height. Krystal let me borrow this absolutely gorgeous deep purple dress that fit me perfectly.

The dance began at eight, and the six of us of us gathered in 612 about an hour and a half before that to complete finishing details. We lent out our jewelry and make-up to each other, gushed over each other's appearances, and took loads of pictures. I was wearing the amethyst necklace that Ilse gave me for my birthday, and an ornate hairpin of Denise's. Krystal had borrowed a pair of my earrings that looked like snowflakes, while Kara loved my blue goldstone necklace in the shape of a wolf. I was glad to be able to lend out as well as borrow.

"Hey, it's snowing!" Bria said, turning from the mirror where she had been adjusting a pearl necklace (Kara's). We all clustered around to see. It wasn't coming down hard, but there would probably be a decent dusting on the ground tomorrow.

"Snow already?" I said, watching the flakes dance.

"It's a little late in the year for the first snowfall up here," Ilse said. "And speaking of late, it's almost time. We should go."

We were almost to the elevator when Felicity exited the lounge. "Violet, can I talk to you? Privately?"

She asked, subdued, looking wary at all the distrustful faces. She was clearly not dressed for the dance, which was odd because she had been very excited about it.

"Yeah, okay. Um, Ilse, could you please tell Tim I'll be a couple minutes?" I strongly doubted Felicity was going to try anything, especially while in the dorm.

Ilse was hesitant, but finally agreed. "Very well, I shall tell your date that you will be there shortly." There was emphasis on the word date, but I figured she was teasing me about Tim and I being friends.

"Is the lounge alright?" I asked. I was willing to give Felicity the benefit of the doubt, but that only went so far.

"Lounge is fine. The floor's pretty empty by now."

We went back to the lounge, but Felicity seemed to be having trouble getting started. I tried to help. "Are you alright? You weren't hurt too badly?"

She startled a little. "Yes, fine. Don't even have much of a headache anymore." Felicity rubbed at the back of her head.

I winced. Head injuries should never be underestimated. "You do know why he knocked you out, right?"

"Yes. And no. I know he saved me. I also know I wasn't his first priority. You were. Also, I wanted to say I'm sorry." She smiled at my confusion. "You know I'm a Werecat? Lion to be precise. Because he's a large cat too, and he's pretty hot," we shared a smile, "I was attracted to him immediately. Pheromones plus a school girl crush. It was obvious, from the beginning, that he only cared about you. So I got jealous. Really jealous. I've done some nasty things because of it. I was tricked by Celeste into giving her information that non-Weres really aren't supposed to have, and you saw what that did. When I left the hall yesterday, Celeste followed me. She said she knew how I could get Adrian's attention. I was to fake being unconscious and she'd get him for help. I was so confused when she got you instead, and then…" She started to cry.

I wasn't sure what to do, but risked giving her a hug. Felicity stiffened in surprise, then relaxed. She backed off quickly though. "Careful, you don't want to ruin your dress. And I'm not quite finished. I spread some of the rumors, the ones about you. Celeste said you were the major suspect for the bombing, and it never even occurred to me to wonder how she would know that. I was the one who wrote that nasty message on your door. The one about Hyde not needing humans. I know I've done some unforgivable things, but I'm very sorry, and going to confess everything to the faculty."

I held up a hand. "You haven't always been the nicest, I agree. And I was hurt by the message, but I'm not seeing the unforgivable part. The worst parts you were tricked into, and the faculty knows about them already, and you aren't still jealous of me, are you?"

"A bit, but not enough to be nasty about it anymore."

"Then don't worry about it. If confessing will make you feel better, I won't stop you, but I won't say anything more about it if you don't." I didn't have any tissues, but the lounge had paper towels, so I handed her one to clean up a bit.

"Thank you. I see why Adrian likes you so much. Good luck. Have fun at the dance."

"Thanks, but I'm not going with Adrian, I'm going with Tim. Aren't you going to come?"

"No, I'm…no."

"You should. If you want to."

"No, I'm a mess today. I really don't think I'm up for it. Have fun with Adrian."

"I told you, I'm going with Tim."

She smiled. "If you say so. Go on; don't keep your date waiting any longer."

She was right, so I hurried down, apologizing before the elevator was all the way open. "I'm so sorry. I need... Adrian? What are you doing here?"

Adrian was standing in the lobby, looking a little awkward, and very handsome in his suit, holding a white rose. "Ilse and Tim told me I was taking you to the dance tonight. In fact, there were some pretty dire threats issued if I refused." I stared at him in confusion. "Unless, of course, you don't want to go with me?"

"No, that's...fine. I'm just surprised." That didn't cover it. "You don't have to, if you don't want to. I know you didn't want to go."

"No, I'm fine. I... want to go to the dance with you." He sounded reluctant to say it, but I don't think he was lying.

"You look nice." This was turning into the weirdest date ever.

He shrugged. "Allison picked out the suit. You, however, look gorgeous. Um, here." He gave me the flower and offered an arm.

The stem was thorn-less, so I tucked it carefully in my hair. "Thank you. Uh, I didn't get a boutonniere. I didn't think Tim would be able to wear one."

"Doesn't matter." He cast a glance outside. "Let's take the tunnels. You'll freeze out there."

"Good idea." I couldn't put a coat on over the dress. We took the first underground level, and were not the only ones to have that idea, but still got to the hall quickly. It was beautiful, if a little noisy and crowded. Even my signs didn't look too bad. Though that might have been because they were in the darker parts of the room. "I should warn you, I really don't know how to dance."

"Neither do I. We'll have to fake it."

It didn't take long to decide that either Adrian did know how to dance, or he was incredibly good at faking it. Ilse and Tim waltzed by at one point, looking perfectly elegant and fitting despite that fact that Tim made Ilse look tiny, and the music wasn't even close to a waltz. I waved at them, and they smiled and waved back. Ilse winked, but didn't say a word.

I did dance a song with Tim, but he wouldn't say much about the exchange. He wasn't upset by it, which I was relieved about, however he wouldn't say how or why he arranged it.

Eventually I insisted on a break before my feet fell off. Adrian grabbed us each a cup of punch and we sat, watching the dancers. Kara came by a moment later, eyes shining, clearly in her element. To my knowledge, she hadn't danced with the same person twice yet. "So, are you glad you came?"

I met Adrian's eye and thought about the dance, the school, and everything the past three months had involved. Adrian seemed to know what I was thinking and smiled at my answer. "Wouldn't miss it for anything."

Now Out!

Moonlit Memories: Book Two

Nightmare's Revenge

By H. J. Harding

Liska is a girl of many faces and more names. Currently she goes by Anna Andrews, a British born college student in West Palm Beach, FL. She prefers to think of herself as Luna Liska, active ninja from the Kikisutai Werefox clan of Japan. It is more comfortable than even her own name.

Liska hoped her second semester of college would be quieter than her first. She was wrong. Within her first week it's clear that last semester's problems aren't over and she isn't fully recovered. Then she has to uncover who betrayed a sworn ally to prove her own innocence. Add in an unexpected encounter from the past that complicates her fledgling relationship with Todd, and classes become the least of her concerns.

And then, there's Nightmare…

Now Out!

The Hyde Chronicles: Book II

Knightfall

By H. J. Harding

Violet Peters doesn't regret her choice to stay at Hyde. Usually. But it has complications. Especially when it comes to relating to her family. Her worlds are separating and Violet finds it harder and harder to straddle the balance. When her own cousin applies to Hyde, even Violet isn't sure if that will help or harm.

She does know that the danger isn't over yet, and someone is using Hyde as their personal chessboard. Violet is determined to do her part to save the school, but even that determination has unexpected consequences. The game is turning deadly, but she can't back down now.

www.ingramcontent.com/pod-product-compliance
Lightning Source LLC
Chambersburg PA
CBHW061130200626
46817CB00016B/590